Guardians Of The Round Table 3
Singed Feathers

Guardians Of The Round Table 3 Singed Feathers

Avril Sabine, Storm Petersen
and Rhys Petersen

Cracked Acorn Productions
Australia

Guardians Of The Round Table 3: Singed Feathers

Published by

Cracked Acorn Productions

PO Box 1365

Gympie QLD 4570

Australia

978-1-925617-73-3 (Kindle)

978-1-925617-74-0 (EPUB)

978-1-925617-75-7 (Print)

Genre: Young Adult Fantasy LitRPG

Happy birthday, Brad. Was this what you were hoping for? Now don't go getting arrested while celebrating.

**When all actions have repercussions,
it isn't really agame.**

While focusing on completing some of their quests, Mallory and her companions travel to new locations, face various creatures, meet more people and discover new information. Something they learn the hard way. As they've been warned, their actions have consequences. Will those consequences be more dangerous than they expected?

.

*

This story was written by Australian authors using Australian spelling.

Name Pronunciation

Like many names there is more than one way to pronounce the following ones. These are the pronunciations used in this story.

Characters

Ahron (ah-ron)

Danae (da-nay)

Edlien (ed-lee-en)

Elodie (ell-oh-dee)

Erym (air-im)

Tyne (tine)

Places

Buckneth (buck-neth)

Eridell (air-a-dell)

Inadon (in-ah-don)

Lilica (lil-e-cah)

Shadhurst (shad-hurst)

Simria (sim-re-ah)

Surith (soo-rith)

Ursen (ur-sen)

Velkden (velk-den)

Wester (west-er)

Wildebay (wild-bay)

Foreword

Opening stats, Mallory's notebook entries recapping the previous adventures and other details can be found at:

www.avrilsabine.com/series/gotrt

The notebook entries will contain spoilers if you haven't read the book they refer to.

Chapter One

Mallory headed for the open front door, dressed in her school uniform, her school backpack slung over one shoulder. "We're going, Mum." She called out loud enough her mum would hear in the kitchen.

"Hurry up." Brodie stood on the patio, also dressed in his uniform and carrying his school backpack. He had the same green eyes as Mallory, but where his brown hair was kept short, Mallory's brown hair that was naturally streaked with copper highlights, fell around her shoulders.

Norine strode towards them, drying her hands on a tea towel. "Why are you leaving so early?"

"It's seven-twenty. Ten minutes isn't early," Mallory said. "I just don't feel like walking fast this morning."

Norine reached for Mallory's forehead. "Are you sick?"

Mallory stepped back before her mum could make contact. "No." The last thing she needed was her mum trying to send her back to bed. She needed to return to Inadon. Even with the trip to buy coffee plant seeds yesterday the day had dragged by at times. All she could think about was the many things they planned to do.

"You look flushed. Are you sure you're not coming down with something?" Norine asked.

Brodie grabbed Mallory's arm, dragging her out the door. "Of course she's not sick. You're going to make us late and then you'll be blaming us for missing the bus when you're the one holding us up." He kept moving towards the edge of the concrete patio.

"Call me if you are coming down with something. I'll organise a lift home for you," Norine called out after them.

Mallory waved, glancing over her shoulder at her mum who remained in the doorway. She waited until they were several houses away before she spoke, keeping her voice low. "I hope she doesn't watch us all the way to the corner. How are we meant to get in the van Ryan borrowed if she does? I told you we shouldn't have left earlier than usual. That it'd make her suspicious."

"It wasn't like we left real early. What happens if

we get stuck in traffic? We can't be late returning to Inadon." Brodie glanced over his shoulder. "She's shut the door. It's all good."

Relief washed over Mallory as she checked the house. Her brother had been right. The door was closed. "Even if we're a little late, it wouldn't be by much. Not with how time works between the worlds." She smiled when she spotted the van parked at the corner. There was a dint in the rear passenger corner, the closed curtains in the rear windows were a faded red and the paint was a dull white, the clear coat flaking away in areas.

"We need a better place to leave from than that van," Brodie said. "Look at it."

The side door slid open as they approached and Callum leaned out. "You're in the back with me, Brodie." He had dark eyes, short dark hair and his lanky body was starting to gain a muscular, wiry look.

Brodie shoved his bag in on the floor. "Good. At least no one will be able to see me in it."

Mallory got in the front of the vehicle. "It isn't that bad."

Ryan chuckled. "Yeah, it is." He leaned close to kiss her, a smile lingering when he moved away. Like his brother, he had dark eyes and hair, but his hair was kept long and tied at the nape of his neck and his tall frame was filled out from hours at the gym, his shoulders broad.

Mallory dropped her backpack on the floor at her feet and buckled up. "Where are we going?"

"Underground parking at the local shopping centre." Ryan pulled out onto the road.

"Callum did you–" Mallory broke off when she turned in her seat to find there was a curtain separating the front and back of the van.

"I wouldn't open that if I were you," Ryan said. "They're getting changed. Or at least that was the plan."

"Don't touch the curtain," Brodie said.

"What were you going to ask me?" Callum asked.

"Did you bring the coffee plant seeds?"

"Yeah. Four of them."

"I still think you should cut your skin and sew one of them inside," Brodie said.

"I'm not cutting myself," Callum said.

"Might be the only way to get one to Inadon," Brodie said.

Mallory thought it was past time to interrupt the conversation that was a repeat of the one that had become rather heated yesterday. "I managed to get hold of Kern and Ewen last night."

"You didn't tell me," Brodie accused.

"I was waiting to tell everyone together." Mallory took her purple notebook out of her backpack.

"What did they say about getting distracted from quests the guardians send us?" Ryan asked.

"That if it doesn't bother those needing the quests done it doesn't bother the guardians. They also said we wouldn't be failed for not completing the quest or failing it. At least not due to a single quest. They wouldn't give me a clearer answer than that. Said some things we need to figure out for ourselves." Placing the purple notebook on her lap, she rummaged in her backpack for a pen.

"Did you ask them about transferring money between here and Inadon?" Ryan asked.

Mallory nodded. It was another topic they'd discussed during yesterday's drive. "You have to be a guardian and they'll transfer it at the current rate. They said we're usually better off earning money on Inadon than transferring money from this world. The exchange rate isn't the best. They also said all party members are paid equally, from the money owed, when a payment is due regardless of how many quests each party member helped with. That if a party member shouldn't be paid then they should be removed from the party before a payment is triggered."

"I don't mind that Danni was paid. She didn't accept any of the other money we earned," Callum said.

"Of course she should be paid," Brodie said. "But we need to work on finding ways to earn money on Inadon."

"Then that's our plan," Ryan said. "Work on getting money and gaining those three CAS points so we can gain a character level. We'll talk to the wagoner about fire drake nests after we escort him to Surith and back."

"I hope we find a nest with eight eggs," Brodie said.

Mallory opened the notebook. "What should I write this time?"

"School," Callum suggested.

Ryan entered the underground parking. "I doubt we'll forget that."

"What about that Mum thinks you're coming down with something and we left ten minutes early," Brodie said.

"Why does your mum think you're coming down with something?" Ryan asked.

"Because of the lame excuse she used when we left early," Brodie said.

Mallory started to argue his statement, but finished writing down the words instead. "Anything else we should make note of?"

Ryan pulled up in a corner park out of the way, turning off the engine. "That'll have to do. Time to dress and return to Inadon."

A shiver of excitement rushed through her and she shoved the notebook into her backpack, taking out her clothes, leather boots and the disc. "I thought we couldn't leave until eight." She checked her phone. "It's seven thirty-five. We still have twenty-five minutes."

Brodie slid the curtains apart. "You've got to get changed, so hurry up." He closed the curtain again and the sound of the door sliding open preceded Mallory's door being opened.

Callum held Mallory's door. "We can leave a few minutes early if we're ready to go."

Chapter Two

Carrying her bundle, and leaving her backpack in the front of the van, Mallory got in the back. Brodie, who stood beside Callum, closed the door as soon as she was in. She dumped her gear on the seat and changed out of her school uniform. It was a chore changing in the cramped space of the van. Jeans weren't the easiest to put on when you were seated. But she managed, slipping on her woollen socks and soft, leather boots. "I'm ready." She checked her phone. It had taken longer than she'd expected. It was seven forty-six.

The door slid open and the rest of the party clambered in, Ryan locking the door behind them. He dropped the keys and his phone on the floor near the door, nodding towards the laptop on the far side of the van. "Someone turn my laptop on?"

Mallory, being the closest, opened the lid and started it up. She waited for it to finish loading and inserted the disc. "We need to come up with a better plan than this." She glanced around the space. "It's too cramped."

"We'll have to remember to sit down before we return here." Callum sat on one of the back seats. "I don't want to think about what might happen if we're standing when we return. That's something we should probably ask Kern and Ewen about."

Brodie looked upwards. "Think it'd cut us in two?"

Mallory inserted the disc into the laptop, placing her phone on her pile of clothes as she waited for the familiar black screen followed by a pale gold circle that slowly brightened, a bow, dagger, staff and sword inside it. Another shiver of excitement raced through her when the image was replaced by gold words on a black screen. She couldn't help reading them out, wanting to savour them. "Do you wish to return to Inadon?"

"Hurry up and select yes," Brodie said.

Mallory's gaze was drawn to the time displayed in the corner of the screen. "Seven fifty-four. That isn't too early? Should we wait the last six minutes?" The time changed as she watched it. "Last five minutes."

"No," Brodie said. "It'll feel like an hour."

"We have to remember to tell Danni she has

money at the Inadon International Bank," Callum said.

"I nearly forgot to tell you," Mallory said. "Kern and Ewen said it's a bank run by neutral demons. They have a branch in every major town and all the capitals."

"I wonder if they have other banks," Ryan said.

Mallory shrugged. "I didn't ask."

"Stop stalling and select yes," Brodie said.

Mallory looked at the time again. A minute until eight. She smiled, wondering if she should make him wait the last minute.

Ryan linked his fingers through hers, grinning. "Stop torturing your brother."

The time changed and, smiling, she chose 'yes'. The world around them went black. Light slowly returned, the dimly lit room of the tavern bedroom coming into focus.

Fang launched herself at Brodie, licking his face. He laughed, patting her. "Guess you missed me, huh?"

Danae sat up in bed. "You're back." She threw back the linen. "It's six thirty already?"

Brodie rose to his feet, holding Fang close. "You were okay?"

Danae nodded. "I was going to be awake before you came back. I didn't mean to sleep in."

Mallory stood up, smiling at Smudge chattering away to Callum who checked his pockets. "We've got plenty of time to get ready." She felt the clothes on their makeshift clothesline. They were damp. She faced Danae. "You were paid for the quests we did last time we were here. Two gold and six silver pieces were deposited in the Inadon International Bank. They gave you a temporary code to access the account. Three thousand eight hundred and seventy-two. You'll need to set up a new code when you first access the money."

"Is there a time limit?" Danae asked. "The closest demonic bank is in Lilica."

"No!" Callum checked through his pockets again. "I can't believe it. Not a single seed."

"We're not going through hell to get you coffee," Brodie stated. "I don't have a revive. And neither does Mal."

"I need coffee," Callum said.

"Why not ask a demon to portal a seed between the worlds?" Danae asked.

"We could do that?" Mallory asked.

Danae nodded. "It won't be cheap, but it is possible."

"Define not cheap," Callum said.

Danae shrugged. "I don't know. Maybe a hundred thousand gold pieces. Possibly more."

Brodie put Fang on the floor. "Should have cut yourself and sewn them inside your skin like I said. Bet that'd work."

Mallory winced. "Can you stop saying that? I don't want to think about it let alone talk about it."

Callum looked down at himself. "I don't think I could do it."

"No one travels through Hellfire unless they're desperate," Danae said, "but if you do go, you should level up your mining and woodcutting so you can bring back some resources with you. You'll also need to put points in farming to give you the ability to grow the seeds once you have them."

"Why level up woodcutter and mining?" Ryan asked.

"Some of the ore and wood there is worth a lot of money. All you need is a pick to unlock mining," Danae said. "The reason you can't bring seeds with you is because they're a living thing. If something is alive, it can only travel between worlds as a member of your party. Unless a demon portals it."

A knock on the door had them turning to face it. Callum was the first to move, opening the door to reveal Ninette. She shifted from one foot to the other, holding a hessian bag. He stepped back. "Come in."

Ninette waited until the door was closed before she spoke. "Are you sure you don't mind giving me a short sword and temporarily adding me to your party?"

Smudge chirruped as he bounded across the room to greet Ninette. She bent down to pat him.

"The offer hasn't changed," Ryan said.

Ninette looked up from where she continued to crouch beside Smudge. "I want to be a warrior. I've wanted to be one for years." Giving Smudge one last pat, she rose to her feet. "Pa won't be happy, but I want to be one." She held out the hessian bag. "Don't tell him. I brought a bag so I can hide the sword. I know he'll find out eventually, but I want to wait before I tell him. Earn some XP first."

Mallory came forward, resting a hand on Ninette's arm. "You're absolutely certain?"

Ninette nodded.

"Accept party member Ninette."

Ninette smiled. "Thank you." She rested her hand over Mallory's. "You can't imagine how much this means to me." She paused a moment. "I've chosen my class if you want to remove me from your party now."

Mallory inclined her head. "Remove party member Ninette."

Ninette continued to smile. "Will you be coming back here?"

Mallory lowered her hand. "We'll be escorting the wagoner back from Surith."

Ryan handed over the short sword. "We have a few more things we want to do in the area before we leave it."

Ninette slipped the sword into the hessian bag. "Let me know if you ever need help. No matter what it is."

"We will," Callum said.

Ninette glanced over her shoulder at the door. "I better go before Pa is wondering where I went." She opened the door. "I'll see you when you return." She bent to pat Smudge who'd followed her. "All of you." With another smile, she stepped into the corridor and closed the door.

Danae waited until Ninette's footsteps could no longer be heard before she spoke. "You never said if there's a time limit for collecting the money from the demonic bank."

"Why are you calling it the demonic bank?" Callum asked.

Danae smiled. "Because it's owned and run by demons."

"I thought it might be," Callum said. "But wanted to check."

"I don't know if there's a time limit." Ryan shrugged. "We told you everything we know."

"If I got a seedling, could I add it to the party?" Callum asked. "Would it be able to travel with us then?"

"It should be able to," Danae said hesitantly. "I mean, it sounds logical."

Brodie clapped Callum on the shoulder. "Great. We'll try that next. Has to be better than going through hell."

"What are you going to call the new party member?" Ryan grinned.

Brodie laughed. "You need a hand coming up with a name?"

"I doubt it. Or at least not anything you're likely to suggest," Callum said.

Chapter Three

Mallory glanced at the damp clothes. "We need to get ready for the day. It'll be seven-thirty and time to leave before we know it."

Brodie eyed the clothes. "We shouldn't have washed them."

"They needed it," Mallory said. "They were stinking of sweat. We really need a couple of changes of clothes."

"We're not wasting money on more clothes," Brodie stated. "You won't let us buy food most of the time so you can't buy things we don't need."

"Talking of food." Callum glanced at the door. "We should see if we can pick up the pie the baker is making for us." He gathered his bow, quiver and leather belt, Smudge remaining at his side.

Brodie's expression brightened. "I'll help." He gathered his weapons and leather belt.

"I'll come with you." Danae took a step towards the door. "That's if you don't need help packing."

Mallory shook her head. "Most of it's packed. Go ahead."

Danae smiled and gathered her weapon, following Brodie and Callum through the door, the companion animals going with them.

Mallory waited until her and Ryan were alone before she spoke. "We'll see what we can buy in Surith. It sounds like it's bigger than Buckneth. If we're going after fire drakes we need more gear."

"If?" Ryan grinned. "I thought you'd already made up your mind."

Mallory's lips slowly curved into a smile. "Okay. When we go after fire drakes."

Ryan chuckled. "That sounds better. You do know your brother is going to complain."

She shrugged. "Probably, but I'm sick of not having enough gear. If we can, I'm selling the mage robe we found in the dungeon and buying clothes. We need them." She gestured towards the ones hanging on the line strung up in the room. "You can't wear damp clothes and we can't wear the same ones non-stop. Even Brodie's extra charisma points wouldn't help with that smell."

Ryan chuckled. "We'll pack everything except the

clothes then visit the wagoner to finalise the escort mission details." He picked up a blanket and folded it.

They packed what they could then geared up, Mallory also plaiting her hair back out of her way. Ryan took the iron key off the chest and locked the door behind them. They ran into the rest of their party outside the tavern, Callum and Brodie arguing about when they should eat the pie.

"Was the wagoner next door?" Ryan asked.

Callum shook his head. "He's collecting the horses and our donkey. Welby is helping him."

"We really need to think of a name for the donkey," Mallory said.

"Bob," Ryan suggested.

"It's a girl," Brodie protested.

Mallory laughed softly. "Beast of burden?"

Ryan grinned. "Yep."

"Then we should call her Bobbi," Callum said.

Ryan shrugged. "Either works for me."

Mallory glanced at each of them. "Bobbi then?"

"That's a stupid name," Brodie muttered.

Mallory shared a look with Ryan. Obviously, her brother didn't get it. Not that it surprised her with how little he'd had to do with role-playing games. "Any other objections to the name?"

Ryan and Callum both shook their heads.

"It's settled then," Mallory said. "We'll call her Bobbi."

"She'll probably get Bob." Callum glanced at Ryan. "Or at least from some people."

Before Mallory could comment, she saw the wagoner and Welby walking along the dirt road. She hurried forward to greet them. "Are you ready to settle on the details of the escort mission?"

"Walk with me around to the back of my place so I can get the horses hitched to the wagon. We can talk while I do that." He nodded to the hitching post near the tavern, looking to Welby. "You can tie the horse and donkey over there."

"How long do you need to stay in Surith and how much are you willing to pay for the escort?" Brodie asked.

"It's approximately two and a half hours by wagon." The wagoner rounded the corner of his home. "I'll need to stay two nights so I can complete all my trades. I can either pay you two gold pieces, which is a bit more than I'd pay for the two guards I need, or I can sell goods on your behalf like I did in Wayholt and not charge you my usual fee. You'd have until midday tomorrow to get the goods to me. I'm afraid I can't lend you a chest this time. They're all full."

Mallory stared at the loaded wagon. No wonder he wanted an escort. As well as the chests that had been on it for the trip to Wayholt, the middle was filled with tall, straw baskets and large, canvas wrapped bundles. There wouldn't be much space for them, unless they sat on top of the chests along the sides.

"Are we limited in the amount of things you'll sell?" Ryan asked.

The wagoner led the horses to the front of the wagon. "As much as you can get to me by midday tomorrow."

Ryan nodded. "Give us a few minutes to discuss it."

Mallory walked beside Ryan as he headed a few metres away from the wagon. "We could gather herbs, but I don't know if that'd help much."

"You could hunt game," Danae said. "You should find a few deer and rabbits between here and Surith. Fresh game always sells well. You wouldn't even need to skin it. There's a butcher at Surith and butchers will take game whole."

"Two gold pieces doesn't seem like much," Brodie said.

"Guards are only paid a silver piece a day. Guards that protect shipments are also paid two copper pieces a kilometre on top of their daily wage," Danae said.

"No way would I be a guard," Brodie said. "How can they afford to eat on those wages?"

"That's why some of them are easily bribed. Ones working for wealthy houses earn more. Adventuring pays better." Danae smiled at him. "Although it is more dangerous."

"Probably a lot more fun than being a guard at a mine or something," Brodie said.

Mallory looked at each of them. "So we get the wagoner to sell things for us?"

Ryan nodded. "Midday tomorrow. That should give us plenty of time to gather some gear. A day and a half."

Once everyone had agreed, they returned to the wagoner to give him their answer, letting him know it wouldn't take long for them to finish getting ready. They carried everything downstairs and met the wagoner out the back of his place once the horse was saddled and the panniers were on the donkey. Danae's clothes, that were damp, were fixed to the sides of the panniers while the rest wore theirs.

Mallory managed not to mention that they needed a second set of clothes and that she needed two sets of clothes, even though she kept thinking it. Brodie would get over needing to spend money on something other than food. A smile slowly formed. Eventually.

The first hour of the journey was quiet. They turned left at the intersection and took turns gathering herbs and hunting game. The slight glimmer to resources made it easier to notice herbs that could be gathered. Except for Danae, who Brodie once more asked to give them a chance to try and catch up. She smiled, but remained on her horse.

They came across a lot more herbs than they did game, only managing to get two rabbits and one deer. As Danae had suggested, they didn't skin them, planning to let the wagoner sell them whole to the butcher. They also shared out the blueberry pie, but not the beef and vegetable pasties from Danae's mother, which everyone except for Brodie agreed to have for lunch.

Chapter Four

Nearing the end of the first hour of their journey, they spotted two wolves on the side of the road, deciding to attack before the wolves could come after them. They managed to take out both before they drew close, even before Ryan could help.

Ryan nodded towards the bodies. "Do we sell them to the butcher or skin them?"

"Butcher. They'll be turned into pet food." Danae slipped an arm and her head through her bow so it hung at her back.

Callum helped Ryan collect the wolves and drape them over one of the chests along with the rabbits and deer. "This isn't too bad. A lot less dangerous than going to Wayholt."

"Did you have to say that?" Brodie muttered. "Now we're probably going to have a horde of hellions come after us."

"Only a horde?" Mallory teased her brother.

"You just wait and see. It always happens. What about that bear?"

Ryan looked at Brodie. "Want to join me in gathering herbs since we're falling behind? Me more than you. Only another forty-five XP and I'll gain a CAS point."

Mallory checked her experience points while Ryan and Brodie gathered herbs. She had sixty-six. Only another thirty-nine to go. Although if she was counting the experience points until her first character level, then she needed to gain two hundred and fifty-two. It seemed like a lot when she looked at it like that. Would they be able to gain enough experience points to earn their first character level before they returned to their world? The task looked daunting. Especially with how long it had taken them to gain their current experience points.

Once Ryan and Brodie had caught up with Mallory and Callum's experience points, they went back to taking turns at gathering herbs. They mostly found calendula and meadowsweet, along with a herb Danae didn't know the name of.

They were half an hour from Surith, and had two experience points until they gained a CAS point, when they spotted four bandits ahead. Brodie drew out his throwing knives. "Check the one with the wooden leg. Give him an eye patch and he could be a pirate. Especially with the way he's dressed."

Danae readied her bow. "He could be a pirate. They do come ashore."

"Focus on the two with bows," Ryan said. "When the other two come close I'll attack them."

"Do you need help?" Welby asked. "I've only got my dagger, but I can help when they come close."

"Help is good." Callum aimed at one of the bandits.

Mallory had her wand in her left hand and dagger in her right. Before she could launch a fireball at a bandit the wagoner, who was behind them, spoke.

"The bandits have twenty health and the pirate has thirty."

Mallory threw a fireball at one of the bandits at the same time as Callum and Danae fired arrows at him. She didn't have time to check over her shoulder to see if the wagoner was using his brass spyglass, but since there was no other way he could have known the stats, she assumed he was.

"He only has five health points left," the wagoner said.

"I've got him." Mallory threw a fireball at the bandit, who crumpled to the ground, while the others attacked the second bandit with a bow. Brodie was able to attack too since the archer had come closer.

"Ten health," the wagoner called out.

Mallory attacked the second archer, wanting to take him out before he could shoot any of them.

"Nice crit," the wagoner said. "Two health left."

"Brodie take out the archer and everyone else focus on the warrior bandit," Ryan said. "I'm going after the pirate."

Mallory wanted to protest. Wanted to tell him they could get the pirate before he reached them. But they couldn't. Not at the pace he was moving. As much as she wanted to help Ryan attack the pirate, focusing on the warrior bandit made more sense. The moment he crumpled from their combined attacks, she faced Ryan who blocked an attack from the pirate with his shield. There was a cracking sound and Ryan tossed the shield aside as he continued to fight the pirate. Mallory launched a fireball at the pirate, sending a second one at him.

An arrow pierced the pirate and he dropped to the ground, Ryan staring down at him. "He broke my shield."

"Things don't last forever." The wagoner remained on the seat, scanning the area with the help of his brass spyglass.

"They have durability which depends on the level of their quality," Danae said.

"You mean my bow could break?" Callum asked.

Danae nodded.

"How do I know when that will happen?" Callum eyed the bow he held.

Danae shrugged. "I don't have the ability to tell the quality or durability of an item."

"Who does?" Ryan crouched beside the pirate. He glanced over his shoulder. "How about you start searching instead of standing around? I'm sure the wagoner would like to get to Surith today."

"And I'd like to go home," Welby said.

Danae helped Callum search the warrior bandit. "Someone who's focused on levelling up bartering. It's one of the abilities you gain."

Mallory searched an archer bandit. "What about my wand? Does it have a durability too?"

Danae nodded. "Everything does. You can help bladed weapons last longer by regularly using a whetstone on them."

"I knew we shouldn't have given that sword to Ninette," Brodie said.

Mallory laughed. "Only you would come to that conclusion."

"Doesn't matter." Ryan held up a cutlass and scabbard. "I'm going to try this out."

"You can use a cutlass?" Mallory asked.

Danae spoke before Ryan could. "It's considered a short sword. It usually has a slightly better attack than a short sword."

Ryan rose to his feet. "Someone want to finish off searching the pirate? I want to swap weapons."

"I'll search him," Brodie said. "Maybe I'll find doubloons."

"What are doubloons?" Danae asked.

Finished searching the bandit, Mallory walked over to the last one. "I guess that means you're not about to find any."

"Maybe gold then," Brodie said.

"Pirates aren't as wealthy as some people think," Danae said.

Brodie held up a wooden leg. "Look what I got."

Callum laughed. "I would have thought that was a letdown after searching for gold."

"It's a pirate leg," Brodie exclaimed.

Mallory slowly shook her head, returning to the wagon to check over what everyone had found. Besides the cutlass and wooden leg, they also found eight copper pieces, one silver piece, four arrows, a pair of worn leather boots and a pair of brown trousers. Two of the arrows were given to Danae to replace the ones she'd lost and Callum took the other two, slipping them into the canvas loops on the outside of his full quiver. He now had three tied to the outside.

Danae brought the broken shield over. "You could get this repaired. It'd be cheaper than buying a new one. Or sell it for a couple of copper coins. There are shops that buy broken weapons and armour and have them repaired so they can sell them on."

Brodie picked up the boots. "Can I have them?"

"Might want to see if they fit first," Ryan suggested.

Brodie sat on one of the chests along the sides of the wagon, taking off his sneakers.

"Are we ready to continue?" the wagoner asked.

Chapter Five

Mallory put the coins in her satchel, cautiously picking up the trousers. "Doesn't anyone believe in washing clothes?"

Ryan chuckled, taking them from her. "Maybe clean bandits don't look as ferocious." He took out a calico bag from one of the panniers and slipped them inside, hanging them from the outside of a pannier. "We'll wash them later. It'll be good to have a spare pair." He looked to the wagoner as he joined the rest of his companions who were seated on the chests, other than Danae who rode Augusta. "We can go now."

Brodie frowned. "They don't fit."

"Let me try." Callum took the boots from Brodie.

Before she checked the stats after their fight, Mallory looked at everyone's health. "Ryan! Drink a health potion." She took one out of her satchel. "You're down to eleven health points."

Ryan glanced at the potion. "He got me twice."

"Take it." Mallory continued to hold out the potion. "And drink it. You can't get through most of the day on such low health." The health potion would take his health back to full, at twenty-one. She'd feel a lot better if she didn't need to worry about him losing his revive.

Ryan took the potion and drank it, putting the empty vial in his backpack. "Is it worth selling the empty vials for now?"

Danae rode beside the wagon. "If you don't want them, I could use them. Eventually."

"When will you be able to make health potions?" Brodie asked.

"Not until level thirty-three and after I learn the recipe. But I'll be able to make herbal infusions and tinctures before that stage. Once I learn the recipes," Danae said. "Vials are used for tinctures too."

"They fit me." Callum stared at the leather boots he wore.

"That's not fair," Brodie muttered, glaring at Mallory, Ryan and Callum when they laughed. "Boots would have been better than this." He nodded to the wooden leg he examined.

Still smiling, Mallory finally managed to check her stats. She'd gained another CAS point and only needed to earn another two before she could gain a character level. She couldn't wait. Although she only had eight experience points of the next one hundred and six she needed to gain. And she still wasn't sure what to put her CAS points in. She had four of them saved up. Was it worth focusing on alchemy if they'd have Danae's help?

She checked everyone's stats, grinning when she noticed only Callum had the same amount as her. Brodie and Ryan were once again falling behind. She glanced at her brother, trying to decide if she should tease him about it.

Brodie frowned.

Callum leaned close, peering at the wooden leg. "Did you find something?"

"I just spent all that time evening out our XP, except for Danni's, and now they're different again," Brodie muttered.

Mallory laughed, catching Ryan's gaze and laughing harder. She slowly shook her head. She should have known she wouldn't need to point it out. "I would have thought you'd realise by now how impossible it is to keep our levels even."

"Obviously it isn't," Brodie said. "Don't we keep managing to get them even?"

Callum chuckled. "He does have a point there."

"Hey, look at this." A section of the leg opened up and Brodie drew out a folded piece of paper. "It's a map."

Ryan took the map from Brodie. "How are we meant to figure out where it's a map of when nothing is labelled?"

"There's an 'x' marked on it." Callum pointed to the letter in between two lines that met at a junction, becoming one as they travelled away from the edge of the map.

"Could be the coastline," Mallory said.

"Did you want me to have a look?" Welby asked. "I know the coast fairly well. At least the coast from Mer Point to Ursen."

Ryan handed the map forward. "Does it look familiar?"

Welby frowned at the map before slowly nodding. "There's a river past Wildebay that forks into two before it reaches the coastline." He handed the map back. "If you want to escort me home, I can show you where that location is once I find out what has happened while I was gone. Normally it wouldn't bother me to travel that distance on my own, but I don't have a bow to protect myself."

"How long will it take to get to Wildebay from Surith?" Mallory noticed the journal icon in the corner of her vision. She checked to find it was a new quest. *Journey Home: The Wildebay hunter will show you where he believes your map leads if you escort him home.*

"Who cares how long it takes." Brodie gestured towards the map. "That's a treasure map. We need to check it out."

"It might not be a treasure map," Callum glanced at the map Ryan continued to hold.

"It must be a treasure map," Brodie argued. "There's an 'x' on it and that always marks treasure."

"Not necessarily," Ryan said. "It's marking a location. That doesn't make it treasure."

"But it was owned by a pirate." Brodie again gestured towards the map.

"Okay, it might be a treasure map," Callum said.

"Only one way to find out." Ryan glanced at each of them. "Who wants to follow it?"

"Me." Brodie spoke before Ryan had barely finished speaking.

Chuckling, Mallory shrugged. It would be good to do another quest and this one seemed simple enough.

"We still don't know how long it takes to travel there and back. We have until lunch tomorrow to get our trade items to the wagoner."

"Around two hours from Surith to Wildebay," Welby said. "Depending on what we encounter along the way."

"And how much further is it to the location?" Mallory asked.

Welby shrugged. "A little hard to judge. There's no actual road. Probably not even a proper track. We can go along the coast and then head inland along the first river until it's possible to cross it. Then head south east from there until we reach the location." He shrugged again. "It's probably nearly eight kilometres, but it'd be close on two hours since there's no clear track."

"Eight hours travel there and back plus anything we might run into and finding the actual treasure," Ryan said.

"We'll be back in Surith before midday tomorrow," Brodie said. "Easily."

"I could probably give you a few extra hours to get your trade goods to me," the wagoner said. "Especially if I don't need to also buy items out of the money for you."

"We don't need anything." Brodie looked pointedly at Mallory. "Not even more clothes."

"How many say yes?" Ryan looked around the group. "Raise a hand." He lifted his hand.

Brodie's hand shot up, followed by a shrug from Callum who also raised his hand.

"I wouldn't mind going treasure hunting." Danae raised her hand.

Mallory grinned. "Unanimous then." She briefly raised her hand.

"Good." Brodie set the wooden leg aside. "Ryan and I can catch up our XP." He jumped off the wagon, heading for the closest herbs, some calendula.

Ryan chuckled as he hopped off the wagon. "XP is always good."

"We don't have much space left for herbs." Callum glanced at the panniers.

"Should be enough to catch up." Ryan strode after Brodie.

Welby turned in his seat to face Mallory. "Why do you need to have your XP at the same amounts?"

"You'd have to ask Brodie," Mallory said.

"But you're helping him keep them at the same level," Welby said.

Callum laughed. "No, we're humouring him for

now. Until he figures out it's impossible to do this forever."

"I heard that." Brodie put some herbs in a pannier.

"Would have spoken louder if you weren't close enough to hear," Callum said.

Brodie gestured towards Callum with his middle finger before he ran towards another cluster of herbs.

Chapter Six

Mallory checked the poppet in her satchel. It was safe. "How far away is Lilica?" She really needed to hand the poppet into a Mages Guild. She didn't want to be the reason the person the poppet was made to harm, died.

"About twelve and a half hours. Probably more since you'll need breaks," the wagoner said.

Mallory sighed. "That's too far away. But I really want to hand in the poppet we found. I keep thinking I'm going to accidentally hurt it."

"I could find a ship's captain heading to Lilica who'd be willing to pay you five silver pieces for the poppet. That way they'd earn five silver pieces when they hand it in to the Mages Guild," the wagoner said.

Ryan returned with some herbs in time to hear the wagoner's comment. "How far away is Lilica?"

The wagoner repeated his earlier information.

"Ship's captain sounds like a good idea. We can't keep dragging it around the countryside," Ryan said.

"What's happening?" Brodie put some herbs in the pannier.

Mallory sighed as she repeated the conversation.

"Sell it to the ship's captain. Then we'll get paid when we go home," Brodie said.

Mallory looked at the rest of them, who nodded. "Lucky you all said yes. Do you know how hard it's been keeping it safe? Someone else would have been looking after it if we didn't sell it to a ship's captain."

Ryan chuckled. "Good thing we said yes then." He returned to gathering herbs.

Mallory scanned her surroundings. There seemed to be more trees in this area, although they were starting to thin out again now. A couple of times as they reached the top of a rise she thought she'd caught a glimpse of the ocean through the trees in the distance. Hopefully, that meant they'd reach Surith shortly. She was looking forward to gaining experience points from visiting another location. And they'd gain more when they reached Wildebay. She doubted there'd be any experience points for finding a location on a treasure map.

Brodie returned with two rabbits, holding them

by the ears. "Look what I got. I really need more throwing knives. Should probably put my CAS points into levelling them up some too. Since my cooking is high enough to make all our recipes."

"You've got four more XP than us," Callum said.

"It was the rabbits," Brodie said. "I didn't think I'd managed to get them. But I had to try. You could gather herbs."

"Nah, I'm sure I'll gain more XP later." Callum absently patted Smudge's head, Fang curled up on the other side of Smudge.

Ryan returned with more herbs. "I'm putting my new CAS point into hunting and getting a hunting bow when we're in Surith. Hunting rabbits has to be better than gathering herbs."

Mallory smiled when she saw his stats. Eight experience points, like her and Callum.

Ryan joined them on the wagon, sitting on the chest next to Mallory. "You have reached level five hunting. You are one percent more likely to gain rare resources from wild animals you have hunted and harvested and can now use a hunting bow."

"What are rare resources?" Brodie joined them on the wagon, sitting beside Fang who looked up at the sound of his voice. She wagged her tail once before closing her eyes.

Welby turned to face them. "Rare resources are things like lucky rabbit feet, drop bear fangs, a wolf heart, bugbear claws and fire drake fangs."

Mallory interrupted him. "People kill fire drakes?"

"Wild adults can cause a lot of problems in settled areas if they're not dealt with," Welby said. "They also lose their baby teeth, which aren't as rare as the adult fangs, but still valuable and can be used instead of adult fangs in alchemy. Two baby teeth for each fang needed."

Brodie's expression brightened. "How much can you make out of baby teeth?"

Ryan chuckled. "We haven't found any yet."

Welby looked at each of them. "You're going after fire drakes?" When they nodded, he slowly shook his head. "Taking on a nesting fire drake is dangerous."

"So we've been told," Ryan said.

"I put that CAS point in my throwing knives weapon affinity. Plus two percent bonus. A pity it won't make a difference. But I will be able to get throwing knives with higher stats, won't I?" Brodie asked.

"Ones that are a better quality, ones from other metals and enchanted ones," Danae said.

"Can I use them yet? Or do I have to level up?" Brodie asked.

"Until you reach level ten you can only use bronze, iron and steel weapons," Danae said. "After that, you can start to use weapons made from other materials. Tools that can also be used as weapons have different requirements."

"Like what sorts of materials?" Brodie asked.

Mallory had been about to ask the same question.

"Glass, blood iron and infernal iron," Danae said.

"Glass." Ryan met Danae's gaze. "I could have a glass sword."

Danae nodded.

Ryan's lips slowly curved into a smile. "I need one of them."

"So do I." Mallory had lost count of the number of times she'd used glass weapons in role-playing games. The thought of being able to actually use them here sent a shiver of excitement through her.

"Glass?" Brodie looked from one to the other. "Won't it shatter?"

"It's made in a special way," Danae said. "It's no more likely to break than any other weapon."

Brodie's expression brightened. "Glass throwing knives. Now that sounds cool."

"We're nearly there." The wagoner gestured to the road ahead, an inn visible in the distance.

Beyond the inn Mallory could see a few farms,

nothing else other than trees visible. "That's Surith?" She'd expected more. It appeared to be smaller than Buckneth.

The wagoner chuckled. "That's the inn on the outskirts. There's a tavern on the waterfront as well, but it can be a little rowdy at times. Some travellers prefer to stay in this one." He checked his pocket watch. "We've made reasonable time. Should arrive around eleven thirty."

"How about an early lunch?" Brodie asked hopefully.

"Might be best," Ryan said. "Save us stopping to eat when we've got other things to do today."

They ate the rest of the beef and vegetable pasties, Danae had brought with her, sharing them with Smudge and Fang while they discussed the items the wagoner would sell for them. All the herbs, the animals they'd gained hunting and the shield since Ryan decided it was no point repairing it when he planned to go dual swords.

"Are you sure you want to sell it?" Danae asked. "You won't be able to wield dual swords until you level up."

"We're going to have to do some grinding. It's taking too long to gain a character level," Ryan said.

"There always seems to be something else to do," Callum said.

Mallory nodded. "Like quests." She'd always found it difficult to resist doing a quest when she stumbled across one. "There are too many interesting quests."

Ryan chuckled. "Tell me about it."

"So we're selling the shield?" Brodie asked.

"Yeah. And buying a hunting bow," Ryan said.

"No wonder we never have any money," Brodie muttered.

Chapter Seven

Mallory couldn't resist grinning at Brodie, noticing Ryan was too. "Anything else we're selling?"

"The hand drum." Callum glanced at Brodie. "Probably too risky to keep it."

"Those skeletons weren't my fault," Brodie protested.

Ryan spoke once the laughter died down. "We should probably sell the fishing pole and get a fishing reel or two. Easier to transport." He turned to the wagoner. "Where's the best place to buy a hunting bow? And quiver for arrows."

"You're not buying arrows so don't even think about it," Brodie said. "Callum and Danni should have some spare. Especially since we regularly get them as drops."

Danae nodded. "I can give you five."

"You can have eight of mine," Callum said. "We

can always buy some later if we figure out that isn't enough."

"Okay." Ryan again turned to the wagoner who hadn't had the chance to speak. "So where should we go?"

The wagoner gestured towards the road they were on, having passed the farms and was now amongst houses spaced well apart. "This road will take us to the harbour. To the right is a general goods shop and to the left is the traders I use. Or if you want, you could try the secondhand shop. Take a left before you reach the traders."

"We'll try the secondhand shop first," Ryan said. "Thanks."

The wagoner inclined his head. "I'll probably have some of your goods sold by this evening if you want to meet up in the tavern along the waterfront after dark."

Ryan glanced at each of them.

Like the rest, Mallory shrugged. They had until midday tomorrow so who knew where they'd be tonight.

"We'll see where we end up," Ryan said. "But we will catch up with you before midday tomorrow."

"I'll probably be with the trader. If I go anywhere else I'll leave word with him where you can find me," the wagoner said. "But you can have a few extra hours to get the goods to me if you need it."

Mallory saw the ocean ahead, sunlight glinting on the waves, several smaller ships docked at the harbour, a couple of larger ones anchored further out. The wagon slowed as they approached the T intersection, another wagon heading in the direction they'd come from and one going past on the road ahead of them. It was a busier village than Buckneth and appeared to have more people than Wayholt. Her gaze was drawn to the harbour that was filled with movement and noise. "Is Surith bigger than Wayholt?"

"Yes and no." The wagoner turned left at the end of the road, driving along the coastline. "Wayholt covers a slightly bigger area, not by much though, and the local population is about the same. Surith has a lot of visitors. Ships calling in and traders from outlying areas."

"Did you see there is a bakers back there?" Brodie nearly fell off the wagon as he tried to see past the building they were passing. "Think we can go back and see what they sell?"

Ryan dragged Brodie back from the edge of the wagon. "We'll see what we earn. But we're not having a look until we're ready to leave."

"Really?" Brodie stared at Ryan, victory punching the air when he nodded. "Hell yeah."

"There's no guarantee," Ryan warned.

"We've got a treasure map," Brodie said.

Callum glanced around the area as they pulled up beside the traders. "Can you say that any louder? Any muggers in the area might not have heard you."

Mallory nodded towards the wooden leg. "We can sell that too."

"No." Brodie grabbed hold of the leg. "It's a pirate leg."

The wagoner jumped down to the ground. "Probably get as much as a gold piece for it."

Brodie looked from the leg to the wagoner. "An entire gold?"

The wagoner nodded.

Brodie turned to Ryan. "Only if we can use the money we make from it to spend at the bakers. Or somewhere else that sells food."

"Deal." Ryan took the wooden leg from him and set it on top of one of the chests. "We'll put the rest of the gear for you to sell in hessian bags and pile it up on the back of the wagon. Will that do?"

Again the wagoner nodded. "I won't be moving from this spot until I've sold most of the goods. Then I'll make the rounds of the rest of the places and the harbour before coming back here and seeing what else the trader might want. I also need to pick up the items some of the people from Buckneth asked me to buy for them." He glanced at the fishing pole. "You want me to pick up some fishing reels for you, or will you deal with that yourselves?"

"We can do that," Mallory said.

"After we buy one, I might do some fishing to get Smudge food." Callum gathered up his companion animal and put him on the ground.

Smudge looked around, squeaking and making the occasional grunting sound as he tilted his head to the side. He took a step towards the ocean.

"Don't go wandering off," Callum said. "I'll take you for a swim later."

Smudge wrapped his arm around Callum's leg, chirruping.

Fang ran over to Callum, wagging her tail.

Mallory laughed. "I think she wants to go for a swim too."

Callum patted both the companion animals on the head. "Soon."

Fang yipped and Smudge made a sound that was very similar.

"Let's get everything sorted and then Callum can

take them for a swim while we finish shopping." Ryan continued to unpack the panniers.

Mallory handed over the poppet, relieved to be rid of the responsibility. "They will take good care of it, won't they?"

"They'll have to. If they let the person die, the poppet will start to disintegrate and they won't earn any money from delivering it."

"Disintegrate?" Mallory's gaze was fixed on the poppet.

"Yes. The seams will break apart as if they're dissolving and the fabric will fray and unravel," the wagoner said.

Mallory looked the poppet over. It was in good condition. "Okay. Thanks." She returned to helping her companions.

Welby approached them as they worked. "I have someone here I wouldn't mind visiting if you can wait an hour before we leave. A friend of my brother's. I should tell them what happened."

"That's fine," Ryan said. "Give us time to get our shopping done."

"Thanks." With a nod, Welby headed down the road.

Once they were finished sorting out what was to be sold, they walked along the road towards the secondhand shop. Mallory checked the journal icon that had been in the corner of her vision since entering Surith. Like she'd expected, it was a notification that she'd gained ten experience points for discovering Surith. Reaching the secondhand shop, they tied Bobbi and Augusta to the hitching post out the front, leaving Fang and Smudge to guard them.

Entering the dim interior, Mallory looked around. She spotted several fishing reels, some in better condition than others. Remembering Danae's comments about durability, she picked out two that seemed to be in reasonable condition.

Callum headed straight for the counter. "Do you sell coffee?"

"I've never heard of it," the shopkeeper said.

Callum sighed. "I didn't think you would, but it was worth a try."

Ryan joined his brother at the counter. "How about a hunting bow or quiver?"

"I have a quiver, but no hunting bow." The shopkeeper made his way to where the quiver was displayed, handing it over to Ryan. "Only came in yesterday."

Chapter Eight

Mallory joined Ryan and Brodie at the counter, bringing the two fishing reels with her. She put them on the counter while she took out the mage robe. "Are you interested in buying this?"

The shopkeeper looked it over. "Unless you're interested in taking more items in trade I can't afford it. The most I could give you would be eight gold pieces and it's worth twenty-five."

"Oh." Mallory returned the mage robe to her satchel.

"We'll take the quiver and two fishing reels," Ryan said.

Mallory counted out coins. The quiver was eight silver pieces and the fishing reels were six copper pieces each. Before she'd finished Callum, who'd been wandering around, called out.

"I found studded leather vambraces." He held them

up. "They're only four gold pieces. I really need them."

"You got boots." Brodie gestured towards the leather boots Callum wore.

"Get them," Ryan said.

"That's not fair," Brodie protested. "You keep telling me no every time I want something."

Ryan glanced at the throwing knives belt and knives. "Really?"

"Nearly every time," Brodie muttered.

Callum put on the vambraces. "They're a perfect fit."

Danae moved closer to him. "I wish I could find a pair."

"You could try the traders," the shopkeeper said. "He might have a pair."

Mallory handed over four gold, nine silver and two copper pieces, mentally calculating how much she had left. Forty-four gold, twenty-five silver and nineteen copper pieces. For once, it didn't feel too bad handing over coins. A smile slowly formed. She didn't feel broke after spending money.

Outside, Danae handed five arrows to Ryan and Callum gave him eight. Ryan put the quiver on his belt so it hung at his left hip beside the axe, adding the arrows to it.

Callum took one of the fishing reels that Mallory carried. "I should have asked where to get bait."

Facing the ocean, Danae gestured towards the right. "Try the fisherman. He's likely to sell bait. Should only be a copper piece or two."

Mallory gave Callum two copper pieces, smiling when her brother's gaze followed the coins. "Don't worry, Callum. I'll ask if they have coffee."

"Thanks. But I'm not about to hold my breath."

Ryan handed over the trousers, they'd got earlier, to Brodie. "You can wash these while Callum catches some fish. Then you can join him." He took the second reel from Mallory and gave it to Brodie.

Muttering under his breath, Brodie followed Callum, their companion animals walking at their sides.

Mallory turned to Ryan. "Are we going to check out the traders now? Or are we going to see what ships are available for Danni?"

Danae gathered Augusta's reins. "I'm not ready to leave. Adventuring is more exciting than I thought it'd be."

Ryan led the donkey as they walked towards the traders. "I'll see if I can get a hunting bow first and then we can head over to the harbour."

There was a hitching post at the front of the traders

where they tied the horse and donkey before heading inside towards the man behind the counter. Mallory stopped partway there, her attention caught by several rows of vials. As well as the usual health and mana potions, she saw there were temporary boosts for things such as strength and dexterity and health regen potions. Her mouth dropped open when she saw a vial of experience points.

"What did you find?" Ryan stopped beside her.

She pointed to the vial.

"We can buy XP?"

Mallory finally noticed the price. "Not at that price we can't." The vials ranged from five to thirty experience points, but the price worked out to be five gold pieces per experience point. "How do they get it?"

Danae joined them. "From people willing to sell their XP. You can't sell more than your current level."

"What do you mean by current level?" Mallory asked.

"You could currently sell eighteen XP. You can't sell any of the XP from your previous CAS levels," Danae said.

"How much would I earn for each XP?" She

couldn't take her gaze off the vials. Was this a way to make a bit of extra money?

"Depends. Anywhere between one to three gold," Danae said. "Some mages pay better than others."

Mallory gestured towards the vials. "I could do this eventually?"

Danae nodded. "I can't remember what level, but it's pretty high and you'd need to buy or find the spell to do it."

Ryan's gaze was fixed on the vials too. "You sure you want to be a warrior as well as a mage?"

She hit his arm with the back of her hand, unable to resist returning his smile. "Don't you start too."

He draped an arm around her shoulders. "Be whatever you want to be. We'll figure out a way to earn money no matter your choice." He glanced towards the counter. "Finished looking?"

She nodded, but couldn't resist looking over her shoulder one more time as they walked to the counter.

"Good morning." The trader smiled.

"Morning," Mallory said. "Do you sell coffee?"

"Does it have any other name?" the trader asked.

"No. At least not as far as I know," Mallory said. "It's a type of beverage."

"Sorry. I can't help you there. Anything else you're looking for?"

"A hunting bow," Ryan said.

"Now that I do have." The trader led the way to where several hunting bows were displayed. "We have these basic quality ones for eight gold pieces that do a low damage of one, normal damage of three and a crit of four. Or this superior quality hunting bow for twenty gold pieces. The low damage on this one is two, normal damage is three and the crit is five."

Ryan ran his hand over the superior quality bow. "It's too expensive."

Mallory took out the mage robe. "Would you be interested in buying this?"

The trader looked the robe over. "If you're interested in buying at least ten gold pieces worth of goods. After the items I've already bought today, I can only afford to give you fifteen gold pieces as well as the goods."

"Did you want to get the more expensive one?" Mallory asked.

Ryan stared at it a moment longer before shaking his head. "The basic one will do for now. We'll have a look at what else we can buy."

The trader gestured broadly. "Browse as long as

you wish and let me know if I can help you with anything else."

They wandered around the shop, pausing to examine some of the goods. Mallory found throwing knives and gathered eight for her brother. They were only a copper piece each so they needed to find something else. She continued wandering. There were plenty of things she would have liked to buy, but they were out of her price range. They finally decided on a two metre square piece of canvas that was a gold piece, to replace the one they'd cut up, and a thick, white blanket that was five silver pieces. Unable to find something to use up the last two copper pieces, they bought a flask of lantern oil for five copper pieces and handed over three copper pieces along with the mage robe so she could receive fifteen gold pieces instead of silver and copper too.

The trader smiled. "Thank you for your business. If you bring your oil flask back when it's empty it can be refilled at a reduced cost."

Chapter Nine

Returning his smile, Mallory helped Ryan gather their new gear and headed outside, putting the items she carried in a pannier.

Danae stared at the harbour. "I suppose I should…" Her voice trailed off.

"We'll go with you and see what ships are in," Mallory said.

Danae nodded, silently leading Augusta to the harbour and tying her up to a hitching post there. Another two horses were already tied up at the hitching post and they left Bobbi with Augusta as they made their way to the building at the start of the dock.

They waited as the man behind the counter dealt with two other queries before he could help them. Danae stepped forward, glancing out the door before she spoke. "I'm needing passage to Simria for myself and a horse."

The man consulted the large, leather-bound book in front of him. "The next ship available that transports livestock will be leaving in four weeks. Sixth day of the third month. Do you want me to make a booking for you?"

"I don't know. I wasn't expecting it to be so far away," Danae said.

"Come back when you know." The man glanced at the book. "There's currently plenty of space available on it."

Danae wandered outside, looking dazed.

Ryan clapped her on the shoulder. "We're not about to desert you here. You can stick with us until there's a ship available. Or maybe they have one in Wildebay that will be leaving soon."

Danae shook her head. "Passenger ships don't leave from there. Only cargo ships and fishing boats."

Mallory smiled when Fang ran towards them, barking to catch their attention. "I think she wants us to follow."

Ryan slipped his arm around Mallory's waist. "Okay. Let's see where she takes us."

They followed Fang further along the dock to where Callum and Brodie were fishing. Three fish lay on the dock behind them while the trousers were spread out beside Brodie to dry in the sun. As they reached the edge of the dock, Smudge surfaced, squeaking up at them.

"Who caught the fish?" Ryan asked.

Callum laughed. "Technically, I caught two."

"Smudge only put that fish on your line because you let it go when he tried to give it to you," Brodie said.

"It still counted as a catch when it came to XP," Callum said.

Mallory laughed. "Now that sounds like a cheat to me."

Ryan grinned. "And cheats are always good to exploit."

Brodie's gaze was drawn to Danae. "When are you leaving?"

"Not for another four weeks," Danae said.

Brodie frowned, his expression almost immediately brightening. "You're staying with us for another four weeks?"

"Of course she's staying with us until she can catch a ship," Callum said. "Did you think we'd leave her on her own?"

"No, but…" Brodie shrugged. "What are we going

to do? Should we take you to Simria? What if you can't catch a ship over to Merrow for ages."

"It's not that I can't catch a ship," Danae said. "It's catching a ship that also transports livestock. That won't be a problem when I go to Merrow. If I can't find a ship that will let me take Augusta, my father can send her over later. That's if he's going to let me take her with me. He might want to keep her." She smiled. "I'm hoping to convince him I need her more than he does."

Mallory looked around the group as a thought struck her. "We didn't sort out somewhere to meet up with Welby." She faced her brother. "Oh, I nearly forgot." She took out the eight throwing knives she'd placed in her satchel since they'd felt awkward to carry. They were obviously not a weapon suited to her class.

"Throwing knives?" He counted them. "Enough to fill my belt." He slotted them into place. "Hell yeah."

"What are we going to do about finding Welby?" Callum wound in the line, setting the reel aside to help Smudge onto the dock. "Must be near on an hour."

Brodie wound in his line. "What are we going to do with the leftover bait?"

Fang and Smudge sat at his feet, Smudge holding out a paw. Both of them looked up at him.

Ryan chuckled. "I guess that's your answer."

Mallory glanced at the three fish. "We should have brought the basket over." She picked up the wet trousers. "You can carry the fish, I'll carry these."

Brodie shared the bait between Fang and Smudge. "I don't know what these fish are called, but they're different to those gold fin we caught on the shore out from Buckneth."

"They're silver tails," Danae said. "The tail is like silver streamers when you see it under the water. They're ready for eating when they're between twenty to fifty centimetres. You won't find them far off the shore."

Ryan picked up one of the fish. "So they're about average size."

"Should keep Smudge and Fang fed for a day or two." Callum picked up a fish, leaving the last one for Brodie to collect. "And they're edible."

Danae nodded as they headed towards the traders, collecting the horse and donkey along the way. "They're nicest grilled. Or at least they are the way my mother does them."

Reaching the traders, they found Welby waiting out the front. "You were gone when I realised we hadn't set a place to meet up." Welby shrugged. "It's not that large a village so I wasn't worried about tracking you down."

Mallory hung the wet trousers from the side of one of the panniers, making sure they wouldn't wet the contents or drag in the dirt. Danae had packed away her clothes earlier. Finished the chore, she turned to Welby. "With how you can read tracks I doubt you ever lose anybody."

"It's different in a built up area than it is anywhere else." Welby looked at each of them, his gaze returning to Mallory. "You ready to go? That's if you're willing to escort me home."

After a glance around, she nodded. "Yeah. We'll take you home. We want to see what's at the end of Brodie's map." She also wanted to complete the quest. They needed every experience point possible if they were to gain a character level before they returned to their world.

They headed east along the coast, passing the rowdy tavern. She looked at each of the buildings they passed and glanced at the numerous people out and about. It was far busier than Buckneth and the waterfront was busier than anywhere in Wayholt. She couldn't help wondering how busy the capital would be if this was only a village. Or even a town like Ursen, Simria or Lilica. She had no idea of the names of any other towns. They were the only ones she'd been told about on Ruby Isle.

Leaving the village behind, Mallory looked out to sea. "Do we stay along the coast the entire way?" It wasn't a bad view.

"We curve inland at one stage, away from a rocky area, then back to the coast again as we come closer to Wildebay," Welby said.

Callum glanced around. "It seems pretty quiet."

"Sometimes it is," Welby said.

"And other times?" Ryan asked.

Welby shrugged. "Depends."

Mallory hesitated. Did she really want to know what it depended on? Glancing around, she noticed no one else looked like they were about to ask. She also noticed that Danae was leading Augusta instead of riding her. "You don't have to walk because we are."

"That's all right. I don't mind walking," Danae said.

"We should get horses," Brodie said.

"We should wait until we go to the mainland," Ryan said. "It'll probably be expensive enough getting us, Bob, Smudge and Fang over there."

"When are you travelling to the mainland?" Welby asked.

Mallory shrugged. "When we've done a few more things on Ruby Isle."

"When we've finished all our quests," Brodie said.

Mallory opened her mouth to tell her brother that wasn't necessary. She closed it. There were probably some things he needed to learn himself.

Brodie glanced over his shoulder. "I thought we were going to get something at the bakers before we left the village."

Ryan shrugged. "We'll be back by tomorrow at the latest. We can buy something then."

Chapter Ten

Mallory caught sight of a large creature surfacing out to sea. "You have whales?"

Welby looked in the same direction. "That's a killer whale. Very territorial. They're worse during breeding season. They've been known to sink ships that have come too close."

"Not like killer whales in our world then," Callum said.

Mallory eyed the creature. Was a ship the only way to the mainland?

They lapsed into silence, one of them occasionally speaking, Callum once asking if they should gather herbs. They ended up deciding to see what was at the end of the map first. Brodie, in particular, insisting they keep space in the panniers for his treasure. They were over halfway to Wildebay when they stumbled upon six goblins, one of them a couple of inches taller than the rest. Not that it gave him a height advantage since the shorter ones were only four feet tall. The dark green creatures appeared as shocked as they were to stumble upon someone. It didn't take them long to raise their clubs and snarl, showing sharp teeth. The goblins ran towards them, their ragged clothes flapping in the breeze off the ocean that was again visible.

Mallory fumbled, nearly dropping her wand, launching a fireball at the taller goblin. She quickly threw a second one at him. He collapsed on the ground, but not soon enough that she was able to attack the second goblin that had come after her. She tried to block with her dagger as she launched a fireball at him. His cudgel struck her arm and she drew in a sharp breath, pain radiating through her. Before she had the chance to attack him again, he was pierced by an arrow and a throwing knife, dropping to the ground to land on her feet. She stumbled backwards.

"You okay?" Ryan reached for her.

Nodding, Mallory checked her stats. "I lost four health." It wasn't enough to make it worth drinking a health potion, but with how little health she had, she was now down to eleven. She should have been paying attention to her surroundings, not admiring them.

Callum held out the waterskin of health tea. "Drink a cupful of this."

She took a large mouthful, the pain instantly ebbing. "Thanks." She continued to drink, glad she hadn't had any water recently or it would have been more of an effort to drink an entire cup of liquid.

Brodie held up a pair of goblin boots. "Look what I found."

Mallory laughed. "I would have been surprised if we hadn't found any."

Ryan held up a pair of goblin boots too. "Second pair."

By the time they'd finished searching the goblins, they'd found six copper coins and given one to Welby who'd helped, three pairs of goblin boots and twenty grams of beef jerky that Brodie grabbed and began to eat. He shared it with Fang and Smudge, muttering about not having bought anything at the bakers earlier.

As they continued on to Wildebay, Mallory checked everyone's stats, relieved to find she'd been the only one to lose any health. "You're falling behind with XP, Ryan."

"The goblins were too close to use my hunting

bow," Ryan said. "And I'm not that far behind. Only three XP behind you and Callum."

"Yeah, but we're five XP behind Brodie," Mallory said.

Ryan shrugged. "I'll get there eventually." He glanced at Brodie. "It's not that big a deal.

Mallory returned his grin.

"Bet you won't be saying that if I reach character level one first," Brodie said.

Ryan shrugged again. "We're not that far behind."

Ahead, Mallory saw the buildings of Wildebay. It wasn't until they drew closer that she realised they were warehouses and a granary, a tavern beyond them. The wharf was diagonally across from the tavern, the area crowded and noisy. The tavern was also where the road split in two, one section going along the waterfront and the other veering away, but also headed in the same direction. "Is this village as large as Surith?"

"Not quite. If you don't count visitors, our population is probably half a dozen less than Surith's." Welby paused a moment. "Maybe a dozen less since the attack on our village." He gestured to the road that went along the waterfront. "Most of the shops are along there. A few on the side streets."

"Where can we get something to eat?" Brodie asked.

"Either in the tavern or from the baker. To visit the baker take the second road on the right and then the first on the left when you go along the waterfront." Again Welby gestured to the road that went along the coast. "I shouldn't be too long. Half an hour at the most. I need to talk to some people so I can learn what happened. Shall we meet in front of the tavern? Then I can guide you to the location on your map. If you're willing to go so late in the day."

Mallory nodded. It wasn't like they hadn't travelled around the countryside in the dark before. "We'll meet you there."

The moment Welby had walked away, Brodie spoke. "Can we visit the baker? Callum has a copper piece left over. We might be able to get something with it. And we don't have to spend that gold piece at Surith. We can spend it here."

"Half an hour isn't going to give us much time to cook anything so we should probably see what the baker has," Ryan said.

"We've got seven apples and jerky left." Mallory somehow managed not to grin when she made the suggestion, glancing at her brother.

Brodie groaned. "That's not gonna be filling."

"We could always see what the prices are like," Callum suggested.

"Okay." Mallory led the way along the road, glancing at the ships at anchor before she checked the journal icon that was in the corner of her vision. It was a notification about discovering a new location. She smiled. Another ten experience points. Her smile widened into a grin as she realised she'd also gained experience points for finishing a quest.

Journey Home: You escorted the hunter safely home. You were rewarded with a promise from the hunter that he would guide you to the location on your map. You also earned twenty experience points each. She checked all their stats. She was a little over halfway to her next CAS point. "Danni, you're only two XP off gaining another CAS point."

Danae grinned. "I noticed that. If we don't earn any XP by the time we reach the location on the map, I'll collect some herbs."

Mallory glanced to her left as the road veered away from the coastline, large sand dunes visible behind the buildings on the left hand side of the road. They passed a general store and a fishmonger. There was a secondhand shop on the right. She was tempted to go inside and see what they had for sale. Reminding herself of how little money they had, she kept walking, passing a rope maker and another fishmonger. The building on the right was a house, a rooster walking in front of it.

Fang barked, chasing after the rooster.

"Fang! No." Brodie ran after her.

Before Fang could catch the rooster, it threw a fireball at her. With a yelp, she tumbled backwards. The rooster threw a second fireball at her.

Brodie grabbed Fang, picking her up. "Now that would make an awesome pet."

Ryan frowned. "Can I smell singed feathers?"

Mallory nodded. "I can smell them too."

The rooster took a step away, turning into a young man. A naked, young man. He dashed for the house. "The charm didn't work again. It's meant to instantly clothe me." The front door slammed shut behind him.

Mallory stared at the closed door of the small timber house. "Well, that was unexpected."

"It is a village with more than the usual amount of shapeshifters in it," Danae said.

"Does that mean there are shapeshifters in every village?" Callum asked.

"Not every village, but a lot of them," Danae said.

The young man stepped outside, leaving the door open, now dressed in brown trousers and a green shirt that matched his eyes, his sandy blond hair sticking up in all directions. He tried to pat it down, but it seemed to have a mind of its own. He looked to be around Ryan's age, possibly twenty. "I am not a pet. I'm a shapeshifter."

Brodie looked him up and down. "Who can turn into a chicken?"

"There's nothing wrong with being able to turn into a chicken." The young man drew himself upright. He was only as tall as Mallory. "And it's a rooster, not a chicken."

A man who'd been walking towards them stopped, making a production of sniffing the air. "Hey, Roast. Smells like you nearly cooked yourself again. Which is a feat in itself since that spell isn't actually meant to set anything on fire."

Roast glared at the other man who appeared to be a few years older than him. "Stop calling me that. How many times do I need to tell you that isn't my name and I don't like it?"

The second man grinned. "I'll stop calling you Roast when you stop trying to be a mage and be something more sensible."

Chapter Eleven

When Mallory spotted Roast drawing out what looked like a twig from his pocket and aim it at the other man, she interrupted, worried a fight was about to break out in front of her. "What is your name? I'm Mallory." She held out her hand.

Roast stared at her hand a moment before putting the twig in his left hand and shaking hers. "Art. Short for Arthur, but my father is called Arthur too so it gets confusing if we're both called that."

"You should be thanking me. Roast is an improvement on Art."

Mallory faced the other young man. "And your name?"

"Erym." He shook her hand.

"And you're complaining about Art's name," Brodie muttered.

Mallory barely managed not to laugh.

"At least I know better than to be a mage. He should become a warrior like me and level up his unarmed," Erym said.

"You're a rooster too?" Callum asked.

Erym looked offended. "I am a duck."

"That's so much better," Ryan said dryly.

Once more Mallory struggled not to laugh. She turned to Roast. "What if you focused on a different element to fire?"

"He tried water," Erym said. "Nearly drowned himself. Air had him launching himself into the air where he nearly impaled himself on a tree branch. Everyone has told him to avoid lightning."

Brodie chuckled. "Lightning would probably have them calling you barbequed."

Roast drew out the twig he'd returned to his pocket. "You–"

Mallory interrupted him. "What is that?" She pointed to the twig.

Roast looked at the twig he held before meeting Mallory's gaze. "My wand. I had it specially made so I can use it while I'm in my animal form."

"Which was a waste of time." Erym grinned. "Give up before you singe more than a few feathers and completely roast yourself." He strode away after another grin for Roast.

"I need to do something to make them forget the nickname Roast." Roast sighed. "What I really need is a fire resist amulet."

"Where would you get one of them?" Callum asked.

"Mer Point. There's a mage there who can make amulets and charms. She uses spells to increase the level of her enchanting so she can make higher level amulets and charms. It's too dangerous to go that far on my own. I tried to hire someone to take me, but they wanted too much. The most I can offer is five silver pieces."

Mallory smiled as she saw the journal icon appear in the corner of her vision. It had obviously triggered another quest, especially with the way Brodie was frowning. "How far away is Mer Point?"

"Are you interested?" Roast asked.

Ryan shrugged. "Could be. Depending on how long it'd take to get there and back. We have other things we need to do as well."

"Maybe I have something else you need. You're clearly travellers. What about always having a place to stay when you're in the area? My home isn't very big, but I'd offer you somewhere to sleep whenever you're in this area if you escort me to Mer Point and back. I also need the mage to look at my charm to see what's wrong with it." Roast took a step towards Mallory. "I'm desperate to travel there. If I had more money, I'd offer it to you. But I also need to be able to afford to buy a fire resist amulet. They aren't cheap. And pay the mage to figure out what's wrong with my charm."

Mallory was tempted to take a step away from him. "We can't make a decision until we know how far away Mer Point is."

"It's past Surith," Danae said. "There's a merfolk colony out from it."

"A bit over an hour from Surith," Roast said.

"We might be able to manage it," Mallory said.

Roast grabbed her hand, clinging to it tightly. "You can? You can take me there?"

She dragged her hand from his grip. "I didn't say that."

Ryan moved closer to her. "We have somewhere to go this afternoon and need to be somewhere else by midday tomorrow. It will depend on how long everything takes today. As it is, we won't be back before dark."

Brodie stood on the other side of Mallory. "And we need to see what the baker has for sale. I'm hungry."

"I have half a cake that my sister made for me. She works for the baker," Roast said.

Mallory nearly groaned when Brodie's expression brightened. "We can't promise you anything. We have other commitments to deal with." She doubted Brodie would want to give up on his treasure hunt. Although the offer of cake would tempt him.

"No expectations," Roast said. "You can have cake and I'll even make sandwiches. It'll give me more time to convince you."

Brodie turned to Mallory. "Say yes."

Ryan chuckled. "Yeah, say yes, Mallory."

Roast frowned. "Did I say something wrong?"

"Probably something right," Callum said. "Or at least according to Brodie."

Roast directed his question to Brodie. "Will you join me for afternoon tea?"

"Come on, Mal," Brodie pleaded.

She looked at each of her companions. Callum and Danae shrugged, Ryan grinned and Brodie nodded enthusiastically. She faced Roast. "We'll join you for afternoon tea as long as you understand this doesn't mean we'll take you to Mer Point. We have something else to do this afternoon and we don't know if it'll be completed today."

Roast nodded, leading the way inside his house once they'd tied the donkey and horse up out the front. "No pressure. I just want the chance to tell you why I need to learn, as quickly as possible, how to be a mage. I thought I'd have plenty of time to figure it out." He gestured to a timber table with four matching chairs. "Take a seat. I've got a couple of stools I can bring over."

When Roast hurried off through the open doorway of a bedroom, Mallory looked around. The floor was made from timber planks, grains of sand caught in the joins. Several windows let in plenty of light and across from the table was a stone fireplace. To the left of the fireplace was a set of shelves covered in an assortment of crockery and food, a workbench to the right of the fireplace. Against the wall, on either side of the entrance door, were two wooden chests. Both were closed and there was a tall cane basket with a lid beside the one on the right.

Mallory sat at the table, wondering what Roast did for a living to have a house that had timber flooring rather than dirt or rough cut stone. While Roast shifted two of the chairs along and set a stool on either side of the table, she read over the new quest. *Singed Feathers: A shapeshifting rooster from Wildebay is in need of an escort to Mer Point. He is offering five silver pieces and a place to stay whenever you and your party are in the area.*

"What is with all the escort missions?" Callum

lowered his voice to ask while Roast rummaged around on the shelves.

"At least they're good XP," Ryan said.

"Are we going to do the quest?" Danae asked.

Mallory shrugged. "We don't know how long it'll take to follow Brodie's map. Just because it isn't far away doesn't mean it won't take ages to get what's at the end of it. For all we know it might lead to a dungeon we need to complete."

"I didn't think about that," Brodie said. "Another goblin dungeon would be good. Look at the amount of jerky I got from the last one. I'm about halfway through it so more would be great."

Mallory grinned. "I swear you only ever think about food."

"I do not," Brodie protested.

"We won't be able to stay long," Ryan said to Roast when he put wooden plates with cake in front of them. "We have to meet someone else soon."

Roast looked over his shoulder as he headed back to the workbench. "It's for Merry. The dark forces took her along with five other people. How can I go after her when all I can do is singe my feathers?"

Chapter Twelve

"They took Welby's brother too," Mallory said. "He's trying to find out where they took them."

"Cutthroat Harbour. They loaded them onto a ship and headed west. Someone overheard a couple of the sailors talking." Roast put a large wooden plate of sandwiches in the middle of the table. "They were from Cutthroat Harbour and were headed home. I need to travel down there and save Merry before they send the prisoners somewhere else. Like the arena in Hellfire."

"Arena?" Brodie took a sandwich, having already eaten his cake.

Roast sat on a stool. "They pit the slaves against each other and against creatures. Some of the matches are to the death and others are until someone is incapacitated. Which often leads to death."

"There are slaves?" Mallory asked.

"Only in the demonic lands," Danae said. "Although not all demons believe in keeping slaves."

"Mostly the demons that don't live in the demonic lands don't believe in slavery," Roast added.

"So you need to learn how to do magic without killing yourself so you can save your girlfriend from the dark forces which means travelling to a place that sounds like it's the home of pirates," Mallory said.

Roast nodded. "Exactly."

"You need to talk to Welby." Mallory picked up a sandwich, guessing she better have a second one before they were gone.

"Is he going to Mer Point?" Roast asked.

"He's going after his brother," Ryan said. "Sounds like he's probably in the same place as your girlfriend."

Roast frowned. "I heard he'd been captured. That he was one of the five people they took along with his brother and Merry's cousin."

"He's back. We rescued him." Brodie took the last sandwich from the plate.

Roast rose to his feet. "Where is he? I need to see him. I need to ask if he'll help me."

Finished her sandwich, Mallory stood up. "We're meeting him in front of the tavern. But he's busy this afternoon too."

"Oh." Roast's shoulders slumped. "How am I meant to save Merry?"

"We're not about to leave anyone behind when we help Welby rescue his brother," Mallory said. "Even if you can't go after her, we'll help her escape."

"You don't know what she looks like." Roast led the way outside.

"Does Welby know what she looks like?" Danae gathered the reins of her horse.

Roast nodded. "What if she's not with Welby's brother? What if she's somewhere else?" He walked with them towards the tavern.

Mallory wasn't sure what to tell him. She wanted to promise they'd find Merry, no matter what. Things weren't that simple. She was relieved to see Welby walk towards them, a satchel at his side and a bow and quiver at his back.

"I wasn't able to learn anything," Welby said. "Everyone kept telling me to be grateful I escaped."

Mallory nodded towards Roast, not sure if she should call him by his name or his nickname. She supposed Welby would know both. "Then you'll probably be glad to hear what Art has to say."

Welby turned to Roast, not needing to ask him anything before he repeated the information he'd told Mallory and her companions. Welby stared at him for a moment before turning to Mallory. "I'll return to Buckneth with you."

"Okay," Mallory said. Before she had a chance to say anything else, Brodie interrupted.

"Are we going to follow the map now?"

Welby brushed his hand against his satchel. "I have everything I need."

Roast continued to follow them as they walked along the road in the direction they'd come from. "Will you be coming back here?"

"We're not going far," Welby said. "We should be back this evening. Tomorrow morning at the latest."

"Will you come and see me when you return?" Roast asked.

After a glance at her companions, Mallory nodded. "When we're back. Then we'll talk about possibly visiting Mer Point."

Roast grabbed hold of her hand. "Thank you. Call on me no matter the hour you return. You're welcome to stay the night. Or whatever might be left of it." He hurried off before anyone could speak.

"We really need to finish up following this map today," Mallory said. "It almost seems wrong going after whatever it leads to when Roast needs help."

Ryan slipped an arm around her waist, the lead rope of the donkey in his other hand. "We'll give it today. If we haven't figured out where it leads, then we'll do it another day."

"That's not fair," Brodie exclaimed. "Why not make the wagoner wait to go home?"

"I need to head south too," Welby said.

Mallory breathed out heavily, trying not to think of all the things that needed to be done. "We have a lantern and a couple of hours until dark. We'll manage somehow."

"Two and a half hours until dark," Welby corrected.

"Plenty of time. We bought lantern oil earlier." Mallory wished she felt as confident as she'd sounded. When no one else spoke, she checked her journal, the icon having been in the corner of her vision since Roast had shared his information with Welby. The quest for Welby had updated. *Captured By Hellions: The hunter has learned his brother was taken to Cutthroat Harbour along with other prisoners.* She stared at the name of the destination. It still sounded like a place filled with pirates. A lot of pirates. Were they a high enough level to take on lots of pirates? If they all had thirty health points like the one they'd faced earlier, they probably needed to do a bit of grinding first. Or a lot of grinding.

They continued along the coastline, at times

walking along the beach, at others along the sparse grass that edged the sand. It wasn't until they reached the river, turning south east to travel along it that the journal icon appeared in the corner of Mallory's vision. Expecting it to be a new location, she checked.

"No! That's not fair," Brodie exclaimed.

Mallory read the message aloud. "The quest Turn A Blind Eye has expired and is no longer available. It may have been completed by another party or individual."

"I wanted to do that quest," Brodie complained.

"I guess they can't remain available forever," Callum said.

"What about the other ones?" Brodie asked. "The staff. The ancient crypt."

"I wouldn't mind if someone did the coffee quest," Callum said. "I could do with a coffee right now."

"What are we going to do about the other quests?" Brodie demanded. "The staff one is three days old. It might expire next."

"We got Turn A Blind Eye the first day we arrived," Mallory said.

"It's still not-" Brodie broke off when an arrow flew past, barely missing him.

"Take cover, they're hiding behind the trees."

Welby ran in the direction the arrow had come from, crossing the ground in a zigzag fashion.

"Ride for cover, Danni." Ryan ran towards the trees, tugging on Bobbi's lead.

Danae mounted her horse, holding out a hand to Brodie who she helped swing up behind her. They rode for the cover of the trees.

A body crashed into Mallory and she hit the ground, the air knocked from her lungs.

Callum rolled off her. "Stay below the height of the grass or you'll be shot."

"I can't take them out while I'm lying in the grass." She tried to raise her head so she could see what was happening.

Callum pushed her back down. "Everyone else made it to the tree line. The archers were focusing on us. Put your head up and you're likely to be impaled."

"It's safe," Ryan called out. "There were two bandits."

This time Mallory was able to rise. "Who got them?"

"We did." Brodie stepped out from amongst the trees. "Me and Danni. They seemed a little harder than usual."

"Sure that wasn't because it was only two of you taking them on?" Callum asked.

"Must have been level two bandits. I earned four XP for each one," Danae said.

"I didn't think to check that," Brodie said.

Mallory checked the stats, smiling to see Danae had gained a CAS point. The half-elf now had three spare points. "What are you going to put your points into?"

"I'm trying to decide if I add more points to glassblowing so I can make my own vials or put them in alchemy," Danae said.

Ryan handed five copper coins to Mallory. "We got six arrows as well."

"We ready to keep going?" Brodie asked.

Chapter Thirteen

Mallory returned Ryan's grin before turning to her brother. "Yeah, we can keep going."

Further along the river, Welby showed them where to cross. Mallory stared at the calf deep water. "Is it okay to walk through this barefoot? I don't want to get my boots wet so close to dark."

Smudge dived into the water where it was deeper, surfacing before going under again. He made excited little yips when he came up once more.

Barking excitedly, Fang joined him.

Callum sat on the riverbank. "Looks safe to me." He pulled off his boots and socks, rolling up the legs of his trousers.

Everyone sat beside him, doing the same. It didn't take long to cross and once their footwear was back on, they continued south east along the river. It was about half an hour before dark when Fang began to growl and Smudge made soft warning sounds. They tied the reins and lead rope to a tree, readying weapons as they crept closer.

Mallory peered around a tree. "It's not treasure, it's a bandit camp." She spotted four of them. One of the bandits was stirring something in a pot over a cooking fire, another was sharpening his sword and two were playing a dice game, arguing with each other. There were three canvas tents on the far side of the clearing.

Brodie, who stood beside Mallory looking around the other side of the tree, whispered, "I was sure it was a treasure map."

"It might have been a map of where the pirate was to meet up with his friends," Danae said.

"That makes sense," Ryan said.

Brodie stared at the camp. "I was really hoping it was a treasure map."

"Retreat." Mallory moved several metres back from the edge of the clearing, gesturing for everyone to join her. "What's the plan?"

"It took two arrows and three throwing knives to take out each of those bandits we encountered earlier," Danae said.

"I should be able to take one out with two shots before they have a chance to move," Welby said. "I could have taken them out with a single shot if the hellions hadn't stolen my good hunting bow."

"You take the one cooking," Ryan said.

Brodie glanced towards the clearing. "Don't let him fall in the cooking pot."

Mallory barely managed to smother her laughter. "I'll attack the one sharpening his sword."

"I'll help you," Ryan said. "Brodie can help Callum attack the one on the left who's playing dice and Danni can focus on the one on the right." He looked around the group. "Everyone happy with that?"

Nodding, Callum turned to Smudge. "Guard Augusta and Bobbi."

Smudge hurried over to where they were tied up.

"Go with him, Fang," Brodie said.

Once Fang had followed Smudge, they headed to the edge of the clearing. Ryan stood beside Mallory. "You count. You're the only one with a spare hand."

Mallory nodded, holding up her closed fist where everyone could see it. She raised three fingers, one at a time, throwing a fireball at the bandit sharpening his sword once she reached three. He was partway across the clearing, and she was drawing her dagger in case he reached her, when her fourth fireball took him out. Heart pounding, she glanced around the clearing seeing that the rest of the bandits were dead. She lowered her wand, heart beating rapidly.

Brodie stepped into the clearing. "So much for X marks the spot." An arrow struck him high on his left arm and he stumbled behind a tree.

"There's someone in the tents," Ryan said. "Maybe more than one."

"How are we meant to get them?" Brodie pulled the arrow from his arm, crying out in pain. "I think that was a bad idea."

"Luckily it's only a minor health wound. I'll get the health tea." Danae was gone before anyone could protest.

Mallory checked Brodie's health. The arrow had cost him four health points. "I could throw fireballs at the tents, but they don't seem to burn things."

"You need a different sort of spell for that," Welby said.

"That doesn't help right now." Mallory eyed the tent, unable to see anyone. The sound of soft footsteps had her turning away from the camp.

Danae returned with the waterskin, giving it to Brodie. "There are three doses left once Brodie has one. I'm going to have to find somewhere to make a new batch soon."

"Someone's trying to sneak out." Callum fired an arrow.

"I'm going to circle around the back to make sure they don't cut the canvas and escape that way," Ryan said.

"I'll go with you." Mallory turned to Danae. "Fire some arrows into the tents to keep them distracted."

Ryan grinned. "You never know, you might get lucky and hit one." He led the way through the trees.

Mallory followed, regularly glancing into the clearing. Nothing moved. She also heard nothing other than the regular thunk of Danae's arrows.

Ryan stepped to the side. "One's escaping. See him?"

Now Ryan was out of the way, she could see the bandit crawling out the back of the tent, a dagger in hand. She launched a fireball at him and he ducked inside. "I really don't want to have to enter the tents."

Ryan took the lead again. "You aren't entering those tents. You don't have a revive and your health is low."

"You're not going to waste your revive going into a tent."

Ryan stopped directly behind the tents. He kept his voice low. "I'm entering the middle one, the one the bandit was trying to escape from. Cover me."

"How am I meant to do that?"

Ryan shrugged. "I'm sure you'll think of something." He started to move away.

She grabbed hold of his arm, her gaze drawn to the ropes keeping the tent upright. Her lips slowly curved into a smile. "I did think of something. We cut the ropes."

"Wait back here. I'll get them." Once again Ryan started to step away.

She drew him back. "We'll do it together. The rest can cover us. First tent I'll cut the ropes on the left and you do the ones on the right. We'll do that to each of the tents, working our way across."

Ryan held her gaze for a moment before he nodded, drawing her close. "Don't get yourself killed." His lips briefly met hers before he drew away heading for the first tent.

She hurried after him, striding towards the ropes on the left of the tent. After a glance at him, she nodded, seeing that he was in place. She sliced through the ropes. The tent collapsed in on itself, no one protesting and none of the forms inside it moving.

They moved to the next tent, the one that they knew contained at least a single bandit. Again she glanced at Ryan before slicing through the ropes.

Two figures tried to escape, fighting against the canvas that closed in on them.

Ryan ran to the next tent. "Don't worry about them."

She joined him at the next tent, slicing through the ropes. A single figure tried to escape. Ryan attacked through the canvas, staining it red.

"Mallory, behind you," Callum called out.

Mallory turned, automatically raising her wand, launching a fireball at the bandit that came towards her, sword up. The fireball struck, three arrows piercing him at the same time. He collapsed on the ground half a metre from her. The other bandit was on the ground in front of the tent, arrows and throwing knives having ended his life. She lowered her wand seconds before Ryan's arms went around her, crushing her against him.

"You're okay?" His arms tightened around her.

She checked his stats, finding he had full health. "Yeah, I'm okay." She checked the rest of the stats. Only her and Brodie weren't at full health. "We're all okay."

Brodie took a step into the clearing, glancing around. "I think it's clear." He touched his fingers to where the arrow had struck him, leaving a tear behind in his shirt.

Ryan glanced skywards. "There's not much light left in the day. We better see what we can find so we can head back to Wildebay."

Chapter Fourteen

Noticing the journal icon in the corner of her vision, Mallory checked. "We gained fifteen XP for finding a bandit camp."

"Cool." Brodie tested the food cooking in the pot. He made a face. "I can do better than this."

"It must be bad then," Ryan said.

"Very funny," Brodie muttered.

By the time they'd finished searching they had a bedroll, a tent, a grey pair of trousers and a brown pair, a pair of leather boots Brodie was excited to find fit him, a short sword, eight arrows, a stamina potion, twelve silver pieces, sixteen copper pieces, a ruby necklace, two dice, a kitchen knife, a ladle, one kilo of flour in a calico bag, six potatoes, a bottle of cooking oil and half a dozen eggs. There was also a wooden chest they couldn't take with them. Brodie insisted on bringing the cooking pot, carrying it by the handle, the food still in it.

Bobbi, who Ryan had fetched along with Augusta and the companion animals, stood patiently while they packed everything in the panniers. The bedroll and tent went on her back, both rolled up. Once everything was packed, Ryan gestured to the pot Brodie carried. "Looks like it was a treasure map after all."

Brodie glared at Callum and Mallory when they laughed.

"The pirate had probably been invited to help them with a job," Welby said. "They gave him a map to their base. For him to have hidden the map it might have been for a large job he didn't want anyone else to learn about."

Mallory eyed the panniers the donkey carried. "You don't think we're making her carry too much, do you?"

"She's capable of carrying about fifty kilos," Welby said. "You've a little way to go yet. But if you do reach her limit, donkeys are capable of pulling more than they are of carrying. She could easily pull three hundred kilos on flat ground. Less if you're expecting her to go up hills."

"We don't have a cart," Callum said.

"You could cut two poles and attach them to the panniers and string a canvas between them." Welby gestured to the panniers as he spoke.

"That's a good idea," Brodie said.

Welby took a lantern out of his satchel. "Better light your lantern and we'll get started for Wildebay. Not much daylight left."

Mallory lit the lantern, carrying it as they headed towards the river and along its bank. They took a break when they were along the coast and ate the stew in the pot Brodie carried, sharing it with the companion animals. He rinsed it and the crockery in the ocean, scrambling back when a coastal crab came out of the waves towards him.

Callum laughed, firing an arrow at the crab.

"I'd like to see you come face to face with a coastal crab," Brodie muttered, keeping hold of the pot and crockery.

Ryan ran forward, his sword held ready. "They're easier to deal with than bandits."

The moment the crab rose, Mallory threw a fireball at it. Beside her, Callum and Danae fired arrows at the same time. The crab collapsed before Brodie had a chance to attack. Even Ryan didn't get the chance to attack.

They ended up with some crabmeat that Fang and

Smudge happily ate, even after the stew they'd eaten. They were down to the last fish for them.

Brodie put the pot and crockery in a pannier. "Let's hope that's it for attacks on the way back to Wildebay. I could do with some sleep so I have the chance to heal." He picked Fang up.

"You're not the only one." Mallory picked up the lantern she'd set on the sand while they'd been eating.

After the companion animals had been put on top of the bedroll and tent Bobbi carried, they continued along the coastline. They needed to stop three more times to take out crabs. The first time there was two and the next two times there was only one. As they entered Wildebay, Mallory checked her stats. She had eighty-seven of the hundred and six she needed to gain her next CAS point. Brodie was ten points ahead of her and Callum only one point ahead. Ryan had eighty-one points. The three of them would need to gather herbs on the way to Surith tomorrow. It'd give them resources for the wagoner to sell and hopefully help them gain a CAS point each.

"You have somewhere to stay the night?" Welby asked.

"We'll stay with Roast," Brodie said.

"Art," Mallory corrected him.

"Roast isn't that bad a name," Brodie protested.

The lantern Mallory carried flickered out. Welby's remained lit.

Welby gestured towards the lantern. "Don't worry about refilling it. I'll walk you to Roast's place to save you worrying about it for now."

"Thanks." Mallory was surprised to find the village was fairly well-lit with people wandering about and lights on in the buildings they passed, some of them with lit lanterns at the front door. "Does this place ever sleep?"

"Sailors tend to want to spend their money when they're ashore," Welby said.

"I don't blame them," Brodie muttered. "Isn't food meant to be terrible on a ship?"

Mallory smiled at her brother's complaint. Reaching Roast's place, she stopped by the front door. "We're going to Mer Point tomorrow. The wagoner will be spending another night in Surith so we'll have time to take Art to Mer Point and bring him home. Even if we need to spend another night here before we return to Surith the next day to escort the wagoner home."

"I plan to ask a few more questions tomorrow now I have more information and see if I can borrow a horse for the journey. There are a couple of people who owe me favours."

The door burst open and Roast stood in the doorway, a lantern on the table behind him. "You'll take me to Mer Point tomorrow?"

Mallory nodded.

Roast grabbed her hand, shaking it enthusiastically. "Thank you. So much. Did you want to stay here tonight? We can leave with the sunrise. I can take your horse and donkey to the inn where you can have them stabled for the night. They normally charge two silver pieces an animal, but I'm sure I can get it for half that. My family owns one of the cargo agencies and we always make sure they have the best possible ale and wine."

Welby glanced at Roast before turning to Mallory. "I'll see you when you've returned from Mer Point." He nodded to Roast. "He knows where I live."

"Thanks for helping us find the location on the map," Mallory said. Her thanks were echoed by those of her companions.

"Thanks for escorting me home." With another nod, Welby strode away.

Roast looked at each of them. "Want me to organise stabling? You can stay here and get settled in. Set up wherever you want in the main room. Have something to eat if you're hungry." He glanced over his shoulder towards the shelves in the corner.

Mallory nodded. Bobbi and Augusta had to stay somewhere. She handed over two silver pieces, shaking her head when Danae had been about to pay for Augusta. "You're a member of our party too."

Once the gear and companion animals were off the horse and donkey, Roast led them down the road while they got sorted. Mallory refilled the lantern, one of the flasks now empty, and they discovered an outhouse out the back. They also rolled the dice to see who'd get to sleep on what, Brodie having put them in his belt pouch earlier.

Mallory handed the dice to Danae, having rolled nine. "Your turn."

"I have blankets." Danae glanced at the rolled up blankets that had been on Augusta, leaning against a bundle wrapped in a blanket and tied with a rope that had also been on the horse.

"They're not as comfortable as the bedroll," Callum said.

Danae took the dice from Mallory, the last person needing to roll. "Thank you." She rolled the dice. They came to a stop, showing a two and a four.

Brodie victory punched the air. "Hell yeah. I get first choice." He dropped onto the bedroll spread out against the wall. His expression fell when Danae looked at the bedroll wistfully. He slowly rose to his feet. "You have it, Danni."

"It's all right. You got first pick." Danae smiled. "Maybe I'll be the lucky one tomorrow night."

"You sure?" Brodie asked.

Danae nodded, her smile widening. "Yes, but thank you." She turned to Mallory. "And thank you for including me."

Mallory returned the half-elf's smile. "You're one of our party."

"Yeah," Brodie added. "You're one of us."

Danae's smile slowly widened. "I like the sound of that."

"Let's get the rest of the bedding set up." Ryan grabbed a blanket and shook it out.

They were stretched out on the various blankets and the bedroll when Roast returned. Callum had the feather pillow and Brodie was eating a piece of cake, Fang sitting beside him and begging for crumbs.

Chapter Fifteen

Mallory sat on the pale blue blanket and wrote the date in her notebook, staring at it for a moment. Day Seven, Second Month, 514 (7 days on Inadon). It seemed impossible that they'd spent so few days on Inadon. Smiling, she thought back over the day before writing in the notebook.

"Can I get you anything else?" Roast asked.

"We're all good," Ryan said.

"You'd let me know if you needed something?" Roast asked.

Finished, Mallory closed her notebook. "You can stop worrying. We'll take you to Mer Point."

"Will you let me go with you when you travel to Cutthroat Harbour?" Roast asked.

Ryan shrugged. "Guess that depends on how our journey to Mer Point turns out. Have you considered that the mage might not be able to help you?"

"She will," Roast said. "She's known for her amulets and charms."

"I hope she can help you." Mallory returned everything to her satchel. "But we won't be taking you south with us if you can't defend yourself. We'd be worried about getting you killed."

"I'm not useless," Roast argued.

"Have you ever faced a hellion before?" Ryan asked.

"Yes. I was here when they attacked," Roast said.

"What happened?" Callum asked.

Roast looked away. "I didn't have a fire resist amulet."

"You roasted yourself." Brodie held his fingers out to Fang who licked them clean.

"It wasn't that bad," Roast protested.

Mallory sighed. "How about we wait and see what happens. We'll talk about it after we return from Mer Point."

Roast nodded. "Let me know if you need anything through the night. There's an outhouse behind my place and fresh water for drinking in the covered jug on the workbench."

"Thank you." Mallory didn't bother telling him they'd already found the outhouse as she lay back on the blanket, wishing she could have a shower. Maybe there'd be time for a wash in the ocean on the way to Surith tomorrow.

"Someone going to put that lantern out?" Brodie asked once Roast was in the bedroom, the door closed. "I'm the furthest from the table."

Ryan, who was by the fire, the only one without a blanket to pull over him if the night should grow cool, rose to his feet and covered the short distance to the table. "Ready?"

"Yeah." Mallory closed her eyes, drawing the thin blanket up, her reply echoed by her companions. She opened her eyes when she heard Ryan return to the blanket beside her. "You sure you'll be warm enough without one of the thin blankets over you?"

Ryan was on his side, facing her, his smile visible in the flickering light from the fireplace. "Why not come a little closer and share your blanket if you're worried?"

"He can put more wood on the fire if he gets cold," Brodie muttered. "Now shut up and let me sleep."

Mallory laughed softly, lifting the edge of her blanket, her gaze on Ryan.

Grinning, he moved closer, draping his arm across her waist as he closed his eyes.

She fell asleep to the sound of the crackling fire, the warmth of Ryan's arm seeping into her, and Smudge making soft noises as he settled in next to Callum who was on the other side of her. She wasn't sure what it was that woke her.

The fire had almost died out and she was alert, her body tense, Ryan's eyes opened as he drew his arm away from her waist. She frowned. "What woke you?"

"Floorboard." Ryan propped himself up on his elbow, looking past her towards the bedroom.

Mallory turned, seeing the door was ajar. She sighed heavily when she spotted Roast peeking through the gap. "We're awake. Or at least we are now."

"No, we're not." Callum drew the pillow over his head. "Go back to sleep."

Roast opened the door further. "It's about an hour until dawn. I could make breakfast. Bacon and eggs."

Brodie sat up, disturbing Fang who yawned widely. "Breakfast?" He frowned. "You can eat eggs? That doesn't make you a cannibal?"

"Being a shapeshifter doesn't make us related to the animal we can shift into," Roast said.

"Unless that bacon and eggs come with coffee, I don't care." Callum's voice was muffled by the pillow.

"It's bacon." Brodie packed up the bedroll, Fang getting in the way.

By the time their gear was packed, they'd visited the outhouse and sat around the table, Roast was serving breakfast. Callum glared at the cup of tea Roast put in front of him, pushing it aside. "We are going to Cape Barren if the next plan doesn't work. I'm living through hell without my morning coffee."

"What about the other many cups you have during the day? Not missing them?" Ryan grinned when his brother glared at him.

"What's coffee?" Roast asked.

"Why does no one know what coffee is around this place?" Callum stabbed the bacon with his fork.

"I'd go without coffee before I'd go without bacon," Brodie said.

Ryan chuckled. "As if you'd choose anything before food."

Roast hurried through his breakfast, leaving them to finish eating while he collected the horse and donkey from the inn, telling them he'd clean up the dishes when he returned.

Mallory glanced at the door, waiting a minute for Roast to leave the vicinity before she spoke. "What are we going to do if he wants to come with us and the fire resist amulet doesn't work?"

"If we got him killed by taking him with us would that upset the guardians?" Brodie asked.

"I don't know." Ryan put down his cutlery, his food finished. "But we can't take him with us if he can't look after himself. It'd be irresponsible to take him to Cutthroat Harbour if he couldn't protect himself."

"What do we do? Drop him home and sneak off before he can follow?" Brodie asked.

"That wouldn't be very nice," Mallory said.

"Neither would getting him killed," Brodie pointed out.

"Are you going to let me go to Cutthroat Harbour with you?" Danae asked.

"If you want to come with us," Brodie said. "You're a good shot and wouldn't get yourself or us killed."

Danae smiled at Brodie, lightly touching him on the arm before she returned to eating her breakfast.

"We won't be able to stay here if we plan to sneak off," Callum said. "And we shouldn't promise him anything either. I bet that would annoy the guardians, lying to him."

"How about we wait and see what happens," Ryan said. "The fire resist amulet might work."

"I hope it does, but we should have a plan in case it doesn't," Mallory said.

"We stay at the inn, or something, and tell him we're thinking about it. Leave him a note," Ryan said.

"Okay. Good." Mallory rose from the table. "I wasn't looking for a detailed plan. Just something basic." She glanced around the house. "We should take our gear outside, speed up the process of getting ready."

They had everything outside by the time Roast returned and quickly put the panniers on Bobbi and saddled Augusta. It was only a little after dawn by the time they were ready to leave. They walked through the village, the harbour already busy and many of the shops open, people wandering the streets.

Chapter Sixteen

Mallory glanced over her shoulder as they left Wildebay behind. "Does the village ever sleep?"

Roast shrugged. "Between the farmers, fishermen, traders and sailors it seems that someone is always awake."

"What about towns and cities? Are they this busy?" Callum asked.

"Busier," Roast said.

At the same time, Danae said, "Wildebay is quiet compared to a town."

"There's more to see and do in a town," Roast added.

"When are we going to a town?" Brodie asked. "Imagine the different types of food we'd find in one."

Ryan chuckled. "Eventually."

Mallory slowly shook her head when she saw her

brother take a piece of jerky from his belt pouch. "You've not long eaten. You can't be hungry already."

"I'm always hungry." Brodie bit off a piece of jerky, tossing the other half to Fang who caught it in midair.

Smudge hurried to Brodie's side, bounding along beside him as he glanced up at him, yipping several times.

Brodie slipped his hand in his belt pouch again. "See. I'm not the only one who's hungry."

"Did you want fish instead of jerky, Smudge?" Callum asked.

Smudge squeaked as he dashed to Callum's side, bounding up his leg to leap into his arms.

Callum grinned, patting Smudge on the head. "I'm going to take that as a yes."

They stopped long enough for Callum to get the last of the fish out of the basket, that had been put in the top of the pannier, and share it between Smudge and Fang. They'd had the other half of the fish at breakfast. After he'd eaten, Smudge tried to clamber up Bobbi's legs. He curled up on the bedroll when Callum placed him on Bobbi's back. Fang continued to trot at Brodie's side, dashing off to check out the various smells along the way.

They were less than halfway to Surith when Fang gave a single bark, running back to them. Smudge sat up on Bobbi's back, making repetitive high-pitched chirping sounds.

Mallory drew out her wand, spotting five goblins. Before she could launch a fireball, Danae had already shot one, insta-killing it. She threw a fireball at one of the three goblins still standing, Callum having taken one out, at the same time as Roast withdrew his twig wand and launched a fireball at a different goblin. He shifted into a rooster, his clothes left in a puddle on the ground along with his satchel, the smell of singed feathers filling the air.

Brodie faced the rooster the moment the last goblin collapsed on the ground. "Roast." He screwed up his face. "Burnt feathers smell disgusting."

Mallory hastily looked away when Roast became human. Naked again. She grinned when she heard her brother's next complaint.

"Roast! Get some clothes on. Even Callum wouldn't enjoy seeing your scrawny body."

"It's Art. Not Roast. Art."

"Whatever," Brodie muttered.

Mallory helped Ryan search the goblins. When she found forty grams of beef jerky, Brodie joined them, taking the jerky from her. They also found seven copper pieces, a pair of goblin boots and a chisel.

"Why can't goblins drop something more valuable than boots?" Brodie asked.

Ryan put the boots and chisel in one of the panniers. "At least it's more things for the wagoner to sell for us."

Mallory put the copper coins in her satchel. "We should gather some herbs for him to sell." She glanced at Brodie before returning her attention to Ryan. "It'll also give us a chance to catch up with Brodie."

Ryan chuckled, holding out the lead rope to Brodie, Smudge once again riding on the donkey. "You can look after Bob."

Before she joined Callum and Ryan in their hunt for herbs, Mallory turned to Roast. "You okay? You didn't hurt yourself with the fireball?"

Roast sighed heavily. "Only my pride."

She had no idea what to say to him. She continued to follow behind Brodie and Danae, glancing around the area. "We probably should have expected the attack. This is about where we were attacked by goblins yesterday."

Roast scanned the area too. "Are you sure?" When she nodded, he asked, "How many attacked?"

"Six. One of them was a leader." She remembered

how much it had hurt when a cudgel had struck her. They'd done a lot better today than yesterday.

"There's probably a goblin village in the area," Roast said. "Someone will need to deal with it before they become a problem."

"Aww, come on," Brodie complained.

Laughing, Mallory checked her journal since the icon was in the corner of her vision. Like she'd expected, it was another quest. *Village Search: The goblin village between Wildebay and Surith needs to be found and dealt with before it becomes a problem for travellers in the area.*

"Traders pay well for the swords of goblin generals as they are sought after by collectors," Danae said.

Callum, who'd brought a handful of herbs back, put them in a pannier. "I wonder how much traders pay for goblin swords."

"The overseer at South Peak Mine better not have ripped us off," Brodie muttered.

"Depends on the condition of the sword and the rarity of the animal engraved on it," Roast said. "Usually anywhere from two gold to fifteen gold pieces. There are a few rare ones that are more expensive."

Brodie looked over his shoulder to Mallory. "We should find it."

"What about Mer Point?" Roast asked.

Ryan returned with herbs in time to hear the end of the conversation. "What are you planning now, Brodie?"

Brodie repeated the information about the swords. "So we should find it. The village. Before someone else does the quest on us."

Ryan shook his head. "We agreed to escort Art to Mer Point so he can get a fire resist amulet. If the quest is available after we've done that, we'll vote on it."

"But it could be worth fifteen gold pieces," Brodie protested. "Or more if it's rare."

"What about Art?" Danae asked.

"I'm not expecting us to ditch him on the side of the road. He can come with us," Brodie said. "It's only a goblin village. We could keep him safe."

"We made a commitment. Discussion over." Ryan strode towards another cluster of herbs. He glanced over his shoulder. "Coming, Mallory?"

She nodded, about to follow him when Roast tugged her back, his hand wrapped around her forearm. "What's wrong?"

Roast slowed his pace waiting until there were a few metres between them and Brodie before he spoke softly. "You won't let your brother leave me behind, will you?"

She smiled. "He'd never do that. He might lead you into trouble, but he'd also do his best to get you out of it."

"I hope you weren't trying to reassure me," Roast said.

Mallory laughed. "No, not exactly." She tugged her arm from his grip. "Don't worry, we usually manage to keep him from doing anything too stupid." She hurried after Ryan, who'd been joined by Callum, checking their stats. She'd better start picking herbs if she wanted to catch up with them.

By the time they could see Surith in the distance, the three of them had caught up with Brodie and had a hundred experience points each. Brodie looked at the handful of herbs they walked past. "We should pick another twelve each so we can level up before we reach Surith."

Mallory glanced around the area. "I don't think there's going to be enough herbs for the four of us to get twelve each."

Callum shrugged. "Probably wouldn't hurt to try." He turned to Roast who was walking behind him. "Could you lead Bobbi for a bit?"

"I suppose," Roast said hesitantly.

Danae smiled at Roast. "Don't worry, you won't be alone." She looked at Mallory. "We'll wait for you on the outskirts of Surith if we reach it before you're done."

Brodie clapped Roast on the shoulder. "It'll be all good as long as you don't try throwing fireballs." He dashed off before Roast could reply, calling over his shoulder, "First one to them gets them."

Callum raced after Brodie. "Cheat."

Chapter Seventeen

Mallory followed at a slower pace, smiling at Ryan when he joined her, slipping his arm around her waist. She nodded at their brothers ahead of them. "I hope they don't think we're going to take a long rest when we reach Surith."

Ryan chuckled. "Don't warn them. They should know by now that all actions have consequences."

She laughed, slipping her arm around his waist. "You'd think." Her gaze was drawn to her brother who'd reached the clump of herbs first. "But we are talking about Brodie."

Ryan chuckled again. "How about we head off that way a bit?"

"Sounds good." Although she supposed anything that didn't involve running around like crazy would sound good.

It didn't take them as long as she'd feared to gather

the herbs and gain another CAS point. She grinned. Only one more CAS point until they reached their first character level. Excitement rushed through her and she checked Brodie and Callum's stats, seeing that each had collected two extra herbs and were a point above them.

"Want to get another two herbs each?" Ryan asked. "There are a few clusters over there." He pointed further south, away from the village.

She looked to where she could see Callum and Brodie striding towards them before glancing in the direction of the village where she assumed Danae and Roast waited. There were a few trees in the way so she couldn't see them. Checking Danae's stats and seeing they were fine, she nodded. "Yeah, he wouldn't let us get ahead."

When they reached the herbs, Ryan bent to pick them, stumbling back when a large snake struck at him, fangs sinking into his arm.

"Ryan!" She drew her wand, throwing a fireball at the snake that tried to attack again.

Ryan managed to get out of the way and draw his sword. "I didn't see it until it moved. It blended in with the grass."

Callum and Brodie ran towards them, weapons ready, their companion animals on their heels.

Mallory backed away, throwing a fireball at the snake, following it up with a second one. "Be careful, Ryan. It took five health from you."

He blocked the attack, unable to strike back. "It's quick."

An arrow struck the snake, followed by a throwing knife. Mallory threw another two fireballs at the snake, drawing her breath in sharply when the snake nearly got Ryan again.

He sank his sword into the snake, another arrow and throwing knife becoming embedded in the creature. "I think it was harder to kill than a hellion."

Mallory frowned when she checked Ryan's stats. "Did it get you a second time?" She could have sworn it missed.

"No, I blocked each–" Ryan broke off. "I'm losing health."

Callum reached them, stopping in the process of gathering his arrows at Ryan's comment. "Was it poisonous?"

"Bring the snake with us, Callum. Maybe someone in Surith will know what it is and how bad its bite is." Mallory glanced around the area. "And be careful. You can't see them until they move." Keeping her wand in her left hand, she slipped her right arm around Ryan's waist. "How do you feel?"

"My vision was only a little blurry to start with, but now it's getting hard to see properly."

"Surith isn't far." Mallory looked between Ryan and the village.

"Should he be walking?" Callum carried the snake, trying to hold it away from his body, which was near impossible since it was about five metres long.

"I'll run ahead and get Danni to ride back for Ryan." Brodie didn't wait for an answer, breaking into a run, Fang at his heels.

Mallory checked Ryan's health. It had dropped again. He had a revive, but she didn't want him to lose it over a snakebite.

"I lose a point every minute," Ryan said.

"Does it hurt?" Callum asked.

"A dull ache, nausea and blurry vision," Ryan said. "Extremely blurry."

When he'd lost ten health, Mallory took a health potion from her satchel and held it out to him. "Have this. Maybe we can keep your health up long enough to find out what to do."

It took Ryan two attempts to take the vial and he had to stop walking to drink it. He handed the vial back. "I feel fine again."

Mallory looked him up and down as she slipped the vial into her satchel. "Really?" The pound of horse hooves had her looking in the direction of Surith. Danae rode towards them on Augusta.

She came to a halt in front of them, swinging to the ground, the waterskin of health tea in her hand. She glanced at the snake. "It's been fifteen minutes?" Her frown was replaced by a smile. "Oh. You had a health potion."

"I'm sure what you said made sense to you," Callum said. "But I have no idea what you're going on about."

"We never should have split up." Mallory slipped her arm around Ryan's waist again. "Is Roast okay? We're meant to be looking after him."

Danae nodded. "Brodie remained with him." Her gaze travelled to Callum. "It's a chameleon viper. Their venom does one health point of damage a minute for fifteen minutes before wearing off. It's not the venom that kills. It's the blurry vision that makes it difficult for you to see their attacks."

"I would have thought you'd need some sort of antivenom to cancel the effect of a snakebite," Callum said.

"That would work too. But for creatures that are only mildly venomous, a health potion, tincture or herbal tea is usually enough to counteract the effects," Danae said.

"So he'll be okay?" Mallory asked. A rush of relief washed over her when Danae nodded. She tightened her grip on Ryan who draped his arm around her shoulders.

"The potion was good thinking," Ryan said.

"What are we going to do with this snake?" Callum asked.

"The butcher might be interested in the viper," Danae suggested.

Callum looked unconvinced. "It's venomous."

"That doesn't make the meat poisonous," Danae said.

"We'll give it to the wagoner to sell for us." Ryan looked to Mallory. "Did you want to collect those last two herbs?"

"Ah, no. I think it's past time we headed into Surith. And next time, we stick together." Mallory couldn't resist looking at the snake, a shudder going through her.

Brodie came to meet them as they drew close to the village, Roast trailing behind him. "Looks like you didn't die. Or at least you've still got your revive."

Ryan chuckled. "Seems it wasn't as bad as we feared."

"It'd help if we knew more about the world. About the animals and creatures we might encounter. I'd love to have some sort of compendium or monster manual," Callum said.

"My father had one of them come into his shop last year." Danae frowned. "I think it was like fifty or eighty gold pieces."

Callum stared at her for a moment. "A book is worth eighty gold pieces."

Danae nodded. "Some are worth more. A lot more. It takes time to copy them out."

"Copy-" Callum broke off. "Oh, of course. Medieval."

Danae frowned again. "What do you mean?"

"Never mind," Ryan said. "How about we find the wagoner and get Art to Mer Point."

They found the wagoner at the traders. He marvelled over the size of the chameleon viper, the trader already making offers for it as they sorted out the rest of the items for the wagoner to sell on their behalf. Four pairs of goblin boots, the herbs they'd collected on the way, a chisel and the cooking pot from the bandit's camp.

"Where are you off to next?" the wagoner asked.

Ryan nodded towards Roast. "Escorting Art to Mer Point."

The trader came forward. "Did I hear you mention Mer Point?"

They all nodded.

"I was expecting the Mer Point wagoner a couple of days ago. Think you can find out what happened to him? He usually brings the salvage those up at Mer Point dredge up each week. Without fail. Can't think of the last time he was running late." The trader paused a moment. "Five copper pieces for information. Useful information. An extra two copper pieces if you can give me a date when he's due to arrive."

Chapter Eighteen

Mallory checked her journal when the icon appeared in the corner of her vision. Another quest. She smiled. This one seemed simple enough. *Information Needed: The Surith trader is willing to pay five copper pieces to learn why the Mer Point wagoner is late. He will pay an extra two copper pieces if you can give him the wagoner's new arrival date.* It might not be much, but they were going that way anyhow. She glanced at her companions who either nodded or shrugged. She turned to the trader. "We can do that."

"Thanks. Appreciate it." The trader gave them a nod before he went to serve a customer.

Before they left, the wagoner handed over the coins for the items he'd sold along with the empty hessian bags everything had been stored in. "Try not to get yourselves killed. I'd hate to have to find another escort home."

Mallory laughed, catching the glint of humour in his eyes. "It's not something we plan to do."

"Like things always go according to plan," Brodie muttered. "Such as treasure maps that turn out to be directions to a meeting point."

As they headed through Surith, towards Mer Point, Mallory counted the coins the wagoner had given her before slipping them into her satchel. She looked up to see her companions waited for an answer. "We did better than I expected. Fifteen gold, nine silver and eight copper pieces."

Brodie glanced over his shoulder. "Why didn't you say when we were still in the village? I'm hungry. And what about the gold piece we're going to spend at the bakers?"

"Have an apple," Mallory said. "It's not lunch yet."

"Is there somewhere we can buy food in Mer Point?" Ryan asked.

"There's a tavern," Roast said.

"We can have lunch at the tavern?" Brodie asked hopefully.

"We won't have time to cook anything," Ryan said.

"Cool." Brodie took an apple out of the pannier, walking alongside the donkey as he did so. "We can buy lunch." He grinned before taking a bite of the apple. His grin faded. "That doesn't mean we'll miss out on buying something from the baker, does it?" He glared at them when they answered him with laughter.

Ryan grinned. "We can buy something at the bakers when we return to Surith, if you want. But maybe we should keep the money for another tavern meal for when we return to Buckneth."

Brodie and Callum discussed the choices for about half an hour until Brodie frowned at the bridge visible ahead of them. "How much further is it to Mer Point. We should have bought something to eat in Surith. I thought you said we weren't going hungry this time."

The bridge came closer and Mallory looked it over rather than pay her brother any attention. It was only wide enough for one horse drawn vehicle to cross at a time, solid timber rails running along each side. "This is a quaint bridge." She ran her hand along the wooden railing as she walked over it, the horse and donkey's hooves loud on the wide timber planks.

"Probably has a troll under it," Brodie muttered.

Roast shook his head. "I hear they got rid of the troll that was camping under it. The merfolk laid in wait for him and dragged him out to sea. Trolls can't swim." He looked at each of them in confusion when

Mallory, Ryan and Callum laughed. "It wouldn't have been pleasant."

Mallory struggled not to laugh again. "Brodie was complaining. He didn't actually think there was a troll under the bridge. He's just hungry and wants something to eat. Something better than apples."

"I brought cake." Roast placed his hand on the satchel he carried.

Brodie's expression brightened. "You did?"

Roast undid his satchel. "You can have a piece if you'd like. I brought more than I'll eat." He held out a cloth wrapped object to Brodie, glancing around at the rest of the group. "I have one other piece to spare. Not enough for everyone I'm afraid."

Brodie, who'd been about to take the item from Roast, lowered his hand. "Oh."

Mallory smiled at his expression. "I don't mind. I'm not hungry."

"I'll have an apple," Ryan said.

Brodie's expression brightened. "I can split it with you, Danni."

"No, thank you." Danae grinned, glancing at Mallory. "I'm beginning to understand your laughter."

Mallory grinned back at her. "I didn't think it'd take you long." She laughed when she caught sight of her brother's expression. He looked like he didn't know if he should be annoyed by Danae's comment.

Callum took the cloth wrapped object from Roast, ignoring Brodie's complaints. "I'll split it with you and the other three can split the other piece later if they want."

Brodie's complaints stopped mid-sentence. "Okay. Sounds fair." He took half the cake from Callum, turning to Roast. "No one said how much further it is to Mer Point."

"About forty minutes." Roast took the empty cloth from Callum, shaking the crumbs from it before tucking it into his satchel. Fang ran over to sniff at the ground and lick up the crumbs.

Mallory tried not to sigh. They really did need horses. Could horses travel far if they carried two people? Or maybe they could buy one and take turns riding. She eyed Augusta. Should she make that suggestion to Danae since the half-elf tended to walk when they were forced to?

"That's ages away," Brodie muttered before calling Fang to his side. "We need horses."

"Not yet," Ryan said. "Later. When we're in Eridell."

This time Mallory did sigh. She knew it was sensible, but right now, she didn't feel like being sensible. She felt like taking a break from walking. What were they going to do when they travelled south, without the wagoner? She had a feeling Cutthroat Harbour was a long way to travel.

In an effort to take her mind off the long walk, she scanned the area. The shoreline, they'd been following, was becoming rockier and the trees were further apart, barely any along the road ahead. Fang no longer ran back and forth, checking out all the smells, and Smudge glanced up from where he was curled up on the bedroll on Bobbi. He made a few soft sounds before returning to sleep.

Mallory smiled. What would a fire drake be like? She hoped she had the chance to find out. And soon.

Brodie picked Fang up, who had whined a couple of times. "You're getting heavier, girl."

"Give it time and she'll outpace us." Callum patted Fang's head, smiling when she licked his hand. "Let me know if you need a hand carrying her. Or she can go on Bobbi with Smudge."

"She's not heavy, just getting heavier and bigger. It won't be long and she'll be bigger than Smudge," Brodie said. "It's a pity she can't catch up to Smudge's XP. But that's impossible since their XP is based off ours."

His words reminded Mallory of the potions she'd

seen yesterday and she realised she hadn't told him about them. Or Callum. She explained what little she knew about the potions, turning to Danae when Brodie started asking questions.

Danae nodded. "Companion animals can use XP potions. Anyone who levels up can use them. And they aren't harmful or have negative side effects."

"When you finally start sharing out the money we earn, I'm going to save up to buy XP potions for Fang."

When Ryan chuckled, Mallory grinned. "You sure you won't be spending your money on food?"

"Very funny," Brodie muttered.

Chapter Nineteen

They fell silent. The rest of the trip to Mer Point was peaceful. Or at least not dangerous. As they approached the small village, Mallory slowed her pace as she caught sight of the merfolk sunning themselves on the many rocks in the shallows, the beach mostly made up of rocks.

Brodie's jaw dropped open and he came to a stop. "Look at the mermaids lying on the rocks. They're as beautiful as the books and stuff back home say."

"You prefer merfolk to other races?" Danae stopped beside him.

"What?" Brodie frowned. "No. Of course not."

"You said they're beautiful," Danae pointed out.

"No. I mean, I did. But that's because I was surprised," Brodie said.

"You wouldn't have said it aloud if you weren't surprised?" Danae asked.

"No. Yes." Brodie glanced at Mallory.

She was tempted to let him flounder. "I think what my brother is trying to say, rather badly, is that he didn't think they'd look like the ones in the books back home. Even I'm surprised that they're beautiful. Not just some of them, but all of them. Or at least all the ones here."

"Yeah, that. Exactly that," Brodie said.

Ryan wrapped his arm around Mallory's waist, drawing her close to look down at her. "Does that mean you prefer merfolk too?"

She smiled up at him, wrapping her arms around his waist as she moved closer. "Tell me you don't admire the beauty of them."

Ryan chuckled. "Only if you want me to lie to you."

"Never." She briefly met his lips.

"They are stunning looking," Callum said. "What are the males called? Surely they aren't mermaids too."

"They used to be referred to as mermaids and mermen, but they dislike those terms. They prefer the gender-neutral term of merfolk. No other race is collectively called by a term that refers to their gender," Danae said.

"I don't mind what they want to be called."

Callum's gaze remained on the merfolk. "I wouldn't mind getting a closer look at the male merfolk. I want to see if they look as good close up."

Ryan chuckled. "Maybe they wouldn't think you look as good close up."

Callum lightly punched his brother in the arm.

Smiling at their antics, Mallory turned in Ryan's arms to stare at the small village in front of them. They'd passed a farm and a thatched cottage before they'd stopped to look at the merfolk. There was another farm off to their left, a tavern in front of them. A handful of buildings were scattered behind the tavern as well as off to the side and a timber boat ramp was at the end of the road that led into the ocean on their right. "So where will we find this mage?"

"On the other side of the village," Roast said. "The second left if you stay on this road."

"Are we going to get something to eat now?" Brodie asked.

"You did hear the part where I said XP is five gold pieces for each point," Mallory said.

"Not my money. Your shout," Brodie said.

"There isn't likely to be any money to share if we eat all our meals at taverns," Ryan said.

Brodie stared slack jawed at Ryan for a moment.

"We won't be able to eat in the tavern?" He glanced down at Fang, who he still carried. "I–"

Again Mallory took pity on her brother. "We'll eat at the tavern today, but how about we finish escorting Art to the mage first."

Brodie looked from Fang to the tavern several times before he nodded. "Okay."

Roast led the way along the road. Mallory glanced at the merfolk several times, noticing some were now sitting up and watching them. Not a single one smiled and she started to worry about what sort of reception they'd receive in the village. A glance around showed the roads were empty. Where was everyone? Even the tavern they passed was quiet. She looked at the road that was parallel to the one they were on, two horses in a round yard, a building on either side. Surely there were more than horses in the village. She eyed the animals. They looked well taken care of so there was obviously at least one person living here.

"Where is everyone?" Brodie asked.

"That's what I was wondering," Ryan said.

Mallory nodded. "The place is too quiet." Before she turned the corner, and followed Roast, she looked ahead to where the road continued, a lighthouse visible about a kilometre away.

"There are only fifty or sixty people who live here," Roast said.

"Yes, but there should be-" Mallory broke off at the sound of voices coming from the second building on the right. It was a large timber building, far more impressive looking than she'd expected to find in a village that appeared to be smaller than Buckneth. Including the thatched cottage on the outskirts of the village, she'd counted eleven buildings, a round yard and two farms. Not big at all. Not big enough for something that might be considered a small manor house.

"That's where the mage lives." Roast gestured towards the manor house.

They came to a stop out the front. The door was open and between it and the several large windows across the front of the building they saw what looked like the entire population of the village inside.

"This can't be good," Callum said.

"Smudge isn't going off like an alarm and Fang isn't growling," Brodie said.

"We're going in there?" Danae nodded towards the door.

Ryan looked from the mage's place to Bobbi and Augusta. "Maybe a couple of us should stay out here. In case there are problems."

Callum had his bow in his hand, no arrow ready yet. "I'll wait out here." He took Bobbi's lead from Ryan.

"I should probably stay here too," Danae said.

Mallory could hear the disappointment in the half-elf's voice. She wished she could tell her that she didn't need to wait behind, but she had managed to get more crits than all of them. She turned to her brother. "You should wait here too. Watch their backs. Two of us will be enough to go inside with Art."

"You just want to go inside," Brodie muttered.

Mallory grinned. "Party leader."

Ryan chuckled, draping his left arm around her shoulders, his right hand resting on the hilt of his sword. "Come on then, leader. Lead the way."

Roast, appearing confused, looked from one to the other. "Are we going inside?"

Mallory nodded, her left hand remaining close to her wand that she left in the canvas loop. As they walked towards the open door, she checked that the icon in the corner of her vision was only a notification of a new location. It was. There'd been no quest updates.

No one noticed them until they were nearly at the door. A large man, with a black beard, wearing a leather vest, his muscular arms filling the armholes of the vest, turned to face them. His gaze narrowed. "Are you one of them?" he demanded. "It's not time for our answer. He gave us until sunset."

"I'm from Wildebay," Roast said. "I've come to see the mage."

"You picked a bad time to visit." The man looked to Mallory and Ryan. "Are you from Wildebay too?"

Before either of them could speak, Roast did. "They're adventurers. They've taken on hellions before and plan to go to Cutthroat Harbour to face more of them."

"Not exactly how I would have put it," Ryan said.

"Nor me," Mallory added.

"Are you adventurers?" the man asked.

A woman joined him, her long dark hair braided back from her face, a dagger at her side, well worn leather boots covering her leather breeches to the knees. "I'm the tavern owner. Elodie." She gestured towards the man standing beside her. "And this is the blacksmith."

"Mallory." She nodded to Ryan beside her. "And this is Ryan."

Elodie met Mallory's gaze. "Have you fought hellions before?"

"Yes."

"Do you plan to go to Cutthroat Harbour and fight them again?" Elodie asked.

Chapter Twenty

Mallory sighed at Elodie's words. "It sounds worse when you put it that way."

Elodie laughed, the deep-bodied sound filling the building and catching everyone's attention. "It always does." She faced the rest of the crowd. "It looks like we have another option." She gestured towards Mallory and Ryan. "Two adventurers have arrived."

"You can't expect so few to be capable of taking on all the smugglers," a woman at the front of the room said. Her fair hair was cut short, her pointed ears claiming her elf heritage.

"There are three more adventurers outside." Roast gestured towards the open door.

Elodie moved forward to look outside. "Two archers and a rogue." She turned to face the room with a smile. "I vote for the adventurers. The most I've ever done is toss drunks out on their rears." She gestured towards the blacksmith. "And making weapons is not the same as wielding them." Her gaze was drawn to the elf at the front of the room. "As a mage you're probably the only one here capable of fighting the smugglers, but even you can't do anything without your staff."

Roast took a single step towards the mage. "Something happened to your staff?"

The mage inclined her head. "The smugglers stole it. I need to get it back so I can use my magic again. I have no other staff or wand with which to focus it."

"I vote for the adventurers too." A man tossed a gold coin to Elodie before striding outside.

Several more people gave Elodie coins, some copper, some silver and another couple of gold pieces, before leaving the building. Mallory stared after them, not sure what was going on. Had they been hired? What if they weren't capable of taking on smugglers? And how many smugglers exactly.

A man who had dirt stained hands removed his dusty felt hat. "Here." He handed it over to Elodie, dropping several copper coins in it. "For the collection." With a nod to Mallory and Ryan, he also walked outside.

The room was nearly empty before Mallory could speak. "We didn't agree to anything."

Elodie tilted the hat so they could see inside it. "They're willing to pay you."

Ryan chuckled. "Better not let Brodie see that."

Mallory stared at the variety of coins and trinkets, momentarily lost for words. "We don't even know what you need done."

Brodie came to the door. "Why is everyone leaving? And why were they smiling and nodding at us?" His gaze landed on the hat. "What's going on?"

Mallory took a deep breath, trying not to feel overwhelmed by the situation. "I can't make this decision alone. All my party needs to vote on it. And we need to know exactly what's going on."

"Bring them in," Elodie said.

"Is there somewhere we can leave the horse and donkey while we talk?" Ryan asked.

"And what about lunch?" Brodie asked. "I'm starving. How am I meant to decide anything on an empty stomach?"

Elodie shared a look with the blacksmith, who nodded. "They can go in the round yard with the wagoner's horses. Then we'll go to my tavern and talk."

It didn't take long to put Bobbi and Augusta in the round yard and the blacksmith threw some hay in for them. They unsaddled Augusta and removed the panniers from the donkey, leaving them in a pile outside the round yard. The blacksmith assured them everything would be fine.

"What about the smugglers?" Mallory asked.

"We've got people watching for them," Elodie said. "They'll let us know if they spot them. You must have come along the main road or they would have told us someone was coming."

"When I first saw you, I thought the smugglers had killed those watching. But they're good at keeping out of sight. Plenty of rocks around here for orcs to hide behind." The blacksmith walked with them to the tavern. "We sent to Lilica for help a few weeks back, but no one has come. Asked them to get rid of the smugglers for us. The mage was talking about going after the smugglers herself when her staff was stolen. That was two days ago."

Mallory noticed the journal icon appear in the corner of her vision when the blacksmith mentioned sending to Lilica for help. Guessing it was a quest, she left her journal unopened, focusing on what Elodie and the blacksmith had to say.

Elodie nodded. "The mage asked the merfolk to harass the smugglers and prevent their ship from getting in so they can't load up whatever items they've stolen. They captured the wagoner in retaliation and gave us until sunset today to get the merfolk to stop or they'll kill the wagoner. From what we can figure out, they're staying in the caves in the cliffs along the western side of the point."

The blacksmith stepped back, gesturing for them to enter the tavern. "We're running out of time and no one wants them to get away with everything they've stolen. Not those of us living in the village and not the merfolk living in the local colony."

Elodie showed them to a table in the corner, light from a nearby window falling across it. "The merfolk can't keep the ship from landing forever. They'll eventually get past and pick up the smugglers and the items they've stolen." She gestured to the blackboard behind the bar. "If you're willing to listen to what we have to say and at least consider helping us, your meal is on the house." She took a step back, tugging the blacksmith with her. "We'll give you a few minutes to decide what you want to eat."

Roast leaned forward the moment they were alone. "I can't help. I want to, but without a fire resist amulet I'm near useless. As it is I don't know how I'll rescue Merry if the mage can't help me. Look at how little help I was with the goblins."

Mallory lightly touched his arm. "It's okay. You can wait here if we go after the smugglers."

"Do you mind if I visit the mage? Maybe she has a fire resist amulet in stock." Roast half rose from his seat.

"Did you want us to order something for you?" Brodie gestured towards the blackboard.

Roast nodded. "Grilled fish and rice."

"That sounds good." Brodie stared at the blackboard. "I don't know what I should get. Everything sounds great."

Mallory waited until Roast had left before she spoke. "If we don't get the mage's staff back, and she doesn't have any fire resist amulets, then we haven't finished the quest for Art."

"Aww, come on," Brodie said. "That isn't fair. Why can't anything ever be easy?"

Mallory opened her journal, reading the quest aloud. "Cry For Help: Mer Point has lost belongings and goods to smugglers who are staying in the local caves. They sent to Lilica for help, but no one answered. The village is willing to pay a reward to whoever will rid them of the smugglers."

"It doesn't mention anything about the missing staff or the captured wagoner," Brodie said.

"They might be separate quests," Callum said. "Or the staff might be one of the belongings it mentions."

"This quest could be updated when we agree to

listen to what they need." Mallory glanced to where Elodie and the blacksmith stood by the bar. "We should decide what we want to eat before Art returns."

"I'm going to have the large meat pie and veggies," Brodie said. "I love pies."

"I'll have that too," Danae said. "It'll be interesting to see if the pastry is as good as my mother's."

"And I'll have an ale," Brodie said.

"In the middle of the day?" Mallory asked.

"What's wrong with having one in the middle of the day." Brodie glanced at the blackboard again. "And I'll get a beef stew for Fang."

"I'll have the pie too." Callum looked down at Smudge who was in his lap. "You want the grilled fish or should I ask for it raw?" He sighed when Smudge chattered to him. "I have no idea if he wants it raw."

At the word raw, Smudge grabbed hold of his hand, rubbing his head against it.

"At a guess, I'd say that was a yes for raw," Danae said.

When Elodie came over to collect their order, Ryan asked for the seafood platter and Mallory ordered goat in a red wine sauce with vegetables.

"Can I try some of your food?" Brodie asked Mallory. "I've never had goat before."

"Neither have I," Mallory said. "Which is why I ordered it."

Brodie's gaze returned to the blackboard. "I never thought about that. I've been choosing my favourite foods. But there are so many foods I haven't tried. I should have picked something else." Brodie exclaimed over some of the different meals he wouldn't mind trying, asking Danae about them. He fell silent when Roast entered the tavern.

Chapter Twenty-One

Mallory looked Roast up and down. From his dejected walk and mournful expression, she guessed he hadn't been able to buy a fire resist amulet. She sighed heavily. "We'll have to go after the smugglers if we want to help Art."

Roast dropped into a seat, slumping. "I'll never be able to save Merry. She'll be lost to me forever."

"We've been talking about dealing with the smugglers," Mallory said.

"The mage said there are probably fifteen to twenty smugglers. Possibly more. How can you survive against so many smugglers?" Roast slowly shook his head. "I should have known."

"Are they all in the one area?" Ryan asked.

Elodie brought over three of the plates of food, the blacksmith heading out the door as she did. "If you're looking for a map of the caves, you should talk to the trader. He has a few maps in his shop. Maybe he has one of the caves."

Mallory picked up the cutlery Elodie placed beside her plate. "Thank you." She checked her journal even though the icon wasn't in the corner of her vision. Elodie's comments hadn't updated the quest.

It took Elodie another two trips before she had served them, including the companion animals. She also placed a jug of water and cups in the middle of the table, giving Roast, Brodie and Callum the ale each of them had ordered.

Mallory slowly shook her head when Elodie strode back to the bar, taking a mouthful of her food rather than comment on Brodie and Callum's choice. "This isn't bad." She gestured to the food with her fork.

"Let me try." Brodie helped himself, not waiting for a reply.

"Want to swap some food?" Callum broke off a piece of the pie, which took up nearly half the plate. "It tastes pretty good."

The meal was spent swapping and sharing the various food and they were almost finished when a boy about twelve-years-old walked in, hesitantly approaching them. He cleared his throat, his gaze fixed firmly on the floor.

"Can we help you?" Callum asked.

"My Pa is the wagoner." His gaze remained on the floor.

"The man who was kidnapped?" Mallory asked.

The boy nodded.

"Are you asking us to rescue him?" Brodie asked.

The boy nodded again.

"Do you know where the smugglers took him?" Ryan asked.

The boy glanced towards Elodie.

Mallory tried not to sigh. She wasn't successful. "Can you tell us anything?"

The boy briefly met her gaze. "Night vision potions." He held out six vials. "Pa carries them when he travels to Surith in case he's caught out after dark." Again he glanced up. "You can have them if you go after him."

Mallory took one of the vials from him, reading the handwriting scrawled across the label. "Strong Night Vision Potion. Single dose. Duration four hours."

"Cool." Brodie took a vial. "How do they work?" He examined the dark green liquid.

"You drink it," the boy said. "You'll only notice the difference when you're in the dark." He thrust the rest of the vials at Mallory. "Here."

"Only five of us are going after the smugglers." She placed the vials on the table in front of her.

The boy gestured to the companion animals. "Half each."

"Oh. Okay." Mallory smiled up at the boy. "Thank you."

The boy nodded. "Don't let him die." Tears glinted in his eyes. "I don't have no one else." Turning, he bolted from the tavern.

Mallory noticed the journal icon was finally in the corner of her vision. She opened the journal, seeing a new quest. *A Son's Request: The Mer Point wagoner's son fears the smugglers will murder his father. He has offered six strong night vision potions to help in the rescue of the Mer Point wagoner.*

"It's a separate quest?" Callum asked.

"Appears that way," Ryan said.

"I thought it'd be the same quest," Danae said.

Brodie grinned. "Normally I hate quests piling up, but this is good. We'll be able to get paid for doing two quests when they're part of the same thing."

Mallory read over the words one more time. "What if they aren't? What if he's somewhere else and that's why they're separate. They might have hidden him somewhere other than their hideout."

"Did you have to say that?" Brodie muttered. "Way to ruin the moment."

Hearing footsteps, Mallory looked towards the

door. A man entered, removing his cap as he did so. He paused in the doorway before striding towards them, his trousers and shirt looking well made, his boots almost new.

"Mind if I pull up a seat?" The man gestured to a chair at a nearby table.

"Not at all," Ryan said.

The man carried the chair over, placing it gently on the floor before sitting with them. "I'm the trader."

"Elodie said you have maps," Mallory said. "Do you have one of the caves?"

"How about one of Ruby Isle?" Brodie asked. "That shows all the villages, towns, cities and the capital."

The trader looked at Brodie first. "I have several maps of Ruby Isle." He turned to Mallory. "I'm afraid I have no map of the caves. The best way to reach them is to go to the lighthouse and take the track down the cliff then walk around the base of the cliffs to the caves. The tide will be at its lowest at midday. As long as you're out of the caves by about six this evening, you won't get your feet wet coming back by way of the lighthouse."

"How much is a map of Ruby Isle?" Ryan asked.

"The smugglers stole crates of goods that I haven't had the chance to open. Each crate has the words

'Mer Point Traders' painted on them. They also stole a barrel of maple syrup. If you can locate my goods and make sure there are no smugglers that will prevent me from having them collected, I'll give you a map of Ruby Isle and a twenty percent discount on all stock you might wish to purchase through my shop. You can have a discount for as long as I own it."

Elodie, who'd drawn closer, chuckled. "According to your sons, they'll be prying the control of that shop from your dead hands."

The trader shrugged. "A body has to have something to fill their hours." He looked from Mallory to Ryan then back again. "What do you say? Do we have a deal?"

Mallory checked the new quest that had appeared when the trader made his offer. *Stolen Stock: Find the stock the smugglers stole from the trader and ensure that none of them will prevent him from having it collected and he will reward you with a map of Ruby Isle and a twenty percent discount on all stock in his shop for as long as he owns it.*

"Do we get some of the maple syrup too?" Brodie asked.

Danae laughed softly, momentarily placing her hand over Brodie's that was on the table.

"What?" Brodie turned to her in confusion.

Danae only smiled, shaking her head once before looking at Mallory. "Maps aren't cheap. But I could draw a very bad picture of Ruby Isle and approximately where the villages, towns and capital are. Shadhurst is the only city on Ruby Isle."

"I'll throw in a bottle of maple syrup as well," the trader offered.

Brodie faced his sister. "Mal. Say yes, Mal. Say yes."

Laughter greeted his comment and Ryan captured her hand, grinning at her. "Yeah, say yes, Mal."

Mallory smiled at Ryan before tugging her hand from his light grip and glancing around the table. "We don't know if the crates have been opened or plundered by the smugglers."

"I'll accept your word that you'll leave the contents that might be in them intact and you won't open any if you find them sealed. But I can't imagine that they'd bother to open them," the trader said. "It doesn't make sense. Not when they want to transport them elsewhere."

Chapter Twenty-Two

Seeing the journal icon in the corner of her vision, Mallory checked to find the quest had been updated. *Stolen Stock: The trader has also offered to reward you with a bottle of maple syrup.* She almost laughed. Glancing around her group, she smiled when everyone nodded. "We'll see what we can do."

The trader rose to his feet. "Thank you. I appreciate it."

Callum spoke before the trader could move away from the table. "Do you sell coffee?"

"What is that?" the trader asked.

Callum sighed heavily. "It might as well be the elixir of life. Why does no one sell it?"

"Oh, I sell elixir of life potions. I've never heard them called coffee before. I also sell fountain of youth potions, timeless potions and fleeting years potions."

Ryan chuckled. "I've got a feeling they aren't exactly what Callum's looking for."

"What are those potions?" Brodie asked.

"Elixir of life is a revive potion, fountain of youth takes away some of the years your body has lived, a timeless potion stops the ageing process and fleeting years adds years to your body," the trader said.

"Why would you want to add years to your body?" Mallory asked.

"Do you think if I had two years added from a fleeting years potion I could join the guardians?" Brodie asked.

"I doubt it," Ryan said.

The mage entered the tavern, drawing their attention as she strode to the table. She nodded to the trader. "You finished?"

He nodded before turning back to Mallory. "Let me know when it's safe to have my goods collected."

"We will." Mallory watched as he left the tavern, turning to the mage as the trader stepped out the door. "Did you want to have a seat? She gestured to the seat the trader had vacated.

"I won't be here that long." The mage nodded towards Roast. "If you can find and return my staff to me, I'll make a fire resist amulet and fix the charm of your companion as well as let you choose two spells for your level." Her gaze fell on Mallory at the last comment.

Mallory checked the new quest in her journal. *Missing Staff: Return the stolen staff to the mage and in exchange, she will repair the charm and give a fire resist amulet to Arthur of Wildebay along with two spells suited to your level.* Mallory smiled. Half tempted to demand that they agree to the quest so she could get new spells. Instead of making her demands, she glanced at each of them, her smile widening into a grin when all of them nodded. "We'll see what we can do."

The mage inclined her head before leaving.

Mallory once more looked at each of her companions, except Roast. "We should get started. It must be close to midday."

Elodie, who was clearing the table, took out a pocket watch. "A few minutes after."

Mallory rose from the chair. "Then it's time to leave. We have a lot of quests to complete before we need to escort the Buckneth wagoner home."

"Will we be able to get them done in time?" Brodie asked.

Mallory shrugged as she headed for the door, smiling and giving Elodie a nod goodbye. "I wouldn't have a clue."

"Then why did we take on so many quests?" Brodie demanded.

Ryan grinned. "Because they need doing."

Roast stopped in the doorway. "I'll wait here for you to return. Unless…" His voice trailed off.

"It's okay," Mallory said. "You wait here. We'll be as quick as possible."

"Will you do the quest for the mage first?" Roast asked.

Again Mallory shrugged. "I don't know. We need to see what's going on in the smugglers' caves. We'll do whatever is logical."

"Or time sensitive," Ryan said.

"Yeah, that too," Mallory agreed.

Roast pointed north. "I was told if you keep following the road through the village, heading that way, you'll eventually come to the lighthouse. Go to the cliff edge and you'll see the steps that have been cut into the rock face leading to the water below.

"I don't suppose you know where there's an outhouse," Mallory said.

Roast nodded. "Behind the tavern."

"Thanks." Mallory followed Ryan, who collected his backpack.

Once they'd used the outhouse, they followed the

road that went north. The village was as quiet as it had been earlier.

Callum carried Smudge, patting him on the head as he spoke to him. "You stay out of the water when we get down there. Who knows what is in the area with all these smugglers."

Smudge chattered at Callum.

"He doesn't sound impressed with that idea." Brodie looked down at Fang who walked at his side. "You stay out of the water too. We don't know this area and I don't want anything to happen to you."

Fang gave a single bark.

Ryan chuckled. "At least she doesn't sound like she's going mad at you. Not that I have any more of a clue about what she said."

"It'd be nice if we could figure it out," Callum said.

"There are spells that allow you to talk to animals temporarily," Danae said.

"Maybe we should have all been mages. Sounds like there's a spell for everything," Brodie said.

"The problem is levelling up enough to use all the different spells you're interested in," Danae said. "And locating a copy of the spell so you can learn it."

Mallory slowed as they approached the lighthouse, her gaze drawn upwards. She counted the row of small, arched windows that were placed one above the other along the rendered wall. Assuming each was on a separate floor, the lighthouse was four storeys tall. At the top, the light was visible even with how bright the day was. "That light must be visible for miles."

Brodie stopped at the foot of the lighthouse. "Can we go in there? I've never been inside a lighthouse before. Not even in our world." He continued to stare up at the lighthouse. "It'd be so cool to live in one."

Ryan stepped forward and checked the door handle. "It's locked."

"We could ask them once we've done the quests," Callum suggested.

Mallory checked her journal since the icon was in the corner of her vision. "We earned XP for discovering another location."

"Cool," Brodie exclaimed. "A lighthouse is worth fifteen XP. At this rate we'll gain our first character level today."

"I really hope so." Mallory walked around the base of the lighthouse, her companions following. She stopped at the edge of the cliff, eyeing the steep, narrow steps leading to the water's edge. "I wouldn't want to walk down there in the rain."

Fang started down the stairs, glancing over her shoulder when no one followed.

"Okay, I'm coming, girl." Brodie followed her down the stairs, going at a slower pace.

Smudge stretched a paw towards the ground, making soft sounds. As soon as Callum put him on the ground he hurried after Brodie and Fang. Callum followed. "Stay out of the water, Smudge."

The otter continued down the stairs, chattering excitedly.

"I mean it," Callum called after him.

Chapter Twenty-Three

Mallory walked slowly down the steps, Ryan and Danae following her. She constantly checked what was in the area. "If we get attacked while we're walking down these stairs we probably won't survive."

"There doesn't seem to be anything in the area," Danae said.

"Let's hope it stays that way," Ryan said.

They managed to reach the bottom of the stairs without mishap, the small beach at the foot of them more mud and rock than sand. Mallory smiled when Callum scooped up Smudge who'd been heading for the water.

"We'll find somewhere safe for you to swim later." Callum held Smudge against his chest, shaking his head when Smudge scolded him. "Later. There are smugglers around here."

They walked around the point, the cliff towering above them, the beach not improving. As they came around to the other side of the point, Mallory drew out her wand at the sight of two merfolk hung by their wrists on the cliff face further along. Their skin was dry and flaking away, the scales on their tails lifted in places and missing in others. They both wore vests that looked to be made from the skin of a sea creature, their long hair hanging in knots around their face and shoulders, blood streaking both their bodies. One was male and the other female.

"Do you think they're alive?" Callum kept his voice low, Smudge now silent in his arms.

"I don't know. I'd be surprised if they are with the state they're in." Mallory scanned the area, seeing no smugglers. Didn't they have anyone on guard? Surely they wouldn't be able to walk straight into the cave she could see ahead of them without being stopped.

"We need a spyglass," Ryan said. "Then we could check out what's ahead. I'm sure I saw something move behind that boulder past the cave entrance."

Mallory stared at the boulder. It was large enough someone could hide behind it. She didn't see any movement as they drew near, but that didn't mean anything. When they were directly under the merfolk she glanced at them, taking a second look when she realised both of them were alive. This close she could see they were gagged by a thick piece of rope that cut into their flesh.

"We have to cut them down." Callum placed Smudge on the ground beside him.

Smudge stared at the large boulder ahead of them, softly making his high-pitched warning cry. Beside him Fang growled, the sound equally soft so it didn't carry far.

Brodie drew two throwing daggers, nodding towards the merfolk. "I bet it's a trap."

Mallory looked from the merfolk to the boulder. "Then how about we don't fall for it?" She again glanced at the merfolk who were now making noises as they tried to speak past their gags. She wanted to reassure them they wouldn't leave them there, but if there was a smuggler hiding behind that boulder, she didn't want to warn him.

"We're leaving then?" Danae demanded.

Ryan turned so his face wouldn't be visible to anyone who might hear from behind the boulder. He winked at Danae, grinning. "It's not like they mean anything to us."

The sounds from the male merfolk increased at Ryan's comment and he struggled weakly. At the same time, a smuggler popped up from behind the boulder, firing at them with a short bow.

Fang jumped up at Brodie, knocking him out the path of the arrow and causing him to drop one of his throwing knives. Mallory, Danae and Callum attacked the archer smuggler. She ducked behind the boulder.

"Now how are we meant to get her?" Brodie picked up the throwing knife he'd dropped.

"Cover me." Ryan ran towards the boulder, holding his sword. Before he could reach the boulder, the archer smuggler rose again, aiming her short bow at him.

Heart racing, Mallory attacked at the same time as Brodie, Callum and Danae. Her relief at taking out the archer had barely formed when two more smugglers came out of the cave. A mage and a rogue.

Ryan, the one they focused on, dived behind the boulder.

"The mage will have the highest attack." Danae fired at the mage who was turning towards them.

Mallory did the same, as did Brodie and Callum. Ryan came out from behind the boulder, his attack on the mage finishing him off. Mallory instantly turned her attention to the rogue who had thrown his throwing knives at Ryan and was drawing a dagger.

He didn't get the chance to draw it. They all attacked him, including the companion animals.

Mallory hurried forward, peering inside the entrance of the cave. Enough sunlight struggled inside for her to see it was empty. No smugglers and no crates of trade goods. At the back of the cave was a tunnel sloping downwards. Seeing the journal icon in the corner of her vision, she checked as she stepped back from the cave, her companions crowding around her. "Fifteen XP for finding the smugglers' caves." She looked to the merfolk who were now still. "How are we meant to cut them down? None of us are tall enough. And there's nothing in the cave we can use to stand on."

Danae walked over to the merfolk, looking up at them. "They won't last much longer. Maybe we could collect some of these rocks and pile them up to stand on."

"Callum could hold Smudge up and he could chew through the ropes." Brodie joined Danae.

"He's an otter, not a beaver." Callum bent to pat Smudge who leaned against his leg, his gaze also fixed on the merfolk as he made soft sounds of distress.

Mallory looked from the merfolk to the cave entrance. "Someone needs to keep watch."

Ryan strode over to Mallory. He glanced at first

Brodie and then Callum as he wrapped his hands around her waist. "Brodie, keep watch at the cave entrance. Danni, search the bodies." He lifted Mallory several centimetres off the ground.

"What are you doing?" She placed her hands on his shoulders.

He lowered her. "You can sit on my shoulders and cut the ropes. Set your satchel aside to make it easier."

"What am I meant to be doing?" Callum asked.

"You can catch them once Mallory cuts through the ropes holding them up there." Ryan helped Mallory onto his shoulders, moving close to the cliff face.

Mallory waited for Ryan to be still before she drew her dagger. Her gaze collided with that of the merfolk she was in front of, seeing a mixture of fear and hope in the green eyes partially hidden by tangled strands of dark brown hair. "I'm sorry we had to wait. We would have cut you down immediately if we could have." She stretched upwards, her grip tightening on the dagger as she tried to reach the rope. "I'm too short."

Callum had his arms wrapped around the tail of the merfolk. "Stretch some more."

"I'm stretched out as much as I can." Mallory lowered her arm.

"Kneel on my shoulders," Ryan said.

Mallory stared at the top of his head. "You've got to be joking. I already feel like I'm going to fall."

"We don't have many options," Ryan said. "Are you going to leave them here to die?"

Her gaze was drawn back to the face of the merfolk. The hope was gone, only his fear remained. "I'm not going to leave you to die." She sheathed her dagger. The merfolk's expression didn't change. Taking a deep breath, Mallory took hold of Ryan's hands that he held up to her. Wobbling, she slowly rose to her knees, gripping Ryan's hands tightly. She took another deep breath once she was on her knees, holding herself still as she slowly reached for her dagger. She continued to grip Ryan's hand with her other one.

"Hurry up," Ryan urged.

Mallory drew her dagger, stretching out again towards the rope. This time she was able to easily reach it. "Ready, Callum?" She held the dagger at the top of the rope where it was wrapped around a rock that jutted out from the cliff face.

"Ready."

Chapter Twenty-Four

Mallory pressed the dagger against the rope, sawing back and forth as the strands separated. When the rope broke and the merfolk slipped downwards, Mallory nearly fell. Her grip tightened on the dagger and she grazed her knuckles on the cliff trying to steady herself. The sting had her drawing her breath in sharply. "This is madness." She spoke the words softly.

"Can I move along?" Ryan asked.

Sheathing her dagger, Mallory gripped his other hand. "Okay." She wobbled as Ryan moved along the cliff face. Her hands ached from how tightly she held onto him. When he stopped at the next merfolk, she steadied herself before drawing the dagger. Meeting the gaze of this merfolk, she was surprised to see only anger in her eyes, her hair a similar shade to the male merfolk. For a moment, she couldn't look away from the bright green eyes. When she did, it was to find Callum. He was helping the other merfolk into the water, having cut through the ropes with his hunting knife, which rested on the ground beside him. "Callum? Are you going to help?"

"You better hurry up. I can't hold Mallory like this all afternoon," Ryan warned.

"You better hurry anyway." Brodie stepped away from the entrance of the caves. "There's a smuggler coming this way. With a short sword."

"You and Danni take care of the smuggler," Ryan said.

Callum left the merfolk half out of the water and ran to hold the other one. "Cut her down."

Mallory tried to ignore the panic that rushed through her, keeping at the same slow pace that she'd used to cut the previous one down. If she fell or dropped the dagger there wouldn't be time to help the merfolk before the smuggler reached them. She sawed through the rope, her hand trembling as she tried not to rush. Again she nearly fell when the merfolk dropped downwards.

"Leave her there, Callum," Ryan said. "Help Danni and Brodie."

Mallory sheathed her dagger before clambering down, slipping.

Ryan caught her, dragging her close. "You okay?"

Mallory nodded, doubting she could speak with the way her heart pounded and how fast her breath came.

Ryan let her go. "Help the merfolk. I'll help the others."

"You better hurry up," Callum said. "We've got another mage here."

Mallory drew her dagger as Ryan ran towards the cave. She cut the ropes from around the wrists of the second merfolk before cutting through the gags on both of them. The first one had managed to wriggle further into the water. Mallory nicked the second merfolk as she cut away the gag. "I'm sorry. It was so tight."

The merfolk stretched out a hand towards the water. She opened her mouth, but no words came out.

Mallory struggled to help the merfolk into the water. "I think I'm the wrong person for this job. Ryan should have done it." The second merfolk was only half in the water when Ryan returned.

He helped to get both of them fully in the water, looking at his trousers and boots and the sleeves of his shirt that were now wet. A wry smile formed. "I think we're going to need more than spare clothes. We might want to think about spare boots too."

"Is everyone okay?" Mallory checked her journal as she asked the question, even though Ryan nodded. She was surprised to find she'd lost one health point, guessing it had been when she'd grazed her knuckles on the cliff face. "That seems a bit excessive."

"What does?" Ryan asked.

She held out a hand, showing him her grazed knuckles. "One health point."

Ryan laughed softly, turning to look at the merfolk who remained fully submerged in the water, lying motionless on their backs. "Are they meant to be doing that? Shouldn't they swim away or something?"

Mallory shrugged as she checked everyone's health points. Only Ryan had lost any. He now had fourteen health points like she currently did. She closed her journal. "Do we leave them here? Will they be okay? Or are we meant to do something for them?"

Before Ryan had the chance to answer, Smudge dived into the water, ignoring Callum's calls to return.

Danae hurried out of the cave. "Don't be so loud or we might have all the smugglers out here." She stopped when she saw the merfolk. "That isn't good."

"What do we do?" Mallory remained in the water,

the waves lapping against her knees. "Should we give them some of the health tea?"

"That should-" Danae broke off as Smudge burst out of the water in front of them, holding up a fish with black scales. She grinned. "Feed them. You're very clever, Smudge."

"How will that help?" Brodie stood at the edge of the water.

Ryan looked towards him. "Aren't you meant to be watching the cave entrance?"

"Callum is taking a turn." Brodie gestured towards the fish Danae took from Smudge. "How will that help?"

"Merfolk gain both sustenance and health from raw, fresh fish." Danae turned to Ryan. "Hold one of them up so I can give them the fish."

Brodie made a face. "They eat raw fish?"

Danae laughed softly. "Have we finally found something you won't eat?" She held the fish out to the merfolk, holding it up to her mouth while she ate it.

Brodie made a face again. "Scales too?"

Mallory laughed, taking the second fish Smudge caught. "Get over here and help me with the other merfolk, Brodie."

He splashed through the water, grumbling, falling silent before he reached them. He held the merfolk up so Mallory could help him eat. "I just can't see how the scales would taste that good. Or the bones. I mean the actual fish meat itself would probably be okay. After all, they have raw fish in some sushi. So that has to mean it's okay."

Mallory felt the skin of the merfolk's fingers, that were wrapped around hers, become less dry and flaky. "It's starting to work." She kept her gaze off the fish he was eating, not sure she wanted to see him consume it. From head to tail. Even the thought of it made her feel queasy. Not that she was about to mention it to Brodie.

The merfolk Ryan held, drew away from him, having finished eating the fish Smudge had brought her. "Thank you. I'm grateful you saved the two of us. There's one more of us who was captured. She was taken into the caves by the smugglers. What can we offer you to rescue her?"

"A shell," Danae said. "A twisted pearl shell."

Brodie frowned. "A shell? What would we want with a shell? Unless it's made completely of pearl."

The merfolk pulled away from Brodie and Mallory, taking the last of the fish from her hands. "Half-elf you–"

The other merfolk interrupted him. "We have little

choice. If that's what they require, then we can give them no less."

"I don't understand what's so important about a shell." Mallory looked from Danae to the merfolk and back again. "Does it do something special?"

"It's a call on us for a future service. A request we cannot refuse no matter how terrible it might be," the merfolk said.

Mallory slowly shook her head, seeing the anger was back in the merfolk's eyes. "No. I don't accept that."

The merfolk's eyes narrowed. "There's nothing more we can give you. Ours is the smallest shoal at the colony."

"Shoal?" Ryan asked.

"Like an extended family tribe," Danae said. "Which means they're the least wealthy ones at this colony. But this is a really wealthy colony because they get a lot of salvage here."

"Do you want our salvage rights for a set period of time?" The merfolk they'd cut down first glared at them.

Chapter Twenty-Five

Mallory sighed. They'd obviously misunderstood her. "I'm not asking for anything." She quickly spoke again, worried they might misunderstand her comment. "We're not asking for anything."

"But you keep saying you don't have enough money and gear," Danae said. "That you need to find ways to outfit yourselves better."

"You're refusing to help us?" the female merfolk demanded.

Ryan chuckled. "Give up, Mallory. They'll figure it out eventually." He started towards the shore.

Brodie looked from one merfolk to the other. "Or make them pay because they want to."

The merfolk grabbed hold of Mallory's arm, his grip tight. "What are you trying to say? Neither of us are leaders of our Shoal so we can't offer everything it has. Only offer what we're entitled to."

She met his gaze, looking into his green eyes and seeing the anger and desperation in them. "Everything you've offered is too much. We're not about to extort your entire wealth from you to save someone from your family. Give us something if you want, but not everything. And even if you gave us nothing, we wouldn't leave someone behind because they had no way of paying us to help them escape." She pulled her arm from his grip. "If they're alive, we'll bring them back to the sea for you." When he continued to stare at her, mouth slightly open, she smiled and headed for the shore.

He caught up with her before the water became too shallow, grabbing her arm again. "You want nothing and you've turned down the offer of a twisted pearl shell and you'll still rescue a merfolk from our shoal."

"Yes." Mallory drew out of his grip again. "You're slowing me down."

"Yeah, we've got a heap of quests to do. Probably too many." Brodie stood on the shore again. "So hurry up, Mal. We're wasting time."

This time it was the female merfolk who prevented Mallory from reaching the shore. She held up a hand, an iridescent, pearl coloured spiral shell in her palm. "No strings. Yours whether or not you find Tyne.

My companion is Gal and I'm Edlien. Speak my name against the shell when you decide what you need my help with and hold it under the water for a minute so I can locate where you are. I'll travel to you as quickly as I can so stay nearby until I find you."

Mallory took the shell. "You don't need to-"

Edlien interrupted her. "I know. But you seem to be the type of person who deserves such a gift."

"She could take the shell and not rescue Tyne," Gal protested.

"I trust her." Edlien smiled. "Good luck." She headed for deeper water before she sank beneath the waves.

Mallory's gaze was drawn to Gal who continued to glare at her. She started to tell him that they'd rescue Tyne, but doubted he'd believe her. She headed for the shore, glancing over her shoulder as she stepped onto the beach. He continued to glare at her.

Ryan joined her, holding out the satchel she'd left on the beach. "He'll soon figure out we mean what we say."

If they managed to find Tyne alive. She kept that comment to herself, taking the satchel and slinging it over her arm and head as she pulled up her journal to check the new quest. *Merfolk In Danger: Edlien of the merfolk colony at Mer Point has asked for your help in rescuing Tyne from smugglers. She has offered you a twisted pearl shell so you may call on her in your hour of need, regardless of if you manage to rescue Tyne.* Mallory smiled as she reached the entrance of the caves where Brodie was muttering about all the quests they had to complete, slipping the shell inside her satchel.

"Think about all the loot we'll gain." Callum stood near Smudge who was sharing a third fish that he'd caught, with Fang.

"We have five quests for here," Brodie said. "Five!"

Mallory's attention was caught by a pile of items inside the cave. "What's all this stuff?"

"What we got from the smugglers," Callum said. "We haven't had the chance to sort it."

Mallory picked up a pair of black trousers that looked to be about her size. She was tempted to change into them rather than continue to wear her jeans that were wet to the knees, but she supposed they'd need washing first. "Finally, clothes that fit me. I was beginning to think we'd only get ones suited to people bigger than me." She rolled them up and shoved them in her satchel to wash later before sorting through the rest of the items. There were seven copper and one silver piece, five arrows that she split between Callum, Danae and Ryan so they now had twenty each after replacing some that had been lost, a deck of cards, a wand that was put in the backpack and a small drawstring bag that contained a pearl ring.

"Are we going to have those potions so we can see in the dark before we go deeper into the caves?" Brodie asked.

"What if it doesn't take us four hours? Callum asked.

"You don't have to have the entire contents of the vial," Danae said. "One dose, four hours means that's how long that particular dose lasts. You can separate it out into one hour doses. Or halve it. You can't do that with all potions, but night vision potions are ones that can be separated into smaller doses."

"Why didn't we get similar amounts of XP since we took out the same amount of smugglers?" Brodie asked.

"I was looking at that," Callum said. "I figured out that the mages are level two."

"Shall we try a two hour dose?" Mallory opened her satchel.

Ryan drew his sword. "Archers."

Letting her satchel close, Mallory grabbed her wand, her gaze drawn to the tunnel that led into the cave. Two archers drew arrows back, aiming in their direction. She launched fireballs at each of them, one after the other, but not before they'd managed to fire their arrows. One arrow struck Danae while Brodie avoided the second one.

One of the archers turned and ran when Ryan attacked his companion. "Don't let him escape," Ryan ordered.

Mallory threw a fireball at the retreating archer, two arrows striking him at the same time. He landed sprawled across the ground and she hurried forward, the archer Ryan had been attacking also dead. She stood over the archer at Ryan's feet. "We can't let any of them escape to warn their mates. Who knows how many we'd face if that happened." She opened her satchel, taking out one of the strong night vision potions and turning to Ryan. "Do you have those empty potion vials in your backpack?"

Ryan nodded. "I thought it was safer than putting them in the panniers where they might get broken." He removed his backpack and rummaged around in it. "The rest of you want to search the bodies while we sort out the potions?"

Mallory took the empty vial from Ryan and retreated to the cave entrance, for more light to complete the task. She had the first dose, not noticing any difference. She held the other half-full vial out to Ryan. "I'm not sure if it's working."

Ryan drank the contents. "At least it doesn't taste bad."

"What does it taste like?" Brodie joined them, carrying a few items.

"Sweet and like some sort of strange mixture of berries." Ryan handed the empty vial to Mallory before facing Brodie. "What did we end up getting?"

"We found a quiver, a sheathed hunting knife, a silver piece and another one of those small drawstring bags." Brodie handed everything to Ryan except for the bag, Callum and Danae having followed him over.

Ryan held the hunting knife out to Danae. "You should take this." He put the quiver in his backpack and handed the silver piece over to Mallory.

Finished sorting out more potion vials, Mallory handed them around. "What's in the bag?"

Brodie tipped a copper bracelet into his hand, several blue gems embedded in it. "What's with the jewellery? First a ring and now this."

"I guess it's some of the items they're smuggling." Callum took a half filled potion vial from Mallory, downing the contents.

Chapter Twenty-Six

Once everyone had a half dose and the companion animals a quarter dose, Mallory took the bracelet from Brodie, returning it to the drawstring bag and putting it in her satchel along with the three full vials of strong night vision potions. She put the empty vials in the backpack. They now had five empty ones. She glanced around the group. "Are we ready to go?"

Ryan checked the compass he held. "The tunnel heads east." He put the compass away. "We should get moving. We only have two hours until the potion wears off."

"If it's working." Brodie strode towards the tunnel. "Can potions be defective? Or do they have a use by date?"

"It's working." Danae walked at his side, Fang on the other side of him.

"How do you know?" Brodie asked. "Everything looks normal to me."

"Exactly," Danae said. "No difference in the amount of light, even back here in the tunnel where it should be darker."

Brodie glanced around. "Cool. I didn't think about that."

Mallory nearly ran into Brodie when he came to a stop. She stepped around him to see a pit trap in front of them. It took up the entire width of the corridor, the tunnel continuing beyond it. Barrels were lined up along one side of the wall past the trap and the tunnel was approximately five metres long and led into a cave at the other end.

Ryan grabbed Mallory's arm, dragging her into the tunnel to the right. It was half the width of the one they'd been in. "Everyone get out of that tunnel. There are smugglers in the cave at the end of the first tunnel." He kept his voice low.

Mallory had been too busy trying to see if any of the barrels belonged to the Mer Point trader. "How many did you see?"

Ryan shrugged. "At least two. But that doesn't mean there weren't more."

"How are we meant to do this without one of them spotting us and giving the alarm?" Brodie asked.

"Pity we don't have someone with high stealth," Callum said. "They could sneak ahead and let us know where the smugglers are."

"Maybe we all should be buying some of those vials of XP," Brodie said.

Mallory looked along the tunnel they were in. It was longer than the one with the barrels. About six metres long and ending in another cave. It didn't appear to be a very deep cave as she could see a barrel directly across from the entrance. "We can't stand here all afternoon. We have a merfolk and a wagoner to rescue."

"And a tonne of quests to do," Brodie said.

"Want me to sneak ahead and see what's in the next cave?" Danae asked.

Mallory shook her head, taking a step further into the narrow tunnel. There was no way she wanted to tell either of Danae's parents that they'd let their daughter go ahead of them into danger and she'd come to harm. "I'll go."

Ryan drew her back, meeting her gaze. "I don't like that idea either."

Mallory started to protest, smiling instead. "I don't like the thought of any of us going ahead. We can take turns. We'll roll the dice to see who goes first."

Callum took the dice off Brodie when he took them out of his belt pouch. "Roll for initiative?"

Mallory tried not to laugh, worried a smuggler might hear. "One will do. Highest number goes first." She took one of them from him, crouching to throw it onto the rocky ground. "Five."

They took turns rolling the dice. Brodie had the lowest and Danae the highest. Brodie looked from the number one he'd rolled to Danae. "Did you want to swap?"

Danae shook her head. "It's fine. This is fair." She smiled. "Maybe I'll level up my luck next character level."

Mallory wanted to protest. Why had she come up with that plan? Taking a deep breath, she tried not to think about all the things that might go wrong. "We'll go part way along this tunnel and leave you to go ahead. Let us know if it's safe to follow."

They remained silent as they headed along the tunnel, stopping about halfway. Danae continued along the tunnel, reaching the end to peer inside the cave. She looked over her shoulder and gestured them forward before entering the cave and stepping out of sight.

Mallory hurried forward, her companions behind her. When she would have stepped into the cave,

Danae held up a hand, pointing to the tunnel that headed out of the cave, in the middle of the eastern wall.

"I don't know what's down the next tunnel," Danae said softly.

Mallory joined Danae where she was pressed up in the corner to the left of the tunnel she entered the cave from. "I'll have a look." Before she moved closer to the tunnel that headed east, she glanced around the cave they were in. It was approximately three metres square with a makeshift bed on the western wall and three barrels lined up along the southern wall. The rest of her companions were crowded around the entrance they'd come through. She crossed the small distance between her and the eastern tunnel, wincing at the sound her wet boots made. She doubted even a stealth class could be quiet in wet boots. She shivered as she peeked around the edge of the cave wall and into the tunnel. It was cooler in here out of the sun, especially with the lower half of her jeans wet.

Another narrow tunnel stretched away from her. It had to be as long as the first tunnel from start to end at approximately ten metres long. She was about to say it was empty when a rogue came into view, carrying a lantern and entering the tunnel. She pressed herself back against the wall, easing away from the entrance of the tunnel. "A rogue is coming this way." She spoke as softly as possible.

Ryan sheathed his sword and readied his hunting bow. "Let's see if we can take him by surprise." He stepped back into the previous tunnel, moving closer to the entrance, only his drawn back arrow showing inside the cave.

Callum joined Ryan, pressed against the other side of the tunnel exit while Brodie crouched at Danae's feet, where she remained in the corner. He held a throwing knife in each hand. Mallory looked around, trying to find the best spot to stand where the rogue would be less likely to see her straight away. She eased back towards the previous tunnel, standing shoulder to shoulder with Danae. A glance towards the previous tunnel showed Fang and Smudge remained in it.

Mallory's gaze remained fixed on the entrance to the third tunnel. Nothing moved. Her grip tightened on the wand she held. Where was the rogue? Had he spotted them and run back to gather reinforcements? There was no sound of footsteps and she couldn't see any change in light from the lantern he carried. Frowning, she tried to figure out if there'd been a difference other than the actual glow inside the lantern. She couldn't recall if there'd been a bright patch on the ground at his feet or if everything had looked the same. When she was about to give up and check along the tunnel again, to see if he was coming, he stepped silently into the cave.

Danae fired first, the arrow followed by a fireball from Mallory. The rest attacked, the lantern falling from the rogue's hand as he sprawled across the ground, unmoving. Mallory remained as still as the rogue. It took a few seconds for it to sink in that the rogue was no longer a threat. She came away from the wall, checking down the third tunnel again. This time it was clear.

Ryan put his hunting bow away and dragged the rogue further into the cave and out of view of anyone who might come along the third tunnel. "Brodie and Callum search the body and the barrels. Mallory and Danae keep watch at this tunnel while I see what's at the other end." He looked at his boots. "Maybe I should go barefoot. I'd be quieter."

"Keep them on." Danae readied another arrow. "Some of the smaller spiders found in caves can be more poisonous and deadly than the larger ones."

Ryan drew his sword before he started along the far tunnel.

Chapter Twenty-Seven

Mallory watched Ryan, wand at the ready. He seemed to move along the tunnel very slowly. She wanted to tell him to hurry up and tell him not to go so fast for fear of what he might stumble into. She leaned forward when he reached the end, holding her breath as she waited to see what would happen. He backed away from the next cave, facing it for nearly a minute before he turned and made his way slowly back to them.

Brodie joined them at the start of the third tunnel. He held up a vial filled with a yellow liquid. "Good thing we took the rogue out before he could attack us. Weapon poison. Eight uses. The lantern is still good and about half filled with oil and we got a thick, grey woollen blanket off the bed. And five copper pieces. I couldn't open the barrels to see what's inside them. Not without making a lot of noise. We'll have to check them later."

Mallory took the coins from Brodie. "You can have the weapon poison since it's something used by rogues." She slipped the coins into her satchel before returning her attention to Ryan.

He reached halfway and beckoned them forward, pressing a finger to his lips.

They joined him in the tunnel, Brodie needing to hush Fang who growled softly. They put the blanket in the backpack Ryan carried and hung the lantern on the outside of it.

Ryan, most of his attention remaining on the cave he'd checked out, gestured towards it. "There are four beds, three of them occupied and the crates and barrels belonging to the trader. A rogue and two mages are in the beds. There are also three tunnels leading out of the cave. We need to take them out before they can warn anyone."

"How are we meant to do that? Brodie asked. "It's not like they're goblins Danni can one-shot."

"At the most, they have twenty health points. We'll assume Danni will do a crit and the rest of us a normal attack." Ryan nodded towards Mallory. "You have the highest normal attack at six. We'll split into two groups and take out the mages first. If we're lucky, we'll get the rogue before he can go far."

"The tunnel is too narrow for us to stand side-by-side," Callum said.

"We have to enter the cave. The three occupied beds are on the northern wall. Entering is the only way to get a clear shot. None of us can afford to miss," Ryan said. "Brodie and I will be with Mallory and Callum will be with Danni. The moment the mages are dealt with, focus on the rogue. Don't wait for anything. Just attack. We'll take the mage that's in the middle bed while Danni and Callum take the one in the far bed, towards the east."

"At best, Danni and I will be able to attack for thirteen if we both get crits, only nine if both of us have a normal attack. That means we'll have to attack at least twice, possibly three times. If it's three, that rogue will escape. Especially since the three of you won't be able to do any better," Callum said.

Ryan nodded. "Have you got a better suggestion? I'm happy to go with another plan if someone can come up with one."

They either shook their heads or murmured no.

Mallory looked at the entrance to the next cave. "Are we going to do this? We can't stand here all afternoon. Or we might end up with the smugglers waking or another one coming our way."

"Was a barrel of maple syrup in there?" Brodie asked.

"Might have been," Ryan said.

Brodie drew out two throwing knives. "Let's do this."

Mallory grinned, following her brother along the tunnel. Her grin faded as they reached the other end of the tunnel and stepped inside. The cave was about five by four metres and the beds were lined up along the northern wall, two males and one female under grey blankets identical to the one on the bed in the previous cave. She attacked the mage, along with Brodie and Callum, attacking a second time before the mage could do little more than throw the blanket aside and half sit up. Fear raced through her as she turned her attention on the rogue as he dashed for the north west exit. Arrows thudded into him and he sprawled across the ground, not reaching the exit. She wanted to sag against the wall next to her at the relief that rushed through her.

"There's three tunnels. Not counting the one we entered through. Anyone could come in here." Brodie gestured to each of the exits, one on the east wall, in the northern corner and two along the western wall north of the one they'd entered through.

"We need to see if anyone is about to enter through one of them," Mallory said.

"Does anyone feel bad about taking them out while they were sleeping?" Callum asked.

Mallory eyed the rogue. "Not since I learned they use weapon poison. We wouldn't stand a chance against that." She couldn't help thinking about the viper that had bitten Ryan. "Brodie, you check the eastern tunnel, Danni the first one on the western wall and I'll check the next one on the west. Ryan can search bodies and the cave while Callum keeps watch." She moved to the tunnel she had to check, peering cautiously into a smaller cave that was two metres wide and three metres long. A single bed was on the far wall and a barrel to her right in the corner. Danae stepped into the cave from the south, running lightly towards her.

Danae glanced over her shoulder as Mallory stepped out of her way to let her back into the larger cave. "There's a large cave to the north of the little one. I saw at least three smugglers sitting around a cooking fire with their backs to me. One of them might have been a hellion. He had a tattoo on his cheek that could have been a skull, but I didn't get a good look at it."

Mallory turned to ask Brodie what had been in the other tunnel. He was nowhere to be seen and Callum was at the entrance to the eastern tunnel. "Where's Brodie?"

"Checking the tunnel. He's on his way back now. Just went to the first tunnel off this one." Callum stepped back so Brodie could enter the cave.

"There's a large cave west of this tunnel." Brodie gestured behind him to the tunnel he'd stepped out of. "About half a dozen smugglers, a cooking fire in the middle and a table with the food spread out on it on the far side of the cave. Looks like they're getting ready to have afternoon tea."

"You saw all that from the next tunnel?" Mallory asked.

Brodie shook his head. "I had to take a left off that tunnel to see the big cave properly." He looked at Danae. "When did you gain another CAS point?"

"At the end of this fight." Danae gestured to the three bodies.

Mallory took several steps towards her brother. "Focus. What else did you see in the big cave? And how big is it?"

Ryan straightened after searching the body of the

rogue. "And where was each smuggler?" He glanced at Danae. "Have a look at the cave Danni saw to see if it's the same one. It probably is, but it's good to make sure."

Brodie strode towards the tunnel Danae had checked. "What did we get?"

"Not much. Six copper and two silver pieces, leather vambraces that have slots for throwing knives and only one blanket. The other two are blood soaked and full of holes." Ryan gestured towards them. "The four crates and barrel all have the Mer Point trader's mark on them."

Danae stepped in front of Brodie before he could enter the tunnel she'd checked. "Use the tunnel Mallory looked in. There'll be less risk of being spotted."

Brodie headed to the other tunnel, pausing at the start of it. "Are the vambraces for me?"

Ryan grinned. "Looks like it."

"Hell yeah." Brodie entered the tunnel, after telling Fang to wait for him, stepping out of sight. He was back in less than a minute. "Same cave. Danni was right. It's a better hiding spot for checking out the cave from that direction."

Finished putting the blanket in the backpack, Ryan

gave the coins to Mallory and the vambraces to Brodie. "Did you see a merfolk in there?"

Brodie put on the vambraces. "No, but the tunnel I took went down further than the tunnel leading to the big cave." He eyed his vambraces. "I need more throwing knives. I don't suppose you were able to get any from the rogue."

"No." Ryan gestured towards the tunnel Brodie had stepped out of. "How hidden a spot is it? Or can you describe the layout and how many smugglers were in the cave?"

"There was one over at the table with the food on it," Brodie said.

Mallory sighed. "He probably didn't see much more than the food. I'll have a look."

"Don't let them see you." Ryan followed her to the entrance of the tunnel.

Chapter Twenty-Eight

Mallory sent Ryan a reassuring smile, wishing she felt as confident as the smile she'd given him. If Danae hadn't mentioned poisonous spiders, she would have removed her boots to cut down on the noise she was making. Entering the small cave, she stayed close to the wall on her right. There was a barrel taking up most of the corner, it was far enough away from the cave wall that she could slip behind it and peer around the corner.

Pressed against the rough rock of the wall, her wand in her left hand at her side, she leaned to the left, peering through the extremely short tunnel that led into a large cave. It was roughly six metres square with a cooking fire a little north east of the middle. Three smugglers were sitting around the fire with their backs to her, talking. In the far north east corner was a bed, a warrior stretched out in it with his sword on the ground beside him. In the northern corner, opposite the bed, was a table with food spread out on it. A warrior helped himself to the food, his left profile visible to her. She recognised the tattoo on his cheek. A skull with dark eye sockets, the edges partially obscured by tendrils of smoke. He was a hellion. About to move away, she froze when the hellion turned and walked back to the fire with a plate piled high with food.

"The lot of you are useless." He pointed at a mage, sitting by the fire, about to pick up a cup. "Touch my coffee and I will kill you. I'll be glad when I return home to Cape Barren. If you lot make me look bad in front of my captain you'll regret it." He sat on the stool by the fire, picking up the cup and having a drink.

"We've done everything you've paid us to do, Rass." The mage's gaze followed the cup. "It's not our fault the ship can't get in. You're the one who picked an area with merfolk."

Rass slammed his cup down. "If we don't beat the other five companies back to Cutthroat Harbour you lot won't get the bonus I promised."

"We'll be back by the nineteenth of this month," the rogue sitting beside the mage said.

"That's the date we leave Cutthroat Harbour for

the Hellfire and Cape Barren border. If we get back to Cutthroat Harbour that late, we won't be the first to return. And you won't get your bonus."

At the venom she heard in his voice, Mallory wanted to retreat. Instead, she remained pressed against the wall trying to learn as much as possible.

Rass pointed first at the mage and then the rogue. "You two find out what happened to your crew. If they're out there hassling the merfolk I'll string them up too. I want them to suffer as long as possible. And when they're dead, we'll take the other one out and string her up."

Both got to their feet, neither saying anything, only sending a glare towards Rass before they headed for the eastern tunnel.

Mallory's legs went weak at her narrow escape. Forcing them to work, she slowly backed away and entered the cave where her companions waited for her. "Rogue and a mage coming that way." She pointed at the tunnel entrance directly across from her.

Three bows were readied and pointed at the tunnel entrance, Brodie drawing throwing knives. He glanced over his shoulder at Mallory. "You okay?"

She nodded, her gaze fixed on the entrance. The mage entered first and was dead before taking a second step, the rogue tripping over the body. Mallory threw two fireballs at him as he tried to turn back the way he'd come from. He had no chance to escape. "There's a warrior hellion and a warrior smuggler sitting at the fire. And a warrior in a bed in the north east corner. The ones at the fire are to be attacked from that tunnel." Mallory pointed across the room to the eastern one. "And the one in the bed can be attacked from this tunnel." She gestured to the one behind her. "We should have brought Art with us. He could have watched one of the tunnels. There aren't enough of us to take on the enemies in the big cave and watch the other two directions."

"Fang can watch our backs." Brodie bent to pat the wolf cub. "Couldn't you, girl?" Straightening, he pointed to the tunnel leading back to the ocean. "She can wait there and bark if someone comes."

"Smudge can watch the tunnel that goes past the eastern entrance of the big cave." Callum looked down at Smudge who leaned against his leg, a foreleg wrapped around his calf. "He's loud enough to warn us of any enemies that might approach."

Smudge continued to hold onto Callum's leg. He chirruped several times, as if in agreement.

"That settles it," Ryan said. "Who's going after the sleeping warrior and who is going east?"

"I'll go east," Callum said.

Brodie gestured towards the rogue and mage at the entrance to the eastern tunnel. "What about checking what they have. I might get lucky and find some throwing knives for my new vambraces."

"Make it quick," Ryan said. "You've got the amount of time it'll take us to sort out a plan of attack."

Mallory watched her brother search the bodies as she thought over the layout in the cave. "Danni and I will focus on the sleeping one while everyone else takes out the warrior smuggler." She looked at Danae. "I don't suppose there's a maximum amount of people for smuggler groups like there are with goblin villages."

Danae laughed softly. "I wish. For all we know there could be another thirteen like we've already taken out. Or double that."

"How about less than that?" Callum asked.

Brodie rose from the bodies he'd finished checking. "As long as there's enough to get my next level, I don't care how many or few there are." He glanced at the rogue. "No throwing knives, but there was another vial of weapon poison. Eight uses." He crossed the cave to hold out a drawstring bag and four copper pieces to Mallory. "Do you think the jewellery is worth much?"

Mallory tipped the contents of the bag into her hand, finding pearl drop earrings in a gold setting. "They're kind of nice." They weren't something she'd normally wear, but they'd suit some of the clothes she'd seen in this world.

"They are pretty," Danae said. "They'd look nice with my good dress. Not that I've had anywhere to wear the dress lately. At this rate, I'll grow too tall for it before I have the chance to wear it again."

"Where do you normally wear it?" Brodie asked.

"I wear it for special occasions. To weddings, fancy parties and out to celebratory dinners," Danae said.

"I'd take you out for dinner if Mallory wasn't so stingy with our money," Brodie said.

"You would?" Danae asked. "What would we be celebrating?"

"Uhmm." Brodie looked from Danae to Mallory and back again.

Ryan chuckled. "Probably celebrating Mallory giving him money."

Brodie glared at Callum and Mallory when both laughed softly. He gestured towards the eastern tunnel. "We doing this? Or waiting for the rest of them to come to us?"

"Doing this." Mallory took a deep breath. "Everyone ready?" When they nodded, she stepped inside the small cave, remaining close to the rock wall. Once again, she slipped behind the barrel before she peered around the corner into the bigger cave. Nothing had changed. Her gaze was drawn to the cup of coffee. Should she have mentioned it to Callum? It was too late to worry about it now.

Danae pressed against Mallory's side. "Should I go to the other side of the entrance? I can't see anything from here. And how will we know it's time to attack?"

Mallory drew back from the edge. "I didn't think about that." She peered around the edge again before drawing back to talk to Danae. "We'll give them five minutes. Or at least what feels like five minutes. If they don't attack by then, we will." She glanced at the other side of the entrance. "It might be best if you were over there."

With a nod, Danae circled around the cave, staying away from the entrance until she was on the other side of it.

Chapter Twenty-Nine

Mallory kept watch.

The hellion finished eating and tossed his wooden plate on the ground at his feet. "Do I have to do everything myself?" He rose to his feet.

There wasn't time to wait. Mallory threw a fireball at the sleeping warrior, speaking softly to Danae at the same time. "Attack."

"We're under attack." The hellion drew his sword, taking a step towards where Danae and Mallory hid.

Mallory tried not to think about the last warrior hellion who'd come close to her. She threw another fireball at the no longer sleeping warrior who reached for his sword on the ground. An arrow pierced him seconds later and he hung half out of the bed, blood forming a puddle on the ground. She turned her attention to the hellion who'd spun to face east when an arrow had struck him in the back.

Ryan ran towards the hellion, his sword drawn, the other warrior by the fire sprawled on the ground.

Mallory stepped into the bigger cave to get a clear shot at the moving hellion, hearing Danae follow her. She threw a fireball at him. It missed.

Ryan and the hellion's swords clashed.

Mallory threw another fireball and once more she missed the hellion. A target that moved around a lot was hard to attack.

Danae fired her bow, the arrow striking the hellion, Callum's arrow also finding its mark.

The hellion blocked Ryan's attack and glanced over his shoulder at Mallory and Danae. He renewed his attack on Ryan, startled when high-pitched sounds came from the eastern tunnel.

Ryan got past his defence. "Brodie, Callum, help Smudge."

Mallory took the opportunity to attack, a fireball finding its target. She quickly launched another one, as Danae's arrow found its mark.

Ryan finished the hellion off, spinning to face the eastern tunnel. "Make sure there's no one else at our back, then follow." He ran for the tunnel, sword still in hand.

Mallory stared at the spot where the hellion had been. "He vanished."

"He must have had a revive. Possibly a location specific one." Danae looked inside the wide tunnel leading west towards the pit trap that had blocked their way earlier. "No one in here."

Mallory continued to stare at the ground after a glance at the tunnel Danae had checked. At the ground where she'd expected to see a body. "He's alive?"

"Somewhere. Only he will know where his revive transported him." Danae moved towards the eastern tunnel. "Are you all right?"

Mallory wasn't certain. With one last look at the empty ground, she headed for the sounds of fighting she could hear in the tunnel. "I never thought about the fact that hellions might be able to revive. That the people we fought could." There was a hellion who knew who they were. One they'd attacked. She entered the tunnel in time to see two warrior smugglers taken out.

Ryan turned to face her. "If there are any other smugglers in the caves, I'd be surprised. Smudge was loud enough to call all of them." He grinned. "I didn't think of that."

"None of us did." Mallory helped search the bodies.

"I was hoping for more," Brodie said. "I'm ten XP off going up a character level."

While they searched the bodies, Mallory told them about Rass vanishing and what she'd overheard earlier. They found two silver pieces, a short sword and scabbard and another drawstring bag.

Heading back to the bigger cave, Mallory tipped the contents of the drawstring bag into her hand. "What are we going to do about a hellion knowing who we are?" Another copper bracelet slipped out. This one had black gems.

Callum strode straight to the hellion's cup, holding it to his nose and breathing deeply. He momentarily closed his eyes. "It was coffee. Rass drank it all."

Brodie checked the pot hanging over the fire, grinning. "Not all of it."

Returning the bracelet to the bag and slipping it in her satchel, Mallory laughed at Callum's excitement. "How much is in there?"

"Two cups." Callum carried the pot with him to the table in the corner of the cave, where he found a clean cup.

Ryan gestured towards the eastern tunnel. We have to find the Mer Point wagoner and the merfolk. "We can search in here later."

"There's no one else in the caves. You said so yourself. They would have come running." Callum had a drink from the cup, smiling. "This tastes so much better than what we have at home. I wonder if it's related to cooking levels too."

Brodie searched through the food on the table, glancing at Ryan. "You and Mallory can find the prisoners while we search in here. Smudge and Fang can stand guard in case anyone else comes. We've only got about half an hour left on our potions. Splitting up makes more sense."

Mallory eyed the food on the table. "Sure it does," she said dryly.

Danae laughed, her gaze on Brodie. She turned to Mallory. "Did you want me to come with you?"

It was Ryan who answered. "We should be okay." He looked at Mallory. "Coming?"

She started to nod, checking everyone's stats before splitting up. "Ryan! You're down to four HP."

"I know. It was the hellion. I was going to see if I could get through the rest of the day–"

Mallory interrupted Ryan, holding out the spare health potion from her satchel. "Drink it. Now. The day is nowhere near finished."

"Probably only about three hours left of daylight." Ryan took the potion and downed the contents, putting the empty vial in his backpack.

"Exactly. The day isn't finished." Mallory checked Ryan's stats, relieved to see his health points were at fourteen. The only other person who'd lost health points was Brodie. He was down to thirteen. Two less than usual. She strode towards the eastern tunnel. "We have to find the staff too. And make sure all the smugglers are dealt with. The only quest we're close to completing is the one for the Mer Point trader."

"I forgot about that," Brodie said. "Even finishing one quest should level me up."

Mallory checked her experience points as she entered the tunnel, keeping hold of her wand in case they encountered smugglers or she stumbled across one of those small, poisonous spiders Danae had mentioned. She had eighty-six experience points. Only another twenty-one to go. A smile formed. Five quests would well and truly level her up. She looked at Smudge as they passed him in the tunnel, her smile widening into a grin at his pose. He reminded her of a soldier standing at attention.

Ryan glanced over at her. "What do you find amusing?"

Not wanting to offend Smudge by her humour at his pose, she focused on her earlier thoughts. "We'll level up today. The quests will level us up with heaps of XP to spare." Reaching the end of the tunnel, she glanced at the crate, barrel and two chests stacked in the corner that was wider than the tunnel.

Ryan glanced at the objects too. "We'll check them later. For now, we need to find the Mer Point wagoner and Tyne."

The tunnel took a sharp left. Another lengthy tunnel stretched out in front of them. "How big is this place?" Mallory eyed the other end of the tunnel that had to be at least thirteen metres away. Would they manage to find the prisoners and staff before the potion wore off?

"Who knows. Let's hope it isn't too big. I don't want to be stumbling around here in the dark," Ryan said.

"Pretty much what I was thinking." Reaching the end of the tunnel, Mallory took a sharp turn to the right, seeing a bed at the other end. It was only a few metres away. She frowned when she heard voices coming from the east, where the tunnel made another sharp turn before the bed, which was in an alcove. For a moment she thought it might be Tyne and the Mer Point wagoner talking. Her steps slowed when she realised it wasn't.

Ryan stopped to peer around the corner. "I can't see anyone, but there must be at least one smuggler left."

Chapter Thirty

Mallory leaned close to Ryan so she could catch his words. "What are we-" She broke off when the smuggler spoke again.

"Better hope that was a creature and not someone coming to rescue you."

"If you keep holding that blade against my throat it won't matter. The other two told you not to kill me until they found out what was going on."

"If someone else steps out of the tunnel and into this cave I'm not waiting around for an order to kill you. You'll be dead before they have the chance to speak."

"What if it's for her? Are you going to slit my throat then? Whatever that noise was, it didn't sound human. You going to slit her throat?"

The smuggler chuckled. "She couldn't be that lucky."

When the smuggler began to talk about the plans for the merfolk, Mallory drew Ryan back around the corner. "We can't go in there. It'll get him killed."

"We can't leave him in there. That will get him killed too. Along with Tyne."

Sighing, Mallory closed her eyes, leaning against Ryan. There had to be something they could do. If only they'd come up with a better way of having Smudge warn them. Opening her eyes, she drew back from Ryan to smile up at him. "I've got it. Wait here. Don't let him kill them." Her lips briefly met his before she hurried back the way they'd come, breaking into a run once she was far enough away the smuggler wouldn't hear her.

Smudge chattered, tilting his head to the side as she ran towards him.

"We need your help. A smuggler has a blade against the Mer Point wagoner's throat." At least she supposed it was the Mer Point wagoner. There was always the chance they had more than two prisoners. "We need you to distract him so we can prevent him from killing the wagoner."

Smudge squeaked several times before bounding along the tunnel towards Ryan's hiding place.

Mallory hurried after him, falling behind. She reached Ryan's side as she saw Smudge going around the corner. "Is he alive?" All she could hear was the smuggler complaining about being stuck with one of the most boring jobs.

Ryan nodded, holding his hunting bow, his sword sheathed. "Let's get closer so we can take advantage of Smudge's distraction."

Mallory crept along the tunnel. It was only about six metres long, but it felt far too long when she saw Smudge enter the cave and they were only a quarter of the way along.

"How did you get in here?" the smuggler demanded. "Get away from me, you mangy creature."

Smudge chirruped repeatedly, the sound suddenly becoming his high-pitched repetitive warning chirps.

"Enough. I'm warning you. Get back here and I'll show you what we do to annoying creatures," the smuggler said.

Mallory broke into a run the moment Smudge began making his high-pitched cry. She hoped the smuggler wouldn't hear the sound of their footsteps over the noise Smudge made. Entering the cave, she prepared to throw a fireball at the smuggler who was advancing on Smudge, sword drawn.

Smudge fell silent when he saw them enter.

The smuggler looked between Mallory, Ryan,

Smudge and the two prisoners tied up and left on the ground beside the bed in the north west corner of the cave. "Who are you?" He took a step back towards the prisoners. "He yours?" He nodded towards Smudge.

Mallory mentally debated what to say. She didn't want to risk getting the Mer Point wagoner killed. "We came for Tyne. Let the merfolk go and I won't attack you." She glanced around the cave. It had no other exit and contained two beds along with a number of crates and barrels stacked mostly in the north east corner.

The smuggler glanced at Tyne. "You're here for her?"

Mallory nodded, trying not to think about how terrible the merfolk looked. Were they too late? Tyne looked worse than the merfolk who'd been hanging out in the sun. "Yes. Let her go."

The smuggler chuckled. "Do you think I'm stupid? I never heard you say he wouldn't attack me." He nodded towards Ryan. "Not that it matters. Rass would kill me if I went against his orders."

"He's dead. I killed him." Ryan lowered his hunting bow, returning the arrow to the quiver at his side.

The smuggler laughed. "You can't fool me with that comment either. I've worked for him long enough to know he has so many location specific revives it'd take an army to kill him. Not that an army would help since no one knows the location of all his revives."

Shock raced through Mallory. They'd made an enemy out of a hellion it'd take an army to kill? What had they done?

Ryan drew his sword. "You had your chance."

The smuggler spun, taking a step towards the Mer Point wagoner.

Mallory wasn't about to let the smuggler kill either of his captives. She threw a fireball at him, throwing another one as soon as she could. She was about to throw a third one when Ryan attacked the smuggler, getting in her way. She hurried along the side of the cave, looking for an opening. There was none. Ryan and the smuggler moved across the cave too quickly for her to attack one without risking harming the other. Keeping an eye on the smuggler, Mallory made her way to the two prisoners. She drew her dagger as she crouched at the side of Tyne who was the closest.

Smudge came over to Tyne, patting the merfolk on the cheek, making soft sounds. Tyne's eyes remained closed.

"I can pay you. Help me escape and I'll reward you," the Mer Point wagoner begged.

Mallory cut the rope that had been used to gag Tyne, along with the rope that bound the merfolk's hands together. The merfolk didn't move even though Smudge kept patting her on the cheek. Mallory glanced over her shoulder to check Ryan was okay before moving to the Mer Point wagoner's side, hoping he'd help her get the merfolk to the ocean. She kept her voice low. "Your son asked us to save you." She cut through the rope around his wrists and ankles. "But we wouldn't have left you here even if no one had asked for our help to rescue you." She kept checking over her shoulder, looking for an opportunity to help Ryan.

The Mer Point wagoner rubbed his wrists. "Thank you. I hope my son offered you a proper reward with what you've had to face fighting smugglers and the hellion who employed them."

Mallory helped the Mer Point wagoner to his feet. "He's already paid us." She turned towards Ryan in time to see him finish off the smuggler. She took a step towards him. "Are you okay?"

Ryan sheathed his sword. "What about Tyne? Is she alive?"

"I don't know what they did to her, but she's

unconscious. We need to get her to the ocean." Mallory looked towards Smudge when he chirruped then bounded from the cave. "What's he doing?"

"I dunno." Ryan turned to the Mer Point wagoner. "Are you okay? Can you help me carry her outside?"

The Mer Point wagoner helped Ryan lift Tyne. "What did my son pay you?"

Mallory followed them out of the cave. "He gave us six strong night vision potions to help us find our way in the caves."

The Mer Point wagoner walked backwards, carrying Tyne under the arms. "So he didn't actually offer you a reward for your help. Only something to help you carry out the task."

"It also helped us with our other quests in here," Mallory said.

"We'll work something out. And I'll have a talk to my son about his idea of rewarding someone." The wagoner looked over his shoulder as they went around the next corner. He came to a stop at the sight of Callum running towards them, his bow in hand.

Callum slowed as he approached them. "What's going on? Smudge came racing through the bigger cave before and wouldn't stop when I called out to him."

Chapter Thirty-One

Mallory shrugged. "I don't know. Smudge was patting Tyne's cheek and took off when she didn't wake."

"Think he's gone for help?" Callum walked ahead of them as they continued along the tunnel.

Again Mallory shrugged. "I don't know. I can't exactly understand what he's saying." She smiled. "Except for when he's giving us a warning. You should have seen him distracting the smuggler that was in the last cave. There are a heap of crates and a few barrels in there as well. I'm not sure how we're going to get all of them out of here. We also didn't get a chance to check the smuggler for items."

"How many barrels and crates are you trying to get out of here?" the Mer Point wagoner asked.

"We didn't count them. Maybe ten barrels and nearly as many crates. There are also these two chests." Ryan got a better grip on Tyne's tail, nodding to the chests they passed. "It's not exactly easy to carry merfolk."

"Need a hand?" Callum asked.

Ryan shook his head. "There isn't enough space to walk side-by-side in this tunnel. You could go back and search that last cave and the smuggler."

Callum stepped past the tunnel that led to the bigger cave, waiting for them to head towards the cave before taking a step back the way they'd come. He frowned, stopping to stare at the ground. "It looks more worn away here."

"It might be a secret door," the Mer Point wagoner said as they continued along the tunnel to the bigger cave.

Mallory laughed softly. "That'll impress Brodie."

"Him and Danni can check it out while I search the last cave." Callum strode along the tunnel.

Mallory hurried after the Mer Point wagoner and Ryan who were partway across the bigger cave. She smiled at Danae and Brodie who came out of the larger tunnel that led west to the pit trap. "Callum said there might be a secret door in the cave wall opposite the eastern tunnel leading out of this tunnel."

"Cool." Brodie headed for the eastern tunnel, walking faster. "We found a couple of planks that were long enough to go over the pit trap. It'll make it easier to get everything out of here if we can figure out a way to do that." He looked over his shoulder. "Want to help me find the secret door, Danni?"

Mallory entered the western tunnel and followed Ryan and the Mer Point wagoner who crossed the planks. She kept a hold of her wand. If there were any smugglers left in the area they would be at a disadvantage carrying Tyne.

"Maybe we can come to some sort of arrangement about the barrels and crates," the Mer Point wagoner said.

"What kind of arrangement?" Ryan asked.

"I pay some of the locals to help me load my wagon each time I take goods to Surith. I can pay them to collect everything and in exchange, I'll receive fifty percent of the value of the goods. I'll also arrange to sell any of your share you don't want to keep, paying you market value upfront so you don't have to wait around for the goods to be sold." The Mer Point wagoner stumbled as he stepped off the other end of the planks.

"I don't know," Mallory said. "I've got a feeling Brodie won't be overly happy with those terms."

"Forty percent," the Mer Point wagoner offered.

Mallory smiled. She hadn't realised she was meant

to be negotiating. Brodie was the one who should be having this conversation. He enjoyed bargaining with traders and the like. "Maybe we should wait until we can discuss this together. The rest might have other ideas about how to get the goods out of the caves."

"Thirty percent. That's as low as I can go," the Mer Point wagoner said.

Ryan chuckled as they stepped out of the cave. "I think even your brother would be happy with those terms."

Mallory grinned. She was pretty certain her brother would be unimpressed if he knew she hadn't been trying to drive a harder bargain. "I'll check with everyone else, but they will probably be happy with that offer. Not all of the goods are ours though. The ones with the words 'Mer Point Traders' painted on them are the trader's property." She remained on the beach as they carried Tyne into the ocean.

When the water was knee deep, Ryan lowered Tyne into it. "Maybe we should give her some of our health tea."

Smudge surfaced, holding out a fish, chattering at Ryan.

"People need to be conscious to eat," Ryan said. "It was a good idea though, Smudge."

Brodie burst out of the cave, followed by Danae, Callum and Fang. "I found it. I found the secret door. Oh, and that potion gives you no warning when it's gonna wear off." He gestured towards Callum who carried a lit lantern. "Luckily we found that in the cave and the fire was still going so Callum could see to light it." His gaze was drawn to Tyne. "She's not dead, is she?"

Before Ryan had the chance to answer, Edlien and Gal surfaced, swimming towards them. Edlien reached Tyne first. "Are all those responsible dead?"

Ryan, who'd been supporting Tyne gave her to Edlien. "We learned that one of them has a location specific revive. Possibly several revives. Rass. A hellion."

"Do you plan to go after him?" Gal demanded.

The image of Rass filled Mallory's mind. "I've got a feeling he'll be coming after us." Unless they could figure out a way to prevent him.

"Will you let us know if the day comes that he has no revives left?" Edlien asked. "We'd be willing to reward those who brought about that event."

Gal took the fish from Smudge. "Or if he's ever in a location where we can take our revenge on him for what he's done to our colony." He held out a shell that was the same shape as the one that had been given to Mallory. Unlike it though, this one was a polished ebony colour. "You can let me know with the help of this message shell."

"How does it work?" Ryan asked.

"The same way as the twisted pearl shell works." Gal slipped beneath the water, swimming away and taking the fish with him.

Edlien continued to support Tyne in the water. "Thank you for all you've done. We'll take Tyne home where she can be healed. You have the gratitude of our entire shoal." She beckoned two merfolk forward. One took Tyne from her and the other handed her a barnacle encrusted sword. She held it out to Ryan. "I know you declined any of our salvage, and this may be worth nothing more than the jewel in its hilt, but take it with our gratitude for saving one precious to us." She slipped beneath the surface the moment Ryan took it from her, arrowing through the water. She was soon out of sight.

Ryan waded through the water, looking at the sword he carried. "I didn't expect this."

"You did save the leader of their shoal." The Mer Point trader joined Mallory on the beach. "Is this all your party? Did you want to ask them about the terms I offered?"

"I levelled up," Brodie exclaimed. "I was the first one of our party to get a character level."

"Technically you were the second. Danni got her character level first," Ryan said.

"That doesn't count," Brodie said.

"Why don't I count?" Danae asked. "Aren't I in your party?"

"You do count. And you are in our party. I mean…" Brodie looked at each of them. "Uhm. I meant you started before us. That's all."

Mallory laughed, not feeling in the least like taking sympathy on her brother. "I don't know, Brodie. I clearly heard you say the first of our party."

Brodie's eyes narrowed as he turned to his sister. "I should make you wait outside the secret room when we search the chests."

"Does this mean you're not interested in accepting my terms?" the Mer Point wagoner asked.

Chapter Thirty-Two

Mallory was tempted to laugh again when she saw the Mer Point wagoner's confused expression. "If you want to wait in the first cave, we'll talk about it while we check out the secret room Brodie found."

The wagoner inclined his head, stepping inside the cave and sitting on a rock not far from the opening.

Mallory half listened to Ryan's explanation to Callum, Brodie and Danae as they walked across the plank that covered the trap. She brought up her journal and read over the details of the quest they'd completed. *Merfolk In Danger: You rescued Tyne and returned her to Edlien and were rewarded with salvage, a barnacle encrusted sword, for your party. You also earned ten experience points each.* Noticing there was a new quest, she grinned. Obviously Brodie had been too busy admiring his new character level to have noticed. *Waiting For Justice: Edlien and Gal want the death of the ones responsible for harming those of their merfolk colony. Including Rass, the hellion who escaped. They are willing to reward anyone who can bring this about.*

They were nearly out of the bigger cave when Brodie exclaimed, "Not another quest."

Mallory laughed. "I wondered when you were going to notice."

"You couldn't have told me?" Brodie demanded.

"Not likely," Callum said. "Who wants to be the bearer of bad news? You do realise that quest is going to be stuck in our journals for ages."

Brodie stopped beside the door to the secret room, the rock walls and ground smoothed to create a space two metres wide and three metres deep. "The lever was a hole in the wall with a mechanism that needed to be pushed inwards."

Mallory stepped into the room, two chests in front of her and an empty weapons rack on her left. "Let's see if this secret room is as profitable as previous ones." She crouched in front of the chests, trying to open them. "They're locked." She eyed the keyholes. "How are we going to get them open?"

"The blacksmith might be able to open them," Danae suggested.

"The other chests down the end of this tunnel are

locked too." Callum stood in the doorway, gesturing towards the left.

"We only accept the Mer Point wagoner's offer if it doesn't include the chests, but he also helps get them out of here for us too," Brodie said.

"What was found in the last cave and the bigger cave?" Ryan asked.

"All the barrels and crates were nailed shut, but I found another grey, woollen blanket and five copper pieces. The mage's staff was under one of the beds. I put the staff and blanket in the bigger cave with the rest of the gear," Callum said. "I also found a satchel and…" He drew the word out as he opened the satchel that he'd slipped the strap of over one arm and his head so it hung at his hip. "I found this." He took out a small pottery jar with a wooden cork in the top and opened it. "Ground coffee beans. Enough for about three cups."

Mallory peered in the jar. "Does this mean we don't have to go through hell for coffee?"

Callum corked the jar and returned it to his satchel. "They're not going to last that long." He handed over the five copper coins to Mallory.

"We found a light padded gambeson and a heap of food," Brodie said. "Danni told us that anyone can wear light padded armour. It's padded armour that only archers can wear. The light stuff can be worn by anyone, including traders and craftsmen. It just looked like a plain, padded jacket to me. With absolutely no style to it."

Arriving back in the bigger cave, Mallory picked up the staff. "We should get these quests completed and escort the Mer Point wagoner home. It'd be nice if we can head back to Surith before dark." She put her wand in the canvas loop so she could hold the staff with both hands. It wasn't as difficult for her to carry as Ryan's shield had been, but it wasn't as comfortable as her wand. It felt like one day she'd be capable of wielding such a weapon. Although that day felt like it'd be a long time coming.

"What about the food?" Brodie gestured towards the spread on the table. "We aren't going to leave it here, are we?"

"Take what we can fit in satchels and the backpack," Ryan said.

They found several calico cloths on the table, guessing they'd been wrapped around some of the food. Mallory wrapped a loaf of bread and put it in her satchel, Brodie wrapped a meat pie and handed it to Danae who'd put a large wedge of cheese in her satchel, having wrapped a calico cloth around it first. Ryan put six apples and four oranges in the backpack and tied the blankets on top. He continued to carry the barnacle encrusted sword. Callum put a half filled jar of honey in his satchel, making sure it was sitting upright, and two metal spoons. He put a plate of cooked fish on the ground for Smudge and Fang to share.

"I would have eaten that," Brodie exclaimed.

"Have this instead." Callum handed him a bowl of berries, grinning.

Brodie glared at him, returning them to the table and taking a small bowl of olives. He ate them as they walked towards the exit.

Mallory was relieved to see the Mer Point wagoner was safe. He rose to his feet when they approached, agreeing to their new terms, the quest updating. *A Son's Request: The wagoner offered to help remove the barrels, crates and chests from the caves in exchange for thirty percent of the value of the barrels and crates. He is also willing to pay you a fair price for any items you wish to sell in thanks for all you have done.* She looked at the tide that had come closer to the cliffs. "We better get back to Mer Point before it's too late in the day to empty the caves." They had a lot to get done before they needed to escort the Buckneth wagoner home.

The walk to Mer Point was silent and Callum carried Smudge who curled up in his arms and slept.

Fang walked at Brodie's side rather than checking out the various smells nearby like she often did. When they reached the foot of the steep stairs, Mallory groaned, her gaze drawn to Smudge. "Right now I envy him."

Ryan chuckled. "The steps do look longer than before." He started up the stairs, glancing over his shoulder. "Weren't you the one in a hurry to beat the tide?"

She sighed heavily before following him.

They didn't manage to reach the village before the Mer Point wagoner's son came running towards them, throwing his arms around his father. "You're alive."

The Mer Point wagoner wrapped his arms around his son, patting him on the back. "I've faced worse than a handful of smugglers before." He drew away from his son, resting a hand on his shoulder. "Round up the men. We have work to do this afternoon."

His son nodded before running back to the village.

The Mer Point wagoner faced Mallory. "I'll let the trader know he can collect his goods. He might want to coordinate our efforts. When everything is up here I'll send my son to fetch you. My place is north of the round yard."

"Okay." Mallory watched him go before

continuing towards the village. "We should probably let Art know we're back."

"What about finishing off the quest for the mage?" Brodie asked. "Don't the rest of you want a character level? I still can't decide what attributes I want to put my points in. I'm going to get level one rogue though."

Mallory continued walking towards the tavern. "I want to make sure Art is okay. We're meant to be escorting him, not deserting him somewhere."

"Why don't they give information in the journal about what all the attributes do?" Brodie paused a moment before he spoke again. "You have reached level one rogue. You can now use stealth. Hell yeah! I've got a revive." He frowned. "What is stealth?"

"Being able to move silently," Danae said.

"How do I use it? Or make it work?" Brodie asked.

"It was in the commands listed in the welcome pack," Callum said.

"Doesn't mean to say I remember the exact wording," Brodie said. "Do you?"

Ryan chuckled. "Of course he does. He probably read it more than all of us combined."

"Activate stealth. How hard is that to remember?" Callum asked.

"There's just so much to remember," Brodie muttered.

Mallory paused at the door of the tavern, looking over her shoulder at her companions. "There is a lot to remember. But we'll get there eventually."

"I wish I had more than the welcome pack to read." Callum followed Mallory inside the tavern.

Chapter Thirty-Three

Mallory stopped when she saw the mage was sitting at a table with Roast.

Elodie beckoned them over to the bar. "How did you go? You deal with the smugglers?"

"We got all of them. A hellion too," Brodie said. "There were eighteen or nineteen of them."

"They were hired by a hellion," Ryan said.

"You got rid of the hellion?" Elodie asked.

Mallory wished she could say yes. "He had a location specific revive. We have no idea where he ended up."

Elodie took a roughly woven cloth, drawstring bag from behind the bar and held it out to them. "They should think twice about coming around here in future. Thank you for your help. You're always welcome in our village."

Mallory took the cloth bag, nearly dropping it. The

bag was a lot heavier than she'd expected. "We're glad we could help." She handed the bag to Ryan. It was too difficult holding it and the staff.

Elodie nodded towards the staff. "I better let you return that."

Mallory crossed the tavern to where the mage and Roast sat, checking her journal as she did. A smile slowly formed. She finally had her first character level. She'd sort it out later. Once she'd finished talking to the mage. Going to the quest bookmark, she read over the details of the completed quest. *Cry for help: You rid Mer Point of the smugglers in the nearby caves. You were rewarded with a bag of loot for your party. You also earned fifteen experience points each.*

Brodie moved closer to Mallory. "When can we see what's in the bag?"

"Later. When we're finished." Reaching the table, Mallory held out the staff, relieved to hand over her burden.

Taking the staff, the mage nodded to Roast. "We've been having a chat while you've been gone."

Mallory tensed. "You have?" She tried to think of why that would be a bad thing.

"Yes, we have. Why didn't you mention that me helping him is of little benefit to you? That he isn't a member of your party. Two spells are nothing compared to what my staff is worth."

"Oh." Mallory had no idea what to say.

"What do you want for returning my staff?"

Mallory frowned, her gaze drawn to the staff the mage held. "But we've already returned it."

The mage slowly shook her head. "I am perfectly aware of that. Now, what do you want for your help?"

Mallory stared at the mage, speechless for a moment. "I don't know."

"We used up one of our health potions in getting the staff," Brodie said.

The mage nodded her head once. "Done. Visit me before you leave the village." She strode from the tavern.

Mallory stared after her. "I didn't think about that. All I was thinking of was what magic things we might need. And she's already said we can choose two spells."

Roast got to his feet. "You don't mind if I go to the mage's place? She said she'd be able to help me out once you'd brought the staff back."

Ryan slipped the bag of loot into the backpack. "Do you know exactly where the trader's place is? We were only told north of the round yard."

Roast nodded. "Two buildings north of here. I'll show you." He walked outside with them, pointing out the building before he headed to the mage's place.

Before going to the traders, they put some of their new gear in the panniers. They found the trader in his shop. He greeted them with a smile. "Thank you for locating my stock." He made a sweeping gesture that indicated his shop. "The twenty percent discount includes everything I have for sale." He put a bottle of maple syrup with a cork stopper on the counter along with a map of Ruby Isle. "They didn't steal all my maple syrup. I had another barrel that was partly filled."

"Can we come back later when we find out what's in the crates, barrels and chests the Mer Point wagoner is bringing back from the caves?" Ryan folded the map so it would fit in his belt pouch then picked up the bottle of maple syrup.

"Whenever you wish," the trader said.

Callum pointed at a book on a shelf behind the trader. "Can I have a look at that book? Understanding The Crafting Ability Diplomacy."

"I'm not about to let you read it without buying it. Then there'd be no point for you to buy it once you unlocked the skill and knew about the different abilities gained for each level," the trader said.

"That book unlocks diplomacy," Brodie said.

The trader nodded.

"Can you get other books to unlock the different crafting abilities?" Brodie asked.

"I have the one for diplomacy and one for sailing. Only eight gold pieces each with the twenty percent discount," the trader said.

"Sixteen gold for the two?" Brodie winced. "That sounds a bit much."

"If you buy several items I might be able to give you a multiple purchase discount like I do for my other customers," the trader offered.

"It's a typical price," Danae said.

"We'll be back later." Brodie strode towards the door with one last glance at the book on display.

Smiling, Mallory followed him, bringing up her journal to check the updated quest. *Stolen Stock: The trader is grateful you located his stolen stock. You were rewarded with a map of Ruby Isle, a bottle of maple syrup and a twenty percent discount on all stock in his shop for your party. You also earned two experience points each.* She stared at the experience earned.

"What?" Brodie demanded, stopping in the middle of the road. "Two experience points? What's with that?"

"Locate quests obviously aren't good if you want to focus on XP gains," Callum said.

"Not good?" Brodie demanded. "They're the worst. If it wasn't for the other quests and finding the food it wouldn't have been worth doing."

"What about the discount at the traders?" Mallory asked.

"Okay, that too," Brodie said.

Callum gestured towards the mage's place. "We going to see what XP we get for finding the staff?"

"It better not be two XP," Brodie muttered. "And when are we going to look inside the loot bag?"

"We can have a look now if you want," Mallory said.

"Yes." Brodie reached for Ryan's backpack.

Ryan stepped away. "I can manage." He took another step back when Brodie tried to look in the bag he took out. "Maybe we should have checked it in the tavern. At least then we could have tipped it over the table so we could all see what was in it."

Mallory took the bag from him, opening it up to peer inside. There was a mixture of coins, jewellery and trinkets. She held it out for everyone else to have a look. "Want to hold it again for me, Ryan, so I can get the coins out?"

Ryan took the bag from her, holding it while she

removed the coins. "Should we see if the Buckneth wagoner will sell this stuff in Surith for us?"

"He'll charge us a selling fee," Brodie protested.

"We might not have time to get everything done and sell it in Surith," Callum said. "It might make sense to have him sell it for us."

Mallory shrugged, busy counting the coins. "Four gold, seven silver and twenty-three copper pieces."

"Can we share it out?" Brodie asked.

Chapter Thirty-Four

Mallory mentally calculated how much money they had. "Okay. We can't share all of it out though."

"Why can't-" Brodie broke off. "Wait. What? We can?"

Mallory laughed, the sound echoed by Ryan and Callum. "Yeah. We can."

"Cool. How much?" Brodie asked.

Mallory gave each of them a silver and four copper pieces, adding the rest to the group funds. They now had a total of sixty-three gold, forty-four silver and seventy-seven copper pieces. "Ready to see the mage now?"

The mage greeted them when they entered, directing them to a counter with two health potions lying on it, a large, leather-bound book beside it. "That book contains a list of the spells I have available for sale. What level are you?"

"Unlevelled," Mallory said.

"You've got a character level you can use to level up your mage," Brodie said.

Mallory started to say she wasn't certain what to do with her point. It would have taken too long to argue it out with her brother so she moved closer to the book. "What spells do you have for an unlevelled mage?"

"All the basic elemental spells, flame and mend spell level one." The mage opened the book, turning a few pages. "Which two would you like?"

"I already have a basic elemental spell. Fire. I should probably get the other two rather than another elemental one," Mallory said. "What does flame and mend do?"

"Mend spell is used for repairing different things. The level one version can only mend cloth. The more you level it up, the larger the damage you can repair and the less mana it costs to repair it." The mage gestured to the tear in the sleeve of Brodie's tunic. "You could mend that with it."

"That sounds useful," Mallory said. "What about the other one?"

"Flame allows you to set things alight. Both those spells are useful, but having one of the basic elemental spells doesn't make the rest of them useless. Different creatures are weak to some elements and other creatures are resistant to them." The mage paused. "Which spells do you want?"

"Flame sounds good for when we have a campfire," Brodie said.

Callum eyed Brodie's tunic. "Mend sounds more useful than any of them."

"I'll go with mend and flame. How much are the elemental spells for unlevelled mages?" Mallory asked.

"They start at fifteen gold pieces." The mage took two scrolls from behind the counter. "Read them aloud to learn them." She picked up the health potion vials. "These are for you too."

Mallory tucked the two health potions and spell scrolls into her satchel. She'd look them over later. "Thank you." She sent a longing glance at the spells she couldn't afford before she turned to Roast who stood off to one side. "What about your amulet and broken charm?"

"They've been dealt with," the mage said.

"Thanks." Mallory glanced over her shoulder. "We should probably see if the Mer Point wagoner has brought the crates, barrels and chests out of the caves." She noticed the journal icon was in the corner of her vision.

"I'll go with you," Roast said. "I guess you'll want

to leave once you've finished with the Mer Point wagoner. There are less than two hours until dark."

"Enough time to at least reach Surith before dark as long as we leave within the next half hour." She headed outside while checking her journal. *Missing Staff: The mage was pleased to have her staff returned and surprised to learn that half of what she offered was for a person not in your party so she offered a different reward including repairing the charm for Arthur of Wildebay and giving him a fire resist amulet. You were rewarded with two spells for an unlevelled mage and two health potions (ten health points each) for your party. You also earned five experience points each.*

"Five XP?" Brodie exclaimed. "That's not much better than the other quest."

"We should focus on escort missions," Ryan said. "Better XP."

Mallory glanced at Roast. If he hadn't been with them, she would have mentioned how much of a pain escort missions could be. She decided to change the topic. "Did you test the charm and amulet, Art?"

"The charm works. I was able to shapeshift and change back without ending up naked," Roast said. "The mage told me I'd damaged it with my magic that went awry."

"What does it look like?" Mallory looked him up

and down, but she couldn't see anything that might be a charm.

"An expandable, plain bracelet I wear around my ankle. It expands or shrinks depending on what shape I'm in," Roast said.

"Cool." Brodie knocked on the door of the Mer Point wagoner's house.

The door was opened by his son. "My father had just sent me to collect you. He's out the back. There are too many barrels and crates to fit everything inside. He sent for the blacksmith to open the chests." The boy stepped outside, glancing up at Mallory before returning his gaze to the ground. "This way."

Mallory followed him. "What about the barrels and crates? Did he get them open?"

The boy nodded. "We pried them open."

Mallory's steps slowed as they came around the corner of the house. There were a lot more barrels and crates than she'd expected. Either that or it looked more when they were gathered together in the one area. She counted them as they continued to walk towards them. Fifteen barrels and nine crates as well as four chests that the blacksmith was working on opening.

"What's in them?" Ryan strode towards the closest barrel.

The boy continued to walk beside them. "Barrels have vinegar, wine, flour, rice, olives, ale, barley and oats. Crates have cloth, carded wool, blankets and one has rag dolls."

Ryan peered into the barrel in front of him. "Olives."

Brodie's gaze travelled across the barrels spread out behind the Mer Point wagoner's house. "Which ones have wine and ale?"

The Mer Point wagoner joined them. "Elodie said she's interested in the wine and ale. The flour and olives too. The rest I can easily sell in Surith when I travel there in a couple of days."

Mallory grinned when the journal icon appeared in the corner of her vision and she checked it to find a quest had been updated. *Information Needed: You have learned the Mer Point wagoner plans to travel to Surith in a couple of days.* Now all they had to do was let the Surith trader know.

"A pity we don't have a caravan or wagon so we can take a lot of this stuff with us." Callum set Smudge on the ground.

Smudge and Fang wandered amongst the crates and barrels, sniffing at them and trying to peer in at the top.

"Do you think Bobbi could carry a barrel of ale?" Brodie asked.

Mallory slowly shook her head. "We can't carry unnecessary stuff."

"Ale is necessary," Brodie protested.

The blacksmith straightened, gesturing to the chest that was open in front of him. "A lot of bits and pieces in it. Waterskins, tools, daggers and pottery jars."

Brodie grabbed one of the waterskins out of the chest. "I can fill it with ale."

Again Mallory slowly shook her head. Before she could say anything, Callum grabbed a waterskin too.

"I need one. I doubt you're going to share." Callum strode to a barrel of wine.

The rest of the chests were soon opened and they found similar gear. Brodie filled a two litre waterskin with ale and Callum filled one with wine. Mallory rolled her eyes when Ryan also filled one with wine, grinning at her. Mallory threw her hands up in the air when Danae filled a waterskin with ale after Brodie suggested she should.

Danae ran a hand over a piece of emerald green cloth. "It'd make a nice dress."

"Do you want it?" Brodie asked.

Danae looked at the cloth a moment longer before she stepped away. "It isn't practical."

"Wine and ale is?" Mallory looked at each of the waterskins they carried.

Ryan chuckled. "Obviously." He turned to the Mer Point wagoner. "What will you pay us for our share?"

"Wait a minute," Brodie protested. "What if I want some of the food? I could make porridge with the oats. Or Anzac biscuits with them and the flour. If I can get some sugar and golden syrup. I wonder what they'd be like with maple syrup instead of golden syrup."

Chapter Thirty-Five

Mallory checked how close the sun was to the horizon before facing her brother. "Make it quick. We still have to visit the traders."

Brodie ended up taking a kilogram of oats, three of rice and two of flour, ignoring Mallory when she said they already had a kilogram of flour from the bandit camp. They also took four thick, grey woollen blankets when Callum suggested they could cut a hole in them and use them as a poncho if the weather grew cold, or shorten them to be used as cloaks.

The Mer Point wagoner took out a small, leather-bound book and filled it with cramped handwriting as he calculated the value of the rest of the goods and gave them their share. Thanking him, they headed towards the traders, Mallory slipping the thirty-seven gold pieces into her satchel. She checked the updated quest. *A Son's Request: You escorted the Mer Point wagoner home. You were rewarded with seventy percent of the value of the barrels and crates and the entire value of the chests for your party. You also earned twenty experience points each.*

"Now that's better XP," Brodie said.

"How much money do we have now?" Callum asked.

"A hundred gold, forty-four silver and seventy-seven copper pieces. Although one of those gold pieces belongs to Smudge. Did you want to carry it for him?" Mallory asked.

"You can carry it for now," Callum said. "Does that mean we can buy both those books? I want the full set. That's what I've been missing. How can I decide what to level up when I don't know all the details? There wasn't anywhere near enough information in the welcome pack. I miss not having a wiki."

"We should probably get armour," Mallory said.

"We're doing okay without it for now," Callum said. "Those books would be handy."

"I want to unlock diplomacy." Brodie stepped inside the traders.

"That's two votes." Callum followed him.

Ryan chuckled as the rest of them entered the shop. "Make that three. We can afford it. And it'll be useful knowing more information."

"Do you have any other information books?" Callum asked the trader. "They don't have to unlock anything."

"I have 'Understanding The Classes Of Inadon: Mage' if you're interested," the trader said. "It gives details about the class, but doesn't unlock it."

"How much?" Mallory looked at the thin book he placed on the counter. Learning more about the class would be good.

"Four gold with the twenty percent discount."

"We'll take the three books." Ryan glanced around the shop. "Anything else we need?"

They had the oil in the lanterns and flasks topped up, bought belt pouches for Mallory and Callum, a wooden bucket, a light brown shirt for Mallory to wear with her trousers, when she managed to wash them, and three spare shirts. A light grey and two black ones.

Mallory handed over the thirteen gold and six silver pieces the trader charged them after he'd given them a twenty percent discount and multiple purchases discount. They headed to the well, they were given directions to, so Mallory could wash the trousers before they left the village. She used their new bucket. "I should have got a second set of clothes."

"We'll get more," Brodie said.

"I'll get our gear and Bob." Ryan turned to Danae. "You coming with me so you can saddle your horse?"

"I'll help too," Brodie said.

Mallory was left on her own, Callum and Roast joining Ryan and Danae, Smudge and Fang following them. Mallory returned to washing the trousers.

Elodie strode towards the well. "The trader said you'd be here when I went over there to find you. We're going to have a celebration tonight. A party. You're all invited. There'll be plenty of food, drink, music and dancing."

Mallory smiled. It was a good thing her brother had gone with Ryan and Danae. "We have to escort Art home and be back in Surith tomorrow to escort the Buckneth wagoner home."

"Are you certain?" Elodie asked. "We'd love to have you stay. Everyone would like to thank you."

Mallory twisted the trousers to wring the water out of them. "We really can't stay. But thank you for the offer." She would have liked seeing what a party was like on Ruby Isle.

Elodie inclined her head. "You're always welcome to visit. Maybe we'll see you another time."

Mallory shrugged. "Maybe." She had no idea where their travels would take them.

"Safe travels." Elodie nodded before striding back to the tavern.

Brodie reached Mallory first. "What did she want?" He gestured towards Elodie who stepped inside the tavern.

"We're welcome back here if we're ever in the area." Mallory debated with herself if she should tell her brother about the offer as she hung the trousers on the outside of a pannier. She waited until they had left Mer Point behind to tell everyone about the invitation, all of them visiting the outhouse before they began their journey to Surith.

Ryan laughed at Brodie's complaints. "Can you blame her? You would have wanted to stay and it's late enough we won't reach Surith until dark."

"I didn't even get to check out the lighthouse," Brodie muttered. "It'd be cool to live in a lighthouse."

"Will we have to stay in Surith tonight? Roast asked. "I have friends we can stay with if we do need to stay."

Ryan shrugged. "We'll talk to the wagoner and see what time he wants to leave tomorrow."

"We gained ten rep at Mer Point." Brodie turned to Mallory. "When are you going to level up your mage so you can heal us? You could probably have all of us at full health by the time we reach Surith."

"I haven't decided if I want to level up mage or put the level in warrior." As much as she wanted to unlock warrior, there were a few benefits to levelling up mage.

"We've already got a warrior. We don't need two," Brodie said. "You could heal us during fights and we wouldn't have to worry about getting killed."

"I'm not going to become a support class." Mallory glared at her brother. "If you're so worried about it, why don't you go support?"

"No. As if," Brodie said. "That sounds boring."

"Then why should I be expected to be support?" Mallory demanded.

"Because you're the one who chose mage," Brodie pointed out.

"Not so I could stand back and keep you alive while you have all the fun." Mallory chose her second class, raising her chin before she spoke again. "You have reached level one warrior. You can now wield dual swords."

"Nice," Ryan said. "That's what I need to do." He grinned. "Done."

Brodie turned to Callum. "You haven't levelled up yet. You could choose mage as a second class. We have a healing spell. Someone needs to be able to use it."

"You have reached level one archer. You can now wield slings and use sling ammunition." Callum grinned at Brodie.

Brodie threw his hands up in the air. "We're going to die. We have a perfectly good healing spell and no one wants to use it."

"Next level," Mallory said. "I'm going to alternate."

"Then we should focus on gaining XP so you can level up mage," Brodie said.

Callum scooped Smudge up off the ground, his steps having grown slower. "I'm going to focus on archer for now. I like the class. I'd love to get my hands on a book for it like the one we got for mage. It'd be interesting to learn more about each class."

"Check traders in each village you visit. It shouldn't take too long to find one. Books on combat classes are fairly common," Roast said.

"Thanks," Callum said.

"What is everyone going to put their attribute points in?" Mallory looked at Ryan, Callum and Brodie. "I'm thinking of adding some to strength and constitution. Other than that, I'm not sure."

"I might put all of mine in the health one," Brodie said. "Or maybe one in dexterity." He grinned. "To compensate for the ale."

Chapter Thirty-Six

Mallory slowly shook her head at her brother's comment, focusing on allocating her five new attribute points. She put two in constitution and one each in intelligence, wisdom and strength. Checking everyone's stats, she saw Ryan had put two in both strength and constitution and one in luck. Brodie had put four points in constitution and one in dexterity and Callum had added two points to both dexterity and constitution and one point to strength. "A bit worried about dying, Brodie?"

Ryan chuckled. "It looks that way."

Brodie glared at them, his gaze returning to Mallory. "You're the one who wouldn't level up mage so you can use the healing spell."

"At least you have a revive now," Callum said.

"It'd be better to have two like you and Ryan," Brodie muttered.

"My crit attack has gone up a point on the cutlass and short sword," Ryan said.

"My bow crit has gone up a point too," Callum said.

Mallory checked her attack stats. "Both the normal and crit attack has gone up by one for my fireball spell."

"Should we be charging people more for quests?" Brodie asked. "The Mer Point mage and wagoner seemed to think we were being underpaid."

"It's a wealthier village," Danae said. "They can afford to pay more for what they need done. You'll find that in bigger towns and the capital too."

"We need to go to the mainland so we can earn more," Brodie said.

Mallory smiled. It finally felt like they were making progress and that they might be able to face higher levelled areas. "When it's time." They had a few more things to do on Ruby Isle. She thought of the fire drake nest and Cutthroat Harbour. Quite a few things to do.

The journey into Surith was uneventful and they needed to light one of the lanterns long before they arrived. They also shared the slice of cake Roast had saved for Mallory, Ryan and Danae while Brodie had some of his jerky. Asking at the traders, they learned the wagoner was three buildings along at the tavern, across from the harbour. They also told the trader the information he was waiting on and collected seven copper pieces. Mallory checked the updated quest details. *Information Needed: You told the trader the information he needed. You were rewarded with seven copper pieces for your party. You also earned five experience points each.*

Before they left, Callum asked the trader, "Do you have any books about the classes of Inadon or crafting abilities?"

"I have all of the combat class books and shipwright," the trader said. "Five gold pieces for each of the class books and ten gold pieces for the crafting ability book."

Callum turned to Mallory. "What do you think? I'd like the crafting book, but I can do without it for now. Just the class ones would be good. Shipwright will probably be as useful to us as wheelwright is likely to be, but it'd be nice to learn it too."

"I want the rogue one," Brodie said. "We got mage for you so we should get ones for the rest of us."

Mallory mentally calculated how much money they'd have left. "Okay. The three class books we don't have." She handed over fifteen gold pieces while

Callum took the slim, leather-bound books, Smudge at his heel.

As they walked to the tavern, Brodie took the rogue book from Callum. "Are we going to take a rest so I can check this out?"

"We have to see what the wagoner's plans are," Mallory said. "We might have to continue to Wildebay tonight." She turned to Roast who had mostly been quiet all afternoon. "Are you okay?"

Roast nodded. "I can't stop thinking about Merry and what she must be going through. Her cousin too."

"We'll go after her and all the others who've been captured and taken to Cutthroat Harbour," Mallory said.

"I want to go with you," Roast said.

Mallory didn't know how to reply. She didn't know if Roast would be a help or a hindrance. So she was relieved when they reached the tavern. "We have to ask the wagoner what time he wants to leave tomorrow."

They found him at a table in the corner, having something to eat. There were only three other chairs at the table. He gestured to the chairs at a nearby table. "Bring some over and sit down."

"We only stopped in to find out what time you want to leave tomorrow," Mallory said.

Ryan nodded towards Roast. "We still have to return to Wildebay."

"I'd like to leave before midday." The wagoner handed Mallory three gold pieces. "What I made for the items you left with me."

"We have some more things you could sell for us," Callum said. "How much is your seller fee?"

"I can do that. Won't even charge my usual fee since the trader was happy I brought you with me after I assured him you'd get the information he needed. You did get it, didn't you?" the wagoner asked.

Mallory nodded. "Yeah. We did."

The wagoner gestured to the table. "Will the items fit here or will they need to be stored on my wagon for the night?"

"They'll fit on the table." Mallory took a step towards the exit. "We won't be long." They headed outside to where Augusta and Bobbi were, gathering the gear they wanted to sell. Back in the tavern, they put the loot bag on the table along with a chisel, a quiver, a ruby necklace Mallory had forgotten to give him earlier and the four pieces of jewellery in their drawstring bags.

The wagoner looked through some of the items. "Should be able to sell this easily."

"Thanks," Ryan said. "We'll see you tomorrow morning."

They said goodbye to the wagoner, traipsing outside, Brodie complaining they should have bought something to eat. They found somewhere out of the way and had the meat pie from the smugglers' caves along with half of the loaf of bread with some of the honey. Roast had his own food he'd brought with him. Before they continued to Wildebay, Mallory strapped on the sheathed short sword they'd got from the caves. She couldn't wait until the trousers were dry and she could dress in clothes suited to Inadon.

Her right hand kept resting on the hilt of her sword, a smile forming each time it did. They walked along the coastal road, leaving the busy harbour behind, the shadowy darkness of the night pressing in on them.

"You never said if I could travel with you to Cutthroat Harbour," Roast said once they'd left Surith well behind.

"You don't need to come with us," Mallory said. "We will rescue Merry."

"I'll go with or without you," Roast warned.

Mallory barely managed not to sigh. They couldn't

let him travel all that way on his own. And especially not to such a dangerous place.

Ryan spoke before Mallory could. "You can travel with us. But no running into danger. There's no point getting yourself killed trying to rescue Merry."

"All right," Roast said. "That sounds fair. As long as we do go after Merry and her cousin as soon as possible."

Mallory talked about the hellion's conversation regarding the boats leaving Cutthroat Harbour on the nineteenth. "We should deal with the hellion encampment where Welby was held. The less who return to Cutthroat Harbour while we're down there rescuing people, the better."

They argued the option as they continued to Wildebay. Brodie wanted to head straight to Cutthroat Harbour where there'd be plenty of the dark forces for them to take on and earn more money in their world. Callum agreed that taking out the encampment first was a good idea and Danae worried she wouldn't have time to do everything before she had to return to catch a ship to Simria.

Chapter Thirty-Seven

They were over halfway to Wildebay when four goblins attacked. Mallory drew both her sword and wand, automatically throwing a fireball at one of the goblins. Beside her, Roast became a rooster, throwing a fireball at one of the other goblins.

The goblins were taken out within minutes and Mallory was almost disappointed she didn't get to use her sword. Scanning the area, she saw nothing moving. Turning to Roast, she smiled when he became human again, his clothes remaining on him. "Both the charm and amulet work."

Brodie grinned. "Now Roast is the perfect name for you. Especially with how you roasted that goblin."

Roast tucked his tiny wand away. "You might be right. It doesn't sound all that terrible when you look at it that way."

Mallory breathed in deeply. "And there are no singed feathers, Art."

Roast smiled. "I don't mind if you call me Roast. Brodie is right. It's actually not such a bad name anymore."

Ryan crouched beside one of the goblins. "Someone going to help me search them?"

"The goblin village must be close." Brodie searched one of the other goblins. "We should look for it."

"In the morning." Finished checking the goblin over, Ryan moved onto the next one.

"I can help you?" Roast asked hopefully.

"Yeah." Mallory grinned at him. "You did pretty good against the goblins tonight."

"I did?" Roast straightened his shoulders when she nodded. "I did." He gave a single nod. "Yes, I did."

They found a pair of goblin boots and six copper pieces. Callum put Smudge on Bobbi's back, Fang wanting to join him. Brodie stared at the donkey for a moment. "Do you think they sell horses in Surith? We should have enough gold for one now."

"We'd be down to almost no money again if we bought one," Mallory said.

"Why don't we wait and see what the wagoner manages to get for us tomorrow?" Ryan suggested.

"How much would he have to make for us to get

a horse?" Brodie asked as they continued towards Wildebay.

"At least twenty gold pieces," Callum said.

"Why twenty?" Brodie asked.

"Enough to cover expenses if we don't manage to make much for a bit," Callum said. "We do have to be able to feed ourselves and our animals."

"Okay. Twenty and then we see what we can buy. How about one we can ride and that can also pull a caravan?" Brodie suggested.

"A heavy horse should be cheaper. Most people prefer a horse that doesn't look like it belongs behind a plough," Danae said.

Mallory smiled as she listened to Danae and Brodie discuss different horse breeds and possible prices, Brodie mainly focusing on the costs.

Ryan walked beside her. "Not what I ever expected to hear." He nodded towards Brodie.

Mallory chuckled. "He's really getting into trading."

"And cooking." Callum walked on the other side of Mallory.

"Yeah, we can't forget the cooking." Mallory grinned when her brother glanced in her direction, narrowing his eyes.

Wildebay was still noisy when they arrived,

especially the waterfront. They made their way to Roast's home where they unsaddled Augusta and took the gear off Bobbi. Roast took the horse and donkey to the inn, thanking them for escorting him to Mer Point and offering to pay for stabling for the night as he gave them five silver pieces. He offered more since he hadn't needed to pay the mage, but they'd declined. Ryan told him he'd need his money on the journey south.

While he was gone, they set up their beds and Mallory checked her journal before sitting down to write in her leather-bound notebook. *Singed Feathers: The shapeshifter was grateful to have been escorted to Mer Point and back and also offered to pay your stabling costs for the night. You were rewarded with five silver pieces for your party. You also earned twenty experience points each.* She smiled as she sat on the blankets, opening her notebook. There'd be no more singed feathers. At least not from Roast's attempts at fighting.

By the time Roast returned, Ryan had used the whetstone on his weapons and Mallory had written in the notebook and learned the new spells. The parchment vanished after she finished learning mend I and once she'd learned flame, the parchment disappeared in a burst of fire that burned itself out.

Brodie finished making flatbread over the fire Ryan

had lit as Roast stepped inside, pleased to have finally tried out one of his recipes. He had the eggs, flour and cooking oil from the bandit's camp and found water and salt in Roast's kitchen area. He cooked up the rest of the eggs and fried an onion for them to have with the flatbread while Callum went fishing to feed Smudge and Fang.

Mallory practised her new spell by mending Brodie's shirt. Even casting it twice wasn't enough to completely mend the shirt, but she didn't have enough mana to cast it a third time as it took seventeen mana and only repaired an area a centimetre square. While she waited the five minutes for her mana to return, she checked out her other spell, seeing the base attacks of four, six and eight for low, normal and critical were improved by her higher attributes so the normal attack was seven and the critical was ten. It also had damage over time. Four every two seconds for six seconds. Once her mana was back, she finished mending Brodie's shirt.

Callum returned with a fish, Smudge at his side, and they shared their meal with Roast, visiting the outhouse before retiring for the night. Mallory had draped her damp trousers over a chair and set it closer to the fire before sitting on the blankets beside Ryan and brushing her hair.

Smudge bounded across the room to hold out his paws, chattering excitedly at her before lying on his back.

Mallory chuckled. "I think he wants to be brushed too."

"Give me the brush and I'll do it." Callum held out his hand.

"This brush is for people, not animals," Mallory protested.

Ryan grinned, glancing at Brodie. "Debateable."

Brodie gestured towards him with his middle finger. "We should get a pet brush."

"Augusta's brush is in my saddlebags. You can use that," Danae suggested.

Smudge rolled over, bounding over to Danae, holding out his paws as he chattered at her.

Danae patted him on the head. "You are so adorable."

Smudge rubbed his head against her hand, closing his eyes for a moment before pulling away and looking in the direction of the gear stacked against a wall.

"All right. I'll get it." Danae rummaged in her saddlebags, handing the horse brush to Callum.

Mallory smiled as she continued to brush her hair, watching first Smudge and then Fang being brushed.

She handed the brush over to Ryan once she was finished with it. "We're starting to be outfitted better."

"And eating better." Brodie handed the horse brush to Danae.

Ryan chuckled. "We should have hunted down a rabbit on the way here."

"We can do that tomorrow," Callum suggested. "On the way to Buckneth."

"What about having a meal at the tavern?" Brodie asked. "Surely we've got something to celebrate. What about the amount of quests we've completed? We still haven't spent the gold piece at a bakers yet. We could use that at the tavern."

Mallory joined in the laughter, speaking when she finally managed to stop. "We'll see how much we spend tomorrow and if you manage not to visit a baker." She returned the brush to her satchel, climbing between the blankets, moving close to Ryan. He draped an arm across her waist. "Now if only we could shower before going to bed. I hope Eridell has taverns with showers."

"We could remain along the coast and wash in the ocean," Callum said.

Mallory shuddered. "I did consider that, but I'm not

sure I'm up to it. I'd be worried there were undines coming after me."

"Great. Did you have to remind me?" Brodie demanded.

Ryan chuckled again. "We're meant to be sleeping. Not talking half the night."

"Thank you for letting me remain with you," Danae said. "Today has been amazing. I'm not sure how I'm going to attend the academy. Not when there are so many interesting adventures to go on."

Chapter Thirty-Eight

Mallory squeezed her eyes closed, not sure if she should say anything. What would Danae's parents say if she remained with them? She didn't want to think about it. At least not yet. They had other things to worry about. Such as Rass. Snuggling further under the blanket, the warmth of Ryan's body seeping into hers, she fell asleep while trying to figure out what to do about the hellion, coming to no conclusion.

They were woken the next morning, when it was barely daylight, by a knock on the front door. Ryan staggered across the room, his cutlass in hand as he swung open the door. "Welby."

"Are we leaving today?"

Ryan ran a hand through his hair. "Yeah. Once we've had breakfast."

Welby handed over a cloth covered basket. "From the baker. Leave the basket by the front door when you're done with it. They'll collect it later. How long will you need to get ready?"

Roast came out of the bedroom, dressed for the day. "I'll fetch your horse and donkey along with my pony. My gear is packed and I can eat on the way. I'm more than ready to go after Merry."

Brodie took the basket from Ryan, drawing back the cloth. "Pastries. Cool." He took the basket to the table, helping himself to one of the sweet pastries. He gave one to Fang who followed him to the table, looking wistfully up at him.

"What about Smudge?" Callum took one from the basket and handed it over to Smudge who'd bounded over to the table, chattering excitedly.

"Shall I return in half an hour?" Welby asked.

Mallory joined Brodie at the table, along with Danae, worried her brother would eat all the food. "That should be enough time."

Callum put a pot of water on to boil, glancing at Brodie when he grabbed a second sweet pastry. "You better not eat all of them. They look like they'll go perfectly with my coffee." He grinned. "You can't imagine how good it is to say that."

Ryan chuckled. "Good thing the rest of us can survive without coffee." He sat at the table, helping himself to a fruit filled pastry, taking a bite. "These are good." He looked at Brodie. "When are you going to learn how to make things like this?"

"As soon as possible." Brodie shoved the last bite in his mouth and reached for a third one.

Somehow, Mallory managed to save some of the pastries for Roast and when Welby returned, they were packed and ready to go, the basket left by the front door. Mallory was dressed in the black trousers that had dried during the night and the light brown shirt they'd bought in Mer Point. She finally felt like she was dressed in the right clothes. From her soft leather boots to the sword and wand at her sides and the leather belt she'd taken out of one of the panniers and the belt pouch she'd put her money into. She noticed that instead of having the axe at his left hip, Ryan had a short sword hanging beside his quiver, the cutlass at his right.

Grinning, she nodded to his weapons. "You'll finally get to dual wield."

He drew her close, his lips brushing across hers. "You finally unlocked warrior."

Chuckling, she drew away from him and stepped outside, her gaze drawn to Roast's pony. Most of his gear was in saddlebags, a bedroll behind the saddle, the rest of his gear in his satchel. Welby had a similar pony he'd borrowed from a friend. Bulging saddlebags contained his gear and a bedroll had been strapped on behind the saddle. The ponies looked similar, Roast's thirteen and a half hands high and Welby's fourteen hands high. They were sturdy looking and both were flaxen, their cream coloured mane and tail standing out against their brown body.

Welby mounted his pony, facing Mallory who was looking over the animals. "They're New Forest ponies. Sturdy and fast."

As they set out for Surith, Mallory noticed the journal icon appear in the corner of her vision. Opening her journal, she noticed a quest had been updated. *Captured By Hellions: Arthur of Wildebay has joined the expedition to Cutthroat Harbour, wanting to rescue Merry.*

"Are we going after the goblin village?" Brodie asked. "We have a quest for it."

"We don't want to leave goblins in the area." Ryan glanced at the horizon. "It's early enough we should be able to deal with them and reach Surith well before midday."

"And sell the goblin general's sword," Brodie added.

"And hopefully buy our first horse." Callum glanced at Smudge who'd made himself comfortable on Bobbi. "Two heavy horses would be enough for now. We could double up."

"We won't be able to afford two," Mallory said. "Not even dealing with the goblin village will be enough to help us buy a second horse."

"What we need to do is take on more of the dark forces encampments and villages." Callum's hand momentarily rested on his satchel. "Outside of Cape Barren, they might be the only places to get coffee."

"Where did you learn that information?" Welby asked.

Between all of them, they told Welby about the previous day's adventures including the tentative plan to go after the dark forces encampment, where he'd been held, to reduce the number of enemies they'd find at Cutthroat Harbour. Welby slowly shook his head. "People don't tend to attack those of the dark forces around here. It's too dangerous. I have no idea what you'd normally find in their encampment. And I wasn't at the encampment long enough to learn much about them."

"Then I guess we need to pay them a visit and see what we can find." Again Callum's hand momentarily rested on his satchel. "It better be coffee."

"Doesn't matter if it is," Brodie said. "We'll still get paid for going after them."

"It does matter," Callum argued.

Mallory dropped back slightly, leaving them to their argument. She smiled at Ryan when he fell into step with her, Welby and Roast riding a little apart from them. "We'll be back in Buckneth this arve."

Ryan grinned. "Back on track again?"

She laughed softly. "Yeah. Or at least that's what it feels like."

He slipped an arm around her waist. "It feels like it to me too."

They walked arm in arm, the day mostly silent around them, other than Brodie and Callum's argument. She looked over their health, all of them at full health. Which was a lot better today. Ryan and Brodie had twenty-seven health while the rest of them had twenty-one. She momentarily wondered what health and stats Welby and Roast might have, but didn't ask. It seemed kind of rude.

At the same location as previous times, they were attacked by five goblins. Having been half expecting the attack, Mallory stepped away from Ryan, drawing her sword and wand. She attacked with flame this time, wanting to know what the new spell was like.

"Did you have to?" Brodie demanded.

Mallory tried not to breathe in too deeply at the stench of charred flesh, the rest of the goblins having been taken out by her companions. "I didn't realise it'd be that bad."

"What did you expect? It's flame. You burned it," Brodie said.

Ryan looked down at the goblin Mallory had taken out. "It might be best if you didn't use that spell if we want to search the body."

"Or want to breathe," Brodie muttered.

"Should be good for lighting campfires." Callum searched the body of the goblin he'd shot.

"Increasing your intelligence and wisdom didn't help." Brodie glanced at the charred goblin.

"They don't work like that," Danae said. "They're related to magic and mana, not general knowledge."

Callum rose to his feet. "Are we going to search for the village?"

"It shouldn't take us long." Brodie glanced at Mallory. "As long as you don't use flame on them."

"I can track where they came from." Welby gestured towards the goblins.

Chapter Thirty-Nine

Mallory glanced at her companions, each of them either nodding or shrugging. She faced Welby. "That would be good. Once we've finished searching these bodies you can help us find the village."

The search gave them another pair of goblin boots and fifty grams of jerky that Brodie took, saying he needed it because he'd finished off his jerky. They also found twelve copper pieces.

"Can we go now?" Brodie looked towards the charred body. "So we can breathe again." He gestured towards Smudge and Fang who were on Bobbi's back atop the canvas tent and bedroll. "Even they aren't game to get down with that stench."

"That's not the reason," Mallory protested. "It's because the fight was over before they could move."

"I found the tracks," Welby said. "Ready to follow them?"

Ryan strode over to Welby. "Let's go."

Callum held Bobbi's lead rope. "Is it likely to be far from the road?"

Welby shrugged, leading his pony as he followed the tracks, eventually stopping fifteen minutes later, holding up a hand to wave them back, joining them and tying his pony to a nearby tree. "The goblin village is over there." He pointed to where he'd retreated from.

Fang jumped down off Bobbi, looking up at Smudge who held out his paws, waiting for Callum to set him on the ground before he followed Fang through the trees. Callum hurried after them. "Don't go in there on your own."

Mallory drew her sword, her wand already in her hand. "Are there many goblins?" Welby's shrug didn't reassure her and she followed Callum through the trees, Ryan at her side, the rest of her companions behind them.

"Don't go using flame," Brodie warned.

"It's not like I knew what it was going to do. Fireball doesn't do that," Mallory protested.

"Might want to be quiet. The village is right through there." Welby pointed to a cluster of trees ahead of Callum.

Reaching the trees, Mallory peered through them.

The village consisted of small, crude wattle and daub huts in a clearing. One hut was slightly larger than the rest and four goblins stood guard at the front of it. Five goblins wrestled over a meaty bone near an unlit campfire in the middle of the village. She winced when she saw it was raw. No wonder Fang had wanted to head into the village.

Her gaze scanned the rest of the village and she counted seven more goblins. There were at least sixteen goblins and a general. She wasn't sure they could take out enough before the goblins could reach them.

"We going to split up the different groups of goblins between us?" Ryan asked.

"You don't think there are too many?" Mallory asked.

Brodie joined them. "Are we attacking or standing around talking all morning?"

"There are seven of us," Ryan said. "Nine if you count the companion animals. And by the way Fang is eyeing off that bone, she's not going to be happy if the answer is no."

"Okay. We'll split up who we target. See if we can take them out before they reach us." Mallory beckoned the rest of the group over and they sorted out who would go after which goblin. She had the two standing guard on the left of the hut, Ryan the two on the right.

"We ready now?" Brodie asked.

Mallory took a deep breath, trying not to think about how many goblins were visible in the village. As long as there weren't a lot of the creatures in the huts, they'd be fine. "Okay. Attack." She launched a fireball at one of the goblins. She managed to throw a second one at him before he could react. By then it was too late for him and he collapsed on the ground. It wasn't too late for her second target who ran towards her, yelling as he shook his cudgel.

It took her four fireballs to take the second goblin out since she missed twice. Regaining her balance from stumbling backwards at his approach, she realised a leader had come out of one of the huts along with a general. Both were bearing down on her. Fear raced through her and she focused on the general, having no idea what her companions were doing and if any of them were going to help. She couldn't take her attention off the general who ran towards her, sunlight glinting on his short sword. She continued to throw fireballs at him, wondering if she should resort to flame. He dropped mid-stride and Mallory stared at him for a few seconds to make sure he was dead before she could bring herself to look away and scan her surroundings. The leader, who'd been running towards her, dropped in mid-stride, several arrows sticking out of his body. The rest of the goblins were scattered around the clearing, sprawled out in the dirt.

Callum lowered his bow. "Should we check the huts to make sure there are none inside?"

"I'll check the first one and you can cover me," Ryan said.

Callum followed his brother forward.

Mallory checked everyone's stats. Not a single one of them had been harmed. A smile slowly formed. They'd managed to take out the goblins before any of them had a chance to get close. How much harder would a hellion encampment be? Should they do some grinding on the way to Surith and gather every herb they saw?

"Clear." Ryan stepped out of the first hut, striding to the next one.

Smudge leaned against Callum's leg, chattering as Callum kept his bow trained on each hut Ryan checked.

"A pity we can't understand him," Brodie said. "For all we know, he's telling us all the goblins are dead."

"Then how about we start searching bodies so we can get to Surith on time." Mallory stopped at the first body, searching it for items, checking the updated quest while she was at it. *Village Search: You found the goblin village and dealt with the general. You earned fifteen experience points each.*

By the time they'd finished searching, they had seven pairs of goblin boots, twenty-two copper pieces, one hundred grams of beef jerky that Brodie shoved in his belt pouch, two chisels, a hammer, the general's short sword and a wooden trinket box with random items in it. A feather, a smooth pebble, a shell, a piece of fur and a muddy ribbon.

"Do these mean anything?" Mallory stared into the open trinket box she held.

Welby checked inside. "Goblins aren't good at recognising if something is valuable. If it catches their attention, they keep it." He tilted the box so the contents fell onto the ground.

Smudge darted in and grabbed the pebble, tossing it up in the air.

"Looks like goblins aren't the only ones who aren't good at recognising if things are valuable," Brodie said.

Smudge picked up the shell that had landed on the ground in front of him and threw it at Brodie.

"Hey." Brodie took a step away.

Callum chuckled. "Did you forget the pearl?"

Still smiling at Smudge's antics, Ryan examined the goblin general's sword. "I don't think this lot are any more artistic than the other ones."

Mallory took the sword from Ryan, having a closer look at the engraving. "I have no idea what it's meant to be. It looks like a mound of dirt sitting on stumps with ice cream cones sticking out to one side."

Brodie moved in close, giving Smudge a wary look before squinting at the engraving. "They might be jaws. There's squiggly lines on the edges of the cones that face each other. Could be teeth."

"I'd hate to see what sort of creature looks like a mound of dirt and has teeth," Mallory said.

"Might be as big as a hill or mountain," Ryan suggested.

"That sounds worse." Mallory lowered the sword.

Roast gestured to the huts, glancing at Mallory. "You should burn them down so no goblins can move in. There's enough cleared ground around them so they won't set any of the forest on fire."

Chapter Forty

Mallory eyed the distance between the huts and the edge of the clearing. "Are you sure the forest won't catch on fire?"

Welby nodded. "Light them up. The air is still and they'll burn down quickly."

"Okay." Mallory launched flames at each of the huts, the fire quickly taking hold.

"That's a better use for the spell." Brodie glanced back the way they'd come.

Mallory started to comment, changing her mind. "Time to get on the road. We've got a lot of kilometres to travel today."

"Don't we always," Brodie muttered.

"I don't think Fang is interested in leaving." Callum nodded towards the wolf cub chewing on the bone.

"Come on, Fang," Brodie called.

Fang picked up the bone, carrying it with her when she trotted over to him.

"You can't carry that all the way to Surith," Brodie said.

Fang trotted towards where the donkey, horse and ponies had been tied up.

"Guess she has other ideas." Ryan grinned, striding after her, carrying several pairs of boots.

Once the gear was in the panniers, Welby led them back to the road and they continued on to Surith. Mallory suggested gathering herbs and Brodie's expression lit up.

"Think we can get another CAS point before the end of the day?"

Mallory shrugged, striding towards a herb several metres from the edge of the road. While they took turns to pick herbs, running back and forth between the road and the herbs they spotted, Welby and Roast rode a little ahead to keep an eye out for trouble. There was none and they stayed on the road once they saw Surith in the distance.

Mallory checked over their stats. Not only did they have herbs to sell, but they also had eighty experience points. Except for Danae who was, as always, well ahead of them with one hundred and seven experience points and being four CAS points ahead of them.

As they walked past the second house along the coastal road a pig ran out in front of them, a man chasing behind the animal. Fang dropped the bone she'd carried all the way to Surith, barking. The pig was white with black spots scattered across it and ears that flopped forward to hang towards its slightly dished nose.

Brodie scooped up the pig he'd almost tripped over, the animal squealing and struggling to escape. "What are you doing to it?"

The man, who'd been chasing the pig, stopped in front of Brodie. "Hand it over."

Brodie took a step back, continuing to hold the pig. "What are you doing to it?"

When the man tried to come closer, Fang growled and he took a step back. "That's my pig. I'm taking him to the butcher now he's big enough to get a decent amount of coins for him."

"How much do you want for him?" Brodie asked.

"You want to buy him?" The man frowned. "Are you a butcher?"

Brodie took another step back. "I'm not going to eat him."

Ryan chuckled. "Should I remind you of this next time you eat pork or bacon?"

"That's different," Brodie exclaimed. "This one managed to escape. He shouldn't be eaten. He's too smart for that. He's not for bacon."

"What are you going to do with him? It's not like we can cart him around the countryside," Mallory said.

"I'll find someone who wants a pig for a pet. Someone who isn't about to eat him." Brodie looked at the man again. "How much do you want for him? And you better not try and rip me off."

"You want to buy a pig and keep him for a pet." The man's tone of disbelief matched his expression.

"Yes," Brodie stated. "Now how much were you going to sell him to the butcher for?" The pig stopped struggling, making snuffling noises now.

"Five gold pieces," the man said.

"Five! You've got to be kidding," Brodie exclaimed.

"It's a fair price," the man said. "I'm not about to haggle over it with you. Take it or leave it."

"How about four gold pieces and a pair of goblin boots?" Brodie asked.

Fang settled down beside Brodie and began to gnaw on her bone.

Mallory tried not to sigh. She didn't want to waste four gold pieces on a pig that Brodie planned to give away. "Brodie, we don't-"

The man interrupted. "What would I do with goblin boots?"

"Give them to your kids to wear," Brodie suggested.

"I don't have kids," the man said.

Danae spoke before Brodie could. "I'm going to see about sending a letter to my mother to let her know what's happening. Shall I meet you at the traders when I'm done?"

"I might say goodbye to my friends if you're going to be a while." Roast glanced at the man as he spoke the last few words.

"I'll visit the tavern and see what rumours I can pick up." Welby took a step away. "Come and get me when you're ready to leave Surith."

The man glanced at the three who wandered off. "Any more interruptions or can we get on with this? I don't have all day."

Mallory wanted to protest, but Brodie was already haggling with the man. It took longer than she would have liked and she shared several long suffering looks with Ryan, disappointed that in the end Brodie was only able to talk the man down to four gold and six silver pieces. She paid over the money, using up some of their copper pieces instead of the silver. The man grumbled about receiving sixty copper pieces, glaring at Brodie when he pointed out the man could return some of them.

Callum patted the pig on the head. "What are we going to do with him? And how are you going to stop him from running away?"

"I need a piece of rope. A thinner piece than the one in the pannier." Brodie shifted the pig in his arms. "And soon. He's getting heavy. Must be about forty kilos."

"There's a rope maker about four buildings along." Mallory gestured along the road. "I remember it from yesterday."

After a short discussion, Mallory and Ryan hurried ahead and bought a length of rope. They bought a two metre length for a silver piece. Again Mallory paid in copper pieces.

Brodie reached the building as they stepped outside and Mallory helped him tie the rope around the pig's neck. "There you go." Brodie patted the pig on the shoulder. "You're safe now."

Fang dropped the bone she was again carrying and licked the pig.

"Are you sure he's safe?" Callum asked.

Ryan chuckled. "Might not be with the way Fang is eyeing him off."

Brodie squatted in front of Fang. "He's not food. Not for bacon. Got it?"

Fang whined and picked up her bone again.

"Good, girl." Brodie patted her on the head before rising to his feet. "Let's see if we can sell the herbs we collected and the goblin boots."

"The wagoner might sell them for us," Callum said.

Ryan led the way down the road. "Doesn't matter who sells them as long as they're sold. They're taking up a lot of room in the panniers and the backpack. Room we'll need for other things we'll get along the way."

They found the wagoner at the traders, taking the thirty-four gold and seven silver pieces from him for the last sales.

"Hell yeah," Brodie exclaimed. "We're going to buy a horse."

Once the wagoner said he'd take care of selling the nine goblin boots, two chisels, hammer, the goblin general's sword and the herbs, they put the items on the counter. Nodding as they listened to the trader tell them which farms currently had horses for sale. He took out a leather-bound book from under the counter and flicked through the pages while he spoke.

Mallory watched the pages turn, pointing to one of the crudely drawn images. "That's the engraving on the first goblin general sword we found."

Callum leaned forward. "It is. What's it worth?"

"Three gold pieces," the trader said.

"Guess we didn't lose out." Ryan nodded towards the door. "We going to look at these horses?"

Danae stepped inside before anyone had the chance to speak and they explained their plans to her. She asked the trader a few questions about the various horses for sale before leading the way outside. "You don't know much about horses, do you?"

"I've only ridden one a few times," Mallory said.

"We've done a fair amount of riding," Ryan said. "One of our relatives has horses. A distant relative we don't see much anymore."

"There's only one horse worth looking at if you were serious about one you can ride and use to pull a wagon." Danae untied the reins from the hitching post. "It's one of the farms not far from the inn. We would have passed it on our way into Surith the day we arrived."

Ryan gathered Bobbi's lead rope. "Let's hope we can afford it."

Callum walked beside his brother. "You know, if we came back after school, as soon as we got home, we'd only be gone an hour and a half from here."

"We're meant to be in each world equal amounts of time," Mallory said. "Until we can afford potions to stop ageing. Or turn back the ageing."

"We should at least leave it until the next day," Ryan said. "We could leave in the morning before you go to school like we did this time."

"How long will have passed if we're only gone twenty-four hours?" Mallory asked.

"Four hours. We could leave after dinner at the Buckneth tavern and be back in time for a sleep," Callum suggested.

"We won't want to sleep. It'll be morning," Mallory pointed out.

They continued to debate the options on the way to the farm, the pig trotting alongside Brodie, Fang on the other side still carrying her bone. Smudge was again curled up on Bobbi, being led by Ryan.

It took them the entire walk to the farm to decide that they'd take turns to nap and leave at two in the morning. They also decided they should see what a pocket watch was worth so they didn't have to keep asking Ahron for the time.

Brodie knocked on the farmhouse door, smiling

when a woman answered. "We've come to see the horse you have for sale."

"It belongs to my oldest boy. Wait here and I'll find him for you." The woman closed the door behind her, striding off behind the farmhouse.

"Reckon she'll take long?" Brodie asked.

Callum shrugged and Mallory looked off in the direction the woman had taken. No one answered Brodie. Fang settled down to gnaw on her bone again and the pig sniffed around the area, tugging on the lead.

The woman returned about twenty minutes later, the young man smiling when he saw them. "You came about the horse?"

Ryan nodded. "The trader said she's good for both riding and pulling carts and carriages."

"She belonged to my sister, but she gave her to me when she moved to Shadhurst late last year. She didn't want the expense of keeping a horse in a city," the young man said.

"Should have stayed here," the woman muttered. "Nothing good ever came of going to the city."

"Mum." The young man gave the woman a pointed look.

"Well, it doesn't." The woman wandered back inside the farmhouse.

"Were you interested in the cart, or only the horse and tack?" the young man asked.

"What were you wanting for the horse and tack?" Brodie asked.

"Eighty gold pieces," the young man said. "She's only six-years-old and a large, sturdy horse capable of pulling a carriage or wagon. My sister was sad to leave her behind."

"Eighty?" Brodie demanded. "How about sixty?"

"Sixty!" the young man exclaimed. "That sounds like robbery."

Mallory grinned. Her brother was in his element. The trade prices went back and forth, Brodie's offer slowly creeping up.

"If it wasn't for the nest of chameleon vipers out behind the farm I wouldn't consider selling her. But those mercenaries down in Wayholt aren't cheap, what with the travel costs and paying them to do the job. The horse is worth every bit of that gold. Bug might not be of some fancy bloodline and the best we can figure out of her breeding is that she's a mixed draft, but she has the sweetest nature, is a dark bay, eighteen hands high, has a solid build and can pull a wagon all day."

"Bug?" Mallory asked.

The young man smiled. "Her name's actually

Moondancer. When we first got her, she'd dance around in the paddock of an evening. My sister named her. When we found out she was chasing the little glow bugs, the name Bug stuck." He shrugged. "Much to my sister's annoyance."

"What if we dealt with the chameleon vipers?" Danae asked.

"The wagoner wants to leave Surith by midday," Mallory said.

"We haven't seen the horse yet," Ryan said.

"Come and meet Bug." The young man led the way to a barn behind the farmhouse.

Mallory stepped inside the dim interior. There were three horses inside, but it was easy to tell which one was Bug. The horse was massive, her back broad and her body solid. She certainly looked more than capable of pulling a caravan. In the corner was a small cart, probably the one Bug usually pulled. "Has she pulled anything larger than that?" Mallory gestured towards the cart. "And has she pulled anything large enough to need two horses to draw it?"

The young man nodded. "A few times. She gets along well with other horses."

"What I want to know, is how are we meant to get on her back to ride her?" Brodie asked.

"She'll stand patiently beside a stump or a rock

so you can mount her." The young man turned to Danae. "Were you serious about dealing with the chameleon vipers?"

"It's not exactly up to me." Danae glanced at Mallory. "But I know that if we had enough time our party would be capable of it."

"How many chameleon vipers are there?" Ryan asked. "And what does a nest of them look like?"

"Are we going to do this?" Callum asked. "I was hoping to have a look at the shops in Surith to see if there are any more crafting ability books before we leave."

"I have a husbandry one I can throw into the deal if you take care of the chameleon vipers as well. I'll also take five gold pieces off the cost of the horse and tack and offer one gold piece for every chameleon viper you kill." The young man gestured to the three horses. "I haven't dared let them out since I first found the vipers. I can't afford to lose them."

"I know we've unlocked husbandry," Callum said. "But I'd like to know more about it."

"How long will it take?" Brodie glanced out the door. "I was hoping we could have lunch at the tavern before we leave. If we have enough time."

"My mum baked apple pies this morning." The young man patted Bug, who walked over to him, nuzzling his face. "I can throw a pie into the bargain as well."

Mallory grinned when Danae laughed. "That'll guarantee Brodie's vote."

Ryan chuckled. "Pretty much."

Brodie glared at them. "It's apple pie."

Callum laughed, clapping Brodie on the shoulder. "Obviously." He turned to Ryan. "What if we give it a couple of hours? Whatever we can get done in a couple of hours. That way we'll still get back in time and hopefully take care of most if not all of the chameleon vipers."

"What if one of us is bitten again?" Mallory asked. "We don't have a lot of health tea left. Three doses."

"I can set more health tea to steep if they don't mind." Danae turned to the young man. "You can have whatever is left over if we don't use all we've got and have no space for it."

"We could always tip out the wine or ale from one of those waterskins," Mallory suggested.

"Are you serious?" Brodie demanded.

Ryan chuckled. "Obviously not."

Mallory rolled her eyes, turning to the young man. "What if we didn't manage to deal with all the vipers in the time we have? How will that work for the initial discount and the apple pie and book?"

They debated the reward, eventually settling on one they were happy with. Mallory opened her journal to read the new quest while the young man took Danae inside so she could set some health tea to steep before they went after the chameleon vipers.

Nest Of Vipers: In return for killing all the chameleon vipers at the back of the property, the farmer's son has offered a discount of five gold pieces off the horse he has for sale as well as one gold piece for every chameleon viper killed. He will also offer one apple pie and a husbandry crafting ability book. If you are unable to deal with all the chameleon vipers, instead of the five gold pieces discount, you will only receive two gold pieces. All other rewards will remain the same.

Ryan stepped close to Mallory. "I wonder what the chances are of there being ten chameleon vipers?"

"Ten?" Mallory exclaimed.

"Ten would be a good discount on the eighty he's charging." Ryan grinned. "Fifteen chameleon vipers would be better."

"How can you say that?" Mallory demanded.

Callum joined them, Smudge following, playing with the pebble he carried. "Because then that would give us the discount Brodie first asked for."

Brodie's expression brightened, Fang lying at his

feet chewing on her bone. "Think there'll be that many?"

Chapter Forty-One

"Have you forgotten what it was like to face one chameleon viper?" Mallory looked at each of them. "How could we face ten, or even fifteen?"

"We'll be expecting them this time. We should be able to take them out from a distance." Ryan draped an arm around Mallory's shoulders. "We've got this. We're also a higher character level this time."

"I'd kind of forgotten that." Her worries eased and she smiled up at him. "You're right. We've got this."

Danae came out of the farmhouse, striding towards them. "The health tea is steeping and he gave me better directions to the chameleon viper nest. Are we ready to go?"

"Hell yeah. I want to find fifteen chameleon vipers." Brodie looked from Danae to the farmhouse. "We don't need to wait for the tea?"

"It's not that far." Danae glanced at the barn. "He

said we can leave Bobbi and Augusta here if we want."

After leaving the horse and donkey in the barn, along with the pig, they followed Danae out behind the farmhouse. Fang carried her bone. There wasn't much left of it.

Ten minutes later, Danae's steps slowed. "See that tree that's been struck by lightning? The nest is behind it."

"How will we recognise the nest?" Callum glanced at Smudge who remained by his side. "Should we have left our companion animals behind? I wouldn't want anything to happen to either of them."

Smudge patted Callum's leg, chattering up at him, tossing the pebble in the air.

"I think he's telling you he's got this too," Ryan said.

Mallory rose up on her toes, trying to see through the long grass around the tree. "What does a nest look like? I don't want to go stumbling into it."

"They don't build nests. They tend to make use of what's in the environment. Hollow logs, holes in the ground, a tumble of boulders that create a bit of a cave. Anything like that." Danae nodded towards the tree. "Or a branch that's fallen from a lightning strike and been half burned away to create a sheltered area for them to nest in."

"Wait up," Ryan said. "A nest. Does that mean we're going after baby chameleon vipers?"

Danae nodded. "They're as dangerous as adult ones. Maybe more so since they move faster. They'll be anywhere between a quarter and a half a metre long and up to thirty in the nest. The mother will also be in the area. They don't tend to move out of the nest until they're close on three quarters of a metre long."

Callum readied his bow. "Are we going to do this?"

Nodding, Ryan moved closer to the tree. "I see it. The branch behind the tree."

Again Mallory rose onto her toes, trying to get a better look. "There's too much long grass around it. And between us and it."

"What if we burn the grass away?" Brodie asked.

"Terrible idea," Ryan said. "We could end up burning down the whole area."

"We need a water spell too," Brodie said.

"I thought you didn't want me to use the flame spell in a fight," Mallory said.

Brodie gestured towards the fallen branch. "That's different. I'm not expecting you to use it on the vipers. Just the grass."

Mallory slowly shook her head. "Ryan's wrong. It's not a terrible idea. It's an absolutely awful one."

Callum took a step towards the tree. "Are we standing around talking or are we going to do this? We're going to run out of time at this rate."

Mallory drew her sword, her wand having already been in her hand. "What if I send a fireball at the branch?" She really didn't want to get too close.

"You could try the area in front so we can take out any that might be sunning themselves." Danae pointed to the location. It was about a metre in front of the branch.

Mallory glanced at each of her companions who nodded or shrugged. "Okay. Everyone ready?" She received the same answer. "I'll take that as a yes." She launched a fireball in front of the branch. For a moment she thought nothing had happened. There was a rustling and the tops of the grass moved.

"We can't see them." Ryan backed up. "Retreat to the less grassy area behind us."

Mallory stumbled backwards, not about to take her attention from the grass in front. Catching a glimpse of a snake, she threw a fireball at it, quickly following it up with another one. As they reached the area where there was less grass, Mallory's mouth dropped open. How many chameleon vipers had she disturbed? She threw another fireball at the one she'd attacked.

Arrows embedded themselves in some of the other vipers, along with throwing knives, and Ryan ran forward with his cutlass and short sword drawn. The chameleon vipers, although smaller than the previous one they'd fought, were fast and struck out at Ryan who spent most of his time blocking.

Heart racing, Mallory threw fireball after fireball at the oncoming vipers, losing track of which one she was meant to focus on. She had no idea how many came after them, didn't have time to count.

Fang dropped her bone and ran towards the snakes.

"Get back, Fang." Brodie threw throwing knives at the snakes, continuing to retreat, Fang returning to his side.

"One got me," Callum called out. Smudge threw his pebble at the viper. "Get away from it, Smudge." Callum retreated.

Ryan sheathed his short sword long enough to throw the canteen of health tea to Callum.

"No wonder they're so deadly." Callum drank a mouthful. "My vision was so blurry they could have got me again before I noticed." Finished the cupful, he started to rejoin the fight.

"They got me too." Danae took the waterskin of

health tea from Callum. "A good thing I set some to steep." She raised the waterskin to her mouth, rejoining the fight the moment she'd finished a cupful.

When the last viper died, Mallory stared at the dead bodies littering the ground. "Do you think that was all of them?"

"That was only thirteen. I hope not." Brodie gathered his throwing knives. "I really need more of these. I've got spare slots in my vambraces."

"Thirteen." Mallory counted the bodies herself. "It felt like more than that."

"There'll be more." Danae gathered her arrows. "None of these are big enough to be the mother."

Once more Mallory looked at each of the dead bodies. "What's a mother chameleon viper like when you've taken out her babies?"

"More aggressive than the one Ryan faced the other day." Danae slipped arrows into her quiver. "I'm down two arrows."

"I'm down three," Callum said. "And I'm not so sure I want to face a mother chameleon viper."

"What if we tell him this is as many as we can do?" Brodie asked. "We'll get a good discount on the horse. And pie."

"That's wrong." Mallory faced her brother. "We

said we'd give him two hours. We haven't done that. It hasn't even been an hour."

"We really need a pocket watch." Ryan walked through the bodies littering the ground. "How about launch the next fireball closer to the branch."

Mallory checked her stats. "Wait a minute. My mana isn't looking so great."

"After the fight I ended up down to only a couple of arrows, what with missing a few times," Danae said.

"Me too," Callum said. "Can you get quivers that fit more than twenty arrows?"

Danae nodded. "They're a lot more expensive."

"I nearly ran out of throwing knives," Brodie said.

"I was down to three mana after that fight. I'm back to full now if you want to see what's left of the vipers," Mallory said.

"I'm ready," Callum said. "I'm one XP off getting a CAS point."

"I gained a CAS point," Brodie said.

Danae spoke at the same time. "I gained a CAS point and now I'm halfway towards my next character level."

Ryan strode forward. "Let's do this then."

Chapter Forty-Two

Taking a deep breath, Mallory followed Ryan. Surely there couldn't be another thirteen chameleon vipers left. As she came closer to the branch, she launched a fireball next to where she'd launched the first one. Nothing happened. "Do you think they're somewhere else? The rest of them, that is."

"Try directly in front of the branch." Ryan nodded at the location, both his hands holding weapons.

Seeing her mana was back to full, Mallory launched a fireball directly in front of the branch. She stared at the spot. Again nothing happened.

"Do you think the mother viper is out looking for food?" Callum asked.

Fang growled, her gaze fixed on the branch. She took a step towards it.

"You stay back, Fang," Brodie ordered.

"I reckon it's in the branch this time," Callum said.

Checking her mana again, and seeing it was full, Mallory launched a fireball at the branch. The viper burst out of the hollow branch, visible for only a moment before it was hidden by the grasses which moved and rustled. She backed up. "I've got a feeling there was more than one in there."

"Retreat again," Ryan said.

When the vipers came out of the long grass, Mallory momentarily froze. The mother was larger than the viper that had bitten Ryan while they'd been gathering herbs. As if that wasn't bad enough, she was accompanied by more of the little ones. Not as many as last time, but more than enough.

Ryan attacked one of the smaller vipers that reached him. "Focus on the babies. They move the fastest."

Mallory threw fireballs at the smaller ones, stumbling back as two came towards her. She struck one with her short sword, grinning to have finally used it. It was a lot better than the close quarters of a dagger.

"One got me," Brodie exclaimed. "I need the health tea, Danni." Brodie retreated, taking the waterskin with him. "No, Fang. Get back here."

Fang attacked the viper that had bitten Brodie, yelping when it got her.

Brodie dropped the canteen, throwing his daggers at the viper and scooping up Fang. He grabbed the canteen off the ground before retreating, putting Fang down once he was at the back of the group. "Why did you do that, girl?"

Fang whimpered, trying to rise to her feet.

"Here. You have it. I've got a revive. You don't." Brodie slowly tipped the tea into a hand so Fang could lap it up. "That's it, drink up. What were you thinking?" He set the empty waterskin aside, stroking Fang's head. "You've only got six health points at full. That almost killed you. Stay back in future. You hear?"

Fang whined, rising to her feet.

Brodie got to his feet, pointing to the ground. "Stay. Don't move from there."

"You go over with Fang, Smudge." Callum continued to fire arrows at the vipers.

Mallory glanced at Brodie, who swayed on his feet. "Have your health potion. You can't fight like that. And we won't be able to get the health tea before you've suffered the full fifteen minutes of damage." She used her sword to block the viper that struck out at her. "I can give you a spare later."

Brodie downed the health potion, tucking the empty vial into his belt pouch. "I need a revive for

Fang. There has to be a way to get them for companion animals." He rejoined the fight.

"I need one for Smudge," Callum said.

Mallory was forced to retreat several steps as the large viper came at her. She launched two fireballs at it, unable to launch a third. Using her sword, she blocked the attack. "I'm out of mana and it's impossible to drink a potion when I'm fighting."

"Put your wand away." Ryan joined her in attacking the large viper. It turned from one to the other, unable to get in a strike.

Mallory renewed her attacks with the short sword. "That's impractical." She blocked the viper, Ryan slashing at it with his cutlass. "Who has the time to put away a wand, have a potion and get the wand back out?" Enough mana regenerated that she was able to throw a fireball at the viper.

Two arrows and a throwing knife struck the viper that collapsed on the ground. Brodie strode forward to stand over the viper. "Think that was it?"

Mallory looked in the direction of the branch. "I'm not checking."

"I'll check." Ryan strode towards the branch while Brodie, Callum and Danae gathered throwing knives and arrows.

Mallory hurried after him, sheathing her sword to grab his arm. "Are you trying to get yourself killed?"

"I won't be killed. Unless I'm bitten a few times. I've got two revives so it isn't that much of a problem." Ryan pulled out of her grip.

His words made her think of Rass and his many revives. "Two is nothing. Not if Rass tracks us down. I've got a feeling he's going to want revenge." She stayed back when Ryan continued forward.

Danae joined Mallory, her bow ready and pointed at the branch. "We can take out anything that might come after him."

"You should send another fireball at it." Brodie stopped on the other side of Mallory.

Callum joined them. "If that first fireball didn't chase everything out, a second one isn't going to.

When Ryan crouched in front of the branch, Mallory took a step forward, her grip on the wand tightening. "What do you think you're doing? You're going to get yourself killed."

Ryan straightened. "There are about two dozen eggs in here. Anyone want to help me smash them?"

Danae hurried forward. "Don't do that. You can sell them."

"Who would buy chameleon viper eggs?" Brodie demanded.

"Quite a few people." Danae glanced over her shoulder. "Those who milk them for making poisons and others who use them in traps." She stopped beside Ryan, her bow and arrow away. "I can carry some of them. It might be best not to put them in the backpack. They could break."

They all came forward to help, putting away weapons so they could carry more of the eggs. Unable to carry all of them, Callum took the pottery jar from his satchel and gave it to Mallory to look after. "Do not let it break."

Grinning, Mallory slipped it into her satchel. "I managed to look after a poppet without smothering it. I think I can handle coffee."

Even after they filled Callum's satchel a few of them had to be carried. Ryan led the way back to where the dead bodies were scattered across the ground. "Do we need to take any of these back to prove how many we killed?"

"We can always bring him here." Mallory gave Brodie a spare health potion.

He tucked it in his belt pouch and gave Ryan the empty vial. "We should come back and collect as many of the vipers as we can to sell in Surith."

"I doubt Bob and Augusta would be able to carry all of them," Ryan said.

"We should still get what we can. And we'll have Bug too." Brodie strode over to Fang who'd been about to pick up her bone, scooping her up and holding her close. "Leave that. It might have viper poison on it. Looks like I need to level you up too."

Ryan picked up the empty waterskin.

"Callum, Ryan and I got a CAS point from that fight." Mallory hurried after her brother. "How far is Fang off levelling up?"

"She has six hundred and seven XP of a thousand," Brodie said.

"She needs a thousand XP to level up?" Ryan asked.

"A little less than what we need for a character level," Danae said.

Ryan slowly nodded. "Makes sense when you look at it that way."

"Smudge needs a thousand XP too." Callum smiled down at the river otter he carried. "I hope he gets better stats when he levels up."

"He'll be able to wear leather armour when he reaches level one," Danae said. "It won't be until he gets to the higher levels as a companion animal that he'll get a lot more health and improved attacking than a wild river otter of the same level."

"I wonder if they have a book for companion animals like they do for the classes," Callum said.

"We need to set up base somewhere before Callum starts to carry a library around," Brodie muttered. He glared at everyone when they laughed.

The young man came to meet them before they reached the farmhouse. "Did you get all of them?"

Chapter Forty-Three

Mallory stepped forward. "There were twenty-two vipers. The mother and twenty-one babies. Although they weren't all that small." She gestured towards the satchel Callum carried as well as the eggs Danae and Ryan held. "The mother had also laid quite a few eggs."

"Ahh, you weren't expecting me to pay for them too, were you?" The young man's gaze was fixed on the eggs.

"No, we plan to take them into Surith to sell them." Mallory glanced over her shoulder at the direction they'd come from. "Did you want us to show you the ones we killed? We're planning on taking as many of the bodies as we can carry to Surith to also sell."

The young man nodded to the bulging satchel. "By the look of how many you've got there, I'm sure you didn't exaggerate. Did you still want Bug?"

"Yeah," Brodie said.

"Are you interested in buying the cart?" the young man asked.

"Only the horse and tack," Ryan said.

"Yeah, we aren't planning to remain on Ruby Isle," Brodie said.

Mallory followed the young man to the barn. "We'll need a second horse eventually, but we can't afford one yet."

The young man entered the barn. "Bug came from a horse breeder out from Ransted. They'll probably have more like Bug if you're interested in another like her." He saddled the horse.

Mallory watched carefully, not sure she was going to remember how to tack up the horse. "So we owe you fifty-three gold for Bug and her tack."

The young man handed over the reins, nodding. "I'll collect the book and pie. You can't imagine how much we appreciate this. It's tough when there are so few mercenaries in this area of Ruby Isle."

Danae went with him, handing Augusta's reins to Callum and offering to set another health tea to steep for the young man since they wouldn't have any spare to leave behind.

Mallory led Bug out of the barn, Brodie leading the pig while Ryan led Bobbi and Callum led Augusta.

While they waited for the young man to return, they put the eggs in the basket, which Callum carried after putting Smudge on Bobbi, and Mallory returned the pottery jar of coffee to him.

The young man came outside with the pie and book, Danae at his side with a waterskin filled with health tea. Brodie put the book and pie in a pannier, sitting the pie carefully on top of everything, while Mallory handed over fifty-three gold pieces. She calculated what they had left. Fifty-two gold, forty-five silver and fifty-four copper pieces. Due to the quest, they weren't as broke as she feared they'd be.

They said goodbye, heading towards where the chameleon viper bodies were left. Mallory checked the updated quest during the walk. *Nest Of Vipers: After killing twenty-two chameleon vipers, you were able to purchase a horse at the discounted price of fifty-three gold pieces. You were rewarded with a husbandry crafting ability book and an apple pie. You also earned fifteen experience points each.*

Reaching the chameleon vipers, Mallory was surprised they were able to collect all of them. The horses and donkey at first shied away from the dead vipers, settling after a couple of minutes.

Returning to Surith, they found the wagoner at the traders. The wagoner gave them the nine gold pieces he'd made for them and the trader's face lit up when he saw the eggs they carried. "You interested in selling them? I wish I could buy all of them, but I don't have the funds to afford all the eggs let alone the vipers too. You interested in purchasing anything?"

"I'm interested in the shipwright crafting ability book. I want more of those types of books," Callum said. "And one on companion animals if you have it."

"How much would we be looking at?" Mallory asked.

"A hundred and twenty-four gold pieces. I could give you fifty of that after all of today's sales. Will you be wanting to sell the pig too?" The trader gestured through the doorway to where the animals were tied up out the front.

"No," Brodie exclaimed. "He's not for bacon."

The trader shrugged. "A hundred and twenty-four gold pieces."

"What about a pocket watch?" Mallory asked. "Do you have one of them?"

"Seventy-five gold pieces. Only one in stock. Are you interested?" the trader asked.

Mallory faced her companions. "We do need one. We can't keep hassling Ahron to find out the time."

"Does that mean we won't be able to buy the book?" Callum asked.

"I guess we could. It's not that expensive," Mallory said.

The trader gestured to outside. "The general goods shop up the road had one on companion animals the other day. If you're interested I can send the lad to see if they have it. Should only be ten gold pieces." He nodded towards the boy who was tidying shelves.

Brodie turned to Mallory. "Now that'd be better than a book for shipwright."

"Why not get both?" Danae asked. "I don't know all the details on companion animals so I'd like to read it over too. I wouldn't mind getting my own companion animal one day."

After some debate, they decided to get both books, the pocket watch and a coat each when Danae mentioned how cold it would be at Cutthroat Harbour of an evening. Danae already had a coat, packed away in the blanket wrapped bundle on the back of her horse. They chose basic, common coats made of thick, dark brown material, wooden buttons marching down the front of the coats that went to mid-thigh. They were four gold pieces each. They'd also be easier to wear than the blankets Brodie pointed out they could use as cloaks.

Mallory winced when she saw the cost of their

purchases, taking the eighteen gold pieces the trader placed on the counter. "Thank you."

"Any time." The trader beamed at them. "It was a pleasure doing business with you."

Outside they put their new purchases in the panniers while the wagoner admired Bug. Ryan slipped the pocket watch into his belt pouch.

"Hey," Brodie exclaimed. "Why do you get that?"

Ryan grinned. "Probably safer than you having it."

"I'll go get the horses hitched up to the wagon then we can be on our way," the wagoner said. "It'll be nice to get home."

They organised to meet him out the front of the tavern where he said Roast was also waiting for them. By the time everyone gathered together at the front of the tavern, it was nearly one in the afternoon, according to the pocket watch when Ryan checked. The five of them tied the horses, pig and donkey to the back of the wagon and sat on the chests as they ate the pie and the rest of the loaf of bread. Brodie complained that they could have stopped at the tavern for a decent meal. Especially after all they'd earned on the trip. The five of them also had fifty grams of jerky each, giving the same to Smudge and Fang. Roast and Welby rode beside the wagon.

Brodie munched on an apple as they handed

around the crafting ability books to unlock the skills. Mallory grinned when she had a notification after only reading the opening paragraph of the book on diplomacy. *You have unlocked diplomacy, a crafting ability that allows you to improve your standing with different classes and in various locations as well as learn information about people with the help of a spyglass.* She handed the book to Ryan, taking shipwright from him. Again it only took the opening paragraph to unlock the crafting ability. *You have unlocked shipwright, a crafting ability that allows you to repair and make various types of watercraft.* She handed that book onto Callum, taking the book on sailing from him.

"This is such an easy way to unlock crafting abilities." Mallory opened the book, once more reading the opening paragraph. *You have unlocked sailing, a crafting ability that allows you to pilot various types of watercraft.*

"It'd be better if they gave us a level too," Brodie said.

They read over the books on the journey back to Buckneth, Brodie saying several times that they should gather resources and level up a bit more. None of them moved. Mallory considered it, but after the last few days of walking around the countryside, it was good to ride in the wagon for a change. They were about half way to Buckneth when it occurred to her that it was not only going to be a very long trip to Cutthroat Harbour, but also a long trip back.

Chapter Forty-Four

Mallory sat up, having been leaning against Ryan who sat beside her. "How are we planning to get everyone back that we're going to rescue?"

"I didn't think about that." Brodie patted Fang who was curled up in his lap.

Ryan looked towards the wagoner. "Do you ever hire out your wagon?"

The wagoner glanced over his shoulder. "It's too expensive to replace to do that."

"Do you ever go south?" Mallory stared at the wagoner's back, willing him to say yes.

The wagoner again glanced over his shoulder. "The furthest I've been is Wester. But I wouldn't mind going to Velkden. They have an essence crystal mine there."

"What are essence crystals?" Mallory asked.

"A source of mana you can automatically draw on.

Mages tend to use it for doing spells above their level of mana. Such as for making portals work. They're also used for enchanting too," the wagoner said.

"For mana." Mallory smiled when the wagoner nodded. "I could use them?"

"They're very expensive." Roast looked over from where he rode on his pony.

Her smile faded. "Oh."

"Can we go back to the question of if you're interested in going south with us?" Ryan asked.

"I'm interested," the wagoner said. "I'd need to talk it over with my wife. It's a pretty big decision and a dangerous area. Although you lot have been very good for our financial situation."

"We wouldn't want you to be right in the thick of things," Mallory said. "There'd be no point having you travel with us only to have you caught by the dark forces so you can't help us get everyone back."

"Roast could stay with you and protect you and the wagon," Brodie suggested.

"I'm not about to stay behind. I'm going after Merry," Roast said.

Mallory spoke before an argument could begin. "We can worry about that part later. For now, we need to figure out who is coming with us and how we'll get everyone back."

"When would you want to travel to Cutthroat Harbour?" the wagoner asked.

"We need to deal with the hellion encampment first," Mallory said.

"What about Merry?" Roast asked. "You can't expect me to leave her there any longer than necessary."

"Taking out that encampment might mean the difference between surviving the visit to Cutthroat Harbour and not making it out of there alive," Ryan said.

"It's been too long," Roast protested.

It took them the rest of the trip to Buckneth to convince Roast that they needed to take out the hellion encampment first. Welby joined them in convincing him. When they pulled up in front of the wagoner's house Mallory clambered off the wagon, surprised it had been a peaceful trip. Apart from the arguments about going after the hellions.

Brodie hopped off the wagon too, glancing around the area. "I was expecting to run into some creatures along the way. To level up a bit more."

Danae joined them on the ground. "Will the same farmer allow me to agist Augusta with him again?"

"And Bob and Bug too," Ryan said.

"What am I going to do with my pig?" Brodie asked.

"Yeah, Not For Bacon," Callum said.

Brodie glared at Callum. "That isn't his name."

The wagoner nodded. "Leave the ones you want agisted out the front and I'll collect them when I take my horses over." He looked to Roast and Welby. "Same goes for you two. Although someone might want to give me a hand."

"I can help," Welby said, Roast echoing him.

Mallory handed over eight copper pieces, waving Danae's coins away. "We're a party, remember?" She glanced around her group. "I'll see if we can book a room for the night."

Welby turned to Roast. "You willing to share a room if the second one is available?"

Roast nodded, following Welby inside the tavern.

Mallory followed them inside, hoping both the rooms were available. While she waited for Ahron to finish talking to Welby and Roast, she checked the updated quest. *Trade Route Guard: You escorted the wagoner safely home. You were rewarded with the wagoner selling items for your party during the journey. You also earned twenty experience points each.* None of them had gained another CAS point. Danae was the closest with eighty-one experience points.

When Ahron was ready to serve her, Mallory paid five copper pieces and organised for a pitcher of water and a washcloth. She couldn't very well turn up at school stinking of sweat. Taking the key, she headed outside to help unload their animals and take the gear up to the room.

That night, after Mallory had written in her notebook, they had roast mutton for dinner in the tavern, the companion animals sharing a bowl of stew and the rest of Mallory's dinner she couldn't eat. Roast and Welby sat with them, having paid for their own meal, much to Mallory's relief after having spent four silver and three copper pieces feeding the five of them and their companion animals.

Brodie handed his empty plate to the waitress before facing Mallory. "A roast dinner was probably a better choice than buying something at the bakers. Especially since we had pastries for breakfast. But we better be planning to have another tavern meal to use up the balance of the gold coin."

Mallory shared a look with Ryan, both of them grinning before she faced her brother again. "I doubt you'd accept anything else," she said dryly.

Ryan took out the map they'd earned in Mer Point, unfolding it and placing it in the middle of the table.

They went over possible routes they could take to reach Cutthroat Harbour.

Mallory spotted Wester, the village the wagoner had mentioned. It was out from Wayholt, on the coast. Not that far south at all. She spotted Velkden. Cutthroat Harbour was probably as far from it as Surith was from Buckneth at a guess. It was a little hard to judge exactly since none of the roads were perfectly straight.

"We should use the route that takes us through the most amount of places we haven't visited before," Brodie said.

"It's not a sightseeing trip," Welby said.

"It doesn't hurt to gain more XP," Brodie protested.

"If we go through Wayholt, I can let my mother know I'm fine," Danae said.

"Didn't you write her a letter?" Callum asked.

"Letters can take a while to arrive. And sometimes they don't make it," Danae said. "We could also have the blacksmith clean up the sword the merfolk gave you."

"Gave us," Mallory said.

Danae smiled at her.

Ryan leaned forward, his gaze remaining on the map. "We don't need to make the decision tonight.

It's just good to have a look and start thinking about what direction we'll take." He leaned back, glancing around the group. "Tomorrow we deal with the hellion encampment. Who's interested in helping?"

"I was thinking of doing some hunting for food to take south with us," Welby said. "Dry some venison over a smoky fire. It'll save us needing to hunt along the way."

"That's a good plan. We do have to eat," Brodie said.

"I'll get enough for all of us." Welby turned to Roast. "Did you want to help?"

Roast alternated between the options, eventually deciding to help Welby.

The hunter rose to his feet. "I'm going to call it a night. I want to get an early start tomorrow."

Nodding, Roast also got to his feet. "That's probably a good idea."

When it was the five of them and the companion animals at the table, Ryan checked the time on the pocket watch. "We should probably start taking turns at sleeping. Otherwise, it's going to be a very long day at school for the three of you."

Callum stood, lifting Smudge out of his lap as he did so. "You should be the one to stay awake and let us sleep since you can have a sleep whenever you want."

"I have other plans for the day," Ryan said. "But that's okay. You lot sleep and I'll wake you either when I get tired or it's time to go."

"What plans?" Mallory asked.

Ryan smiled. "Plans." His smile widened into a grin. "Don't worry, I'll let you know eventually."

Chapter Forty-Five

After using the outhouse they traipsed upstairs, except for Ryan. Danae and Mallory each got one of the beds while Callum used the bedroll and Brodie the blankets. Mallory felt like she'd no sooner fallen asleep than Ryan was waking her. Stretching, she stumbled out of bed. "What time is it?"

"We have twenty minutes to get ready to return," Ryan said.

"That's heaps," Brodie said. "Oww. Or it would be if I had some light to see what I'm doing."

Mallory could barely see the shadowy figures and shapes in the room from the moonlight coming in the window. "Let me try something." She picked up the wand she'd set beside her bed before going to sleep and used the flame spell to light the candle. She grinned. "That is so amazing."

Brodie shrugged. "A little. I guess."

"A little?" Mallory demanded. "I think you mean a lot." She chased them out of the room so she could get dressed, using the pitcher of water. Once she was finished, she waited in the hallway as everyone took turns dressing in their modern clothes. She used the mend I spell on Ryan's shirt, repairing most of it before it was time to leave. She smiled at Danae. "Take care of everything."

Danae nodded. "I'll see you at six." She glanced at the pocket watch Ryan had left on the chest between the two beds. "Wake me when you arrive?"

Mallory nodded before she spoke the commands to leave Danae, Smudge and Fang behind, making sure they were sitting down and finishing with, "Save progress and transfer party home." Sensation, sound and sight went, returning moments later. She glanced around the cramped space of the van, picking up her purple notebook to check there wasn't anything they'd forgotten. "I can't wait until we can stay longer on Inadon."

"We need revives for Fang and Smudge before we worry about those kinds of potions," Brodie said. "And we've got a tonne of quests to do. We should get them done before someone else does them. Especially the staff one."

"There are only six. That's not exactly a tonne."

Callum looked at the floor, sighing heavily. "All the coffee seeds I tried to take with me are still here. At least we can sometimes get it from the dark forces."

"We should do the staff quest before someone else can do it," Brodie repeated.

"You lot better get ready for school." Ryan checked his phone. "You don't want to be late."

Brodie opened the door. "Don't we?"

Callum and Ryan followed Brodie outside, leaving Mallory to change. She stepped out of the van once she was dressed for school. The smells of the modern world assaulted her. "I don't miss the smell of car fumes."

Ryan slipped an arm around her waist. "Neither do I."

It didn't take long before the three of them were dressed in their school uniforms and Ryan drove them to school. Mallory checked the first message on her phone, reading over the headlines before she read them aloud. "Lost individual found and brought home, woman saved from kidnappers, gang war ended, dubious heroes foil thieves attempt, valuable item returned to owner preventing loss of work, son welcomes missing elderly father home, information prevents costly mistake, unexpected help allows student to overcome years of bullying, vermin problem eliminated to the relief of a coastal town, snake catchers descend on an overrun farm to relocate numerous venomous snakes, man arrives home after being escorted safely out of a war zone."

"Dubious heroes," Brodie muttered. "What's with the insults? Last time we were an unlikely group. Now we're dubious heroes."

Ryan chuckled. "At least we did more quests this time."

Callum looked up from Ryan's phone. "For the eleven quests, poppet and level three hellion we killed, we earned two hundred and thirty-six dollars each. Not bad at all."

Mallory nodded to the phone she held. "And they put four gold, six silver and twelve copper pieces in Danni's bank account." She checked the previous message regarding Danae's payment, adding up the two figures. "Danni now has six gold, twelve silver and twelve copper pieces in her account."

"What's the point of a bank account?" Brodie asked.

Mallory shrugged. "I guess we'll have to ask Danni when we return to Inadon."

"Talking of returning," Callum said. "Can you buy me a coffee seedling today while I'm at school, Ryan?"

Ryan chuckled. "You planning on adding it to our party?"

"Whatever it takes," Callum said.

"You know, we don't have to sleep in our world. We can do schoolwork and sleep while we're on Inadon," Brodie said.

"Why waste time on Inadon using it to sleep when it's better than this world?" Callum asked.

"I guess," Brodie said.

Ryan glanced at Mallory. "We might need to have our first date back on Inadon since we don't spend much time in this world." He grinned. "I wonder what they do for first dates on Ruby Isle since they don't have movies."

Mallory returned his grin. "Go hunting coastal mud crabs."

Chuckling, Ryan pulled up in front of their school. "That wasn't our first date." He got out of the van to say goodbye to Mallory, wrapping his arms around her. "I'll pick you up this afternoon."

"See you this arve," Callum called out as he and Brodie entered the school grounds.

Mallory looked up at Ryan, her arms around his waist. "Are you going to tell me what your plans are? Other than buying a seedling for Callum."

Ryan grinned. "What if I was working on a surprise for you?"

"Are you?"

He chuckled. "In a way."

"How long until I find out what it is?"

His lips briefly met hers. "This afternoon. Tomorrow morning at the latest." He grinned. "Think you can last that long?"

She returned his grin. "Possibly."

"I'm sure you can."

"How about a clue?"

Ryan chuckled. "Okay. A clue." He paused a moment. "It's something we said we need." He opened the door of the van.

She watched him climb in the driver's seat, raising a hand as he drove away, thinking about all the things he might be doing. Something they needed. That was a pretty big list. Her lips curved into a smile. Although not as big as it previously was. They were starting to gain gear, coins and experience points. Turning, she strode towards her class, her smile remaining in place. It was time to see if they could face tougher challenges. Her smile didn't dim and a shiver of excitement ran through her. Like a hellion encampment. Or a fire drake nest.

Final Stats

Character weight does not include any backpacks,
satchels, their contents or items carried by livestock.

Mallory

Character Level: 1
Health: 21
Stamina: 35
Mana: 40
Weight: 5kg 527g/50kg

CAS XP: 48/109
Available CAS Points: 7
Available Class Points: 0
Level Progress: 1/10

Attributes

Strength: 5
Constitution: 7
Intelligence: 8
Wisdom: 8

Dexterity: 5
Charisma: 5
Luck: 5

Class

Mage: 0
Warrior: 1

Class Skills
None

Spells

Fireball: 0
Flame: 0
Mend I: 0

(Expand For More Details)

Weapon and Armour Affinity

Dagger: 1 (+1% damage)
Wand: 1 (+1% damage)
Cloth Armour: 0
Short Sword: 0

(Expand For More Details)

Crafting

Alchemy: 1
Wheelwright: 1

(Expand For More Details)

Reputation

Global: 0
Local Areas:
Ruby Isle
(Expand For More Details)

Buffs and Negative Stats

None

Available Revives 1

Mallory

Spells Expanded

*All attack spells have +25% damage to base attacks.

Level 0

Fireball: 0
Mana cost: 3
Cooldown: 2 seconds
Damage: low 3, normal 5, critical 7
Duration: Instant

Flame: 0
Mana cost: 5
Cooldown: 3 seconds
Damage: low 4, normal 6, critical 8
Damage Over Time: 4 every 2 seconds
Duration: Non-flammable materials 6 secs,
flammable materials until runs out of fuel

Mend I: 0
Mana Cost: 17
Cooldown: 5 seconds
Area Of Effect: 1cm2
Duration: Instant

Weapon and Armour Affinity Expanded

Dagger: 1 (+1% damage)
Wand: 1 (+1% damage)
Cloth Armour: 0

Chain Mail Armour: 0
Short Sword: 0
Shield: 0
Dual Swords: 0

Crafting Expanded

Alchemy: 1
Bard: 0
Bartering: 0
Cooking: 0

Diplomacy: 0
Fishing: 0
Hunting: 0
Husbandry: 0

Languages: 0
Sailing: 0
Scribe: 0
Shipwright: 0

Wheelwright: 1
Woodcutter: 0

Reputation Expanded

Ruby Isle:
Buckneth 24

Mer Point 10
South Peak Mine 5

Surith 5
Wayholt 4

Wildebay 10

Ryan

Character Level: 1
Health: 27
Stamina: 45
Mana: 20
Weight: 11kg 187g/90kg

CAS XP: 42/109
Available CAS Points: 3
Available Class Points: 0
Level Progress: 1:1/10

Attributes

Strength: 9
Constitution: 9
Intelligence: 5
Wisdom: 4

Dexterity: 5
Charisma: 5
Luck: 6

Class

Warrior: 1

Class Skills
None

Spells

None

Weapon and Armour Affinity

Chain Mail Armour: 0
Short Sword: 1 (+1% damage)
Shield: 1 (+1% damage)
(-1% damage taken)
Dual Swords: 0

Crafting

Hunting: 5
Wheelwright: 1

(Expand For More Details)

Reputation

Global: 0
Local Areas:
Ruby Isle
(Expand For More Details)

Buffs and Negative Stats

None

Available Revives 2

Ryan

Crafting Expanded

Alchemy: 0
Bard: 0
Bartering: 0
Cooking: 0

Diplomacy: 0
Fishing: 0
Hunting: 5
Husbandry: 0

Languages: 0
Sailing: 0
Scribe: 0
Shipwright: 0

Wheelwright: 1
Woodcutter: 0

Reputation Expanded

Ruby Isle:
Buckneth 24

Mer Point 10
South Peak Mine 5

Surith 5
Wayholt 4

Wildebay 10

Brodie

Character Level: 1
Health: 27
Stamina: 45
Mana: 25
Weight: 5kg 652g/50kg

CAS XP: 52/109
Available CAS Points: 3
Available Class Points: 0
Level Progress: 1:1/10

Attributes

Strength: 5
Constitution: 9
Intelligence: 4
Wisdom: 5

Dexterity: 8
Charisma: 7
Luck: 5

Class

Rogue: 1

Class Skills
Stealth: 0 (30 seconds,
1 hour cooldown)

Spells

None

Weapon and Armour Affinity

Stiletto: 1 (+1% damage)
Throwing Knives: 1 (+1% damage)
Leather Armour: 0

Crafting

Bartering: 1
Cooking: 3
Wheelwright: 1

(Expand For More Details)

Reputation

Global: 0
Local Areas:
Ruby Isle
(Expand For More Details)

Buffs and Negative Stats

None

Available Revives 1

Bradie

Crafting Expanded

Alchemy: 0
Bard: 0
Bartering: 1
Cooking: 3
Diplomacy: 0

Fishing: 0
Hunting: 0
Husbandry: 0
Languages: 0
Sailing: 0

Scribe: 0
Shipwright: 0
Wheelwright: 1
Woodcutter: 0

Reputation Expanded

Ruby Isle:
Buckneth 24
Mer Point 10
South Peak Mine 5

Surith 5
Wayholt 4
Wildebay 10

Callum

Character Level: 1	CAS XP: 54/109
Health: 21	Available CAS Points: 8
Stamina: 35	Available Class Points: 0
Mana: 25	Level Progress: 1:1/10
Weight: 5kg 477g/60kg	

Attributes

Strength: 6	Dexterity: 9
Constitution: 7	Charisma: 4
Intelligence: 5	Luck: 7
Wisdom: 5	

Class / Spells

Class	Spells
Archer: 1 Class Skills None	None

Weapon and Armour Affinity / Crafting

Weapon and Armour Affinity	Crafting
Short Bow: 1 (+1% damage) Hunting Knife: 1 (+1% damage) Studded Leather Armour: 0 Sling: 0 Slingshot	Wheelwright: 1 (Expand For More Details)

Reputation / Buffs and Negative Stats

Reputation	Buffs and Negative Stats
Global: 0 Local Areas: Ruby Isle (Expand For More Details)	None

Available Revives 2

Callum

Crafting Expanded

Alchemy: 0
Bard: 0
Bartering: 0
Cooking: 0
Diplomacy: 0

Fishing: 0
Hunting: 0
Husbandry: 0
Languages: 0
Sailing: 0

Scribe: 0
Shipwright: 0
Wheelwright: 1
Woodcutter: 0

Reputation Expanded

Ruby Isle:
Bbuckneth 24
Mer Point 10
South Peak Mine 5

Surith 5
Wayholt 4
Wildebay 10

Danae

Character Level: 1
Health: 21
Stamina: 35
Mana: 25
Weight: 5kg 459g/60kg

CAS XP: 81/113
Available CAS Points: 5
Available Class Points: 0
Level Progress: 5/10

Attributes

Strength: 6
Constitution: 7
Intelligence: 5
Wisdom: 5

Dexterity: 9
Charisma: 4
Luck: 7

Class

Archer: 1

Class Skills
None

Spells

None

Weapon and Armour Affinity

Short Bow: 1 (+1% damage)
Hunting Knife: 1 (+1% damage)
Studded Leather Armour: 0
Sling: 0
Slingshot
Unarmed: 1 (+1% damage)

Crafting

Alchemy: 3
Bartering: 1
Cooking: 1
Glassblowing: 1
(Expand For More Details)

Reputation

Global: 0
Local Areas:
Ruby Isle
(Expand For More Details)

Buffs and Negative Stats

None

Racial Bonus

Archer +10% damage
Mage capable of using spells
one level above class level

Available Revives 1

Danae

Crafting Expanded

Alchemy: 3
Bartering: 1
Clothier: 0
Cooking: 1
Diplomacy: 0

Fishing: 0
Glassblowing: 1
Husbandry: 0
Languages: 0
Sailing: 0

Scribe: 0
Shipwright: 0
Wheelwright: 1
Woodcutter: 0

Reputation Expanded

Ruby Isle:
Buckneth 6
Mer Point 10
Simria 22
South Peak Mine 5

Surith 5
Ursen 0
Wayholt 12
Wildebay 10

COMPANION ANIMALS' FINAL STATS

Smudge 8HP (Callum)

670XP/1000XP

Fang 6HP (Brodie)

643XP/1000XP

Free Ebook

Subscribe to Avril's newsletter and receive a free ebook. This ebook is exclusive to those on her mailing list. To find out more about this offer visit:

www.avrilsabine.com/free-ebook

*

We value your privacy and will not sell, rent, exchange or loan your email address to third parties. Your information is confidential and you are under no obligation to remain on the mailing list and can unsubscribe at any time.

Acknowledgements

As always, there are a lot of people to thank. You all know who you are and we hope you should all know how grateful we are for your help.

To The Reader

If you enjoyed this book, why not consider leaving a review to help other readers discover it too? Reader engagement is one of the few ways that lets an author know readers want more books in a particular series or genre. So leave a review and tell friends, not only about this book but also about other ones you've enjoyed, so you can continue to enjoy books by your favourite authors for years to come.

Dreams are meant to be lived,

Avril, Storm and Rhys.

About The Authors

Avril is an Australian author who lives with her family on acreage in South East Queensland. She writes mostly young adult and children's speculative fiction, but has been known to dabble in other genres. You can find more information about her at www.avrilsabine.com where you can also subscribe to her newsletter to be kept informed about new releases, current projects, blog posts and exclusive news.

Storm has a wide range of interests from gaming and blacksmithing to cooking and sewing. It's not unusual to find him cooking at any hour of the day or night, particularly after a long gaming session.

Rhys loves books and gaming and has thoroughly enjoyed combining two of his favourite things. He has been running tabletop gaming sessions for the past few years and enjoys creating characters and doing in depth worldbuilding.

Titles By Avril Sabine

Stories about strong characters and characters who discover their strengths.

SERIES

Assassins Of The Dead- Young Adult Fantasy/ Paranormal

Book 1: Dark Blade

Book 2: Dragon Touched

Book 3: Society Against Vampires

Book 4: King's Request

Dragon Blood- Young Adult Urban Fantasy (with elements of romance)

(5 book series)

Book 1: Pliethin

Book 2: Wyvern

Book 3: Surety

Book 4: Knight

Book 5: Mage

Dragon Mage- Young Adult Urban Fantasy (with elements of romance)

(Series two of Dragon Blood series)

Book 1: Promise

Dragon Blood Chronicles- Young Adult Urban Fantasy (with elements of romance)

(Companion stand alone series to Dragon Blood)

Book 1: Oath

Book 2: Betrayed

Guardians Of The Round Table- Young Adult Fantasy LitRPG

(Co-written with Storm and Rhys Petersen)

Book 1: Dexterity Fail

Book 2: Goblin Boots

Book 3: Singed Feathers

Book 4: Frog Mage

Book 5: Crystal Mine

Book 6: Cursed Harp

Rosie's Rangers- Young Adult Western Steampunk

(6 book series)

Book 1: Justice

Book 2: Vengeance

Book 3: Treachery

Book 4: Accused

Book 5: Wanted

Book 6: Corruption

Mark Of Kings- Children's Fantasy

(Upper middle grade/preteen)

(4 book series)

Book 1: The Arena

Book 2: The Island

Book 3: The Assassin

Book 4: The King

STAND ALONE SERIES

Demon Hunters- Young Adult Urban Fantasy/ Horror (with elements of romance)

Book 1: Blood Sacrifice

Book 2: Retribution

Book 3: Tainted

Book 4: Premonition

Book 5: Cursed

Book 6: Feud

Book 7: Extrication

Plea Of The Damned- Young Adult Urban Fantasy/Paranormal

(6 book series)

Book 1: Forgive Me Lucy

Book 2: Forgive Me Aiden

Book 3: Forgive Me Jena

Book 4: Forgive Me Kobe

Book 5: Forgive Me Marti

Book 6: Forgive Me Dawson

*Realms Of The Fae- Young Adult Urban Fantasy
(with elements of romance)*

The Sword (short story in Like A Girl Anthology)

Heart Of Stone

Book 1: A Debt Owed

Book 2: Marked By The Hunt

Book 3: The Magic Collector

Book 4: An Unexpected Betrayal

Book 5: Imprisoned By Iron

Fairytales Retold (Short Stories)

Snow-White And Rose-Red

The Twelve Brothers

The Light Princess

Beauty And The Beast

Sleeping Beauty

Aschenputtel

The Golden Bird

The Frog Prince

The Death Of Koshchei The Deathless

Myths And Legends Retold (Short Stories)

Ion, Son Of Apollo

Sir Gawain And The Maid With The Narrow Sleeves

Princess Ilse, The Giant's Daughter

YOUNG ADULT NOVELS

Young Adult Fantasy (with elements of romance)

Elf Sight

Earth Bound

Young Adult Urban Fantasy

Stone Warrior (with elements of romance)

The Jungle Inside

Young Adult Contemporary (with elements of romance)

Through Your Eyes

The Ugly Stepsister

Perfect Little Princess

Young Adult Contemporary/Paranormal

Whispers In The Dark (with elements of romance and same sex relationships)

Over Too Soon (with elements of romance)

Young Adult Sci-Fi

Experiment X-One-Six (Urban Sci-Fi/Superheroes)

An Endless Dawn (Post Apocalyptic Sci-Fi)

CHILDREN'S BOOKS

Dragon Lord (Preteen/early teens) (Fantasy)

The Irish Wizard (Upper middle grade) (Urban Fantasy)

SHORT STORIES

Urban Fantasy

Eternally Late

Dealings With Joe

Glimpses (short story in That Moment When Anthology)

Contemporary

The Brat Next Door

Fantasy LitRPG

(Set in the same world as Guardians Of The Round Table Series)

Tales Of Inadon 1: The Disc (Co-written with Storm and Rhys Petersen) (short story in Game On! Anthology)

Post Apocalyptic Sci-Fi

Compulsive Directive

NONFICTION

A Year Of Weekly Writing Exercises (Creative Writing)

Cooking For Families With Allergies (Cooking) (Co-written with Storm Petersen)

Tell Me A Story, Grandma (Memoir)

For the most up to date details on available titles visit:

www.avrilsabine.com/books/bibliography

Guardians Of The Round Table Series

To learn more about this series visit:

www.avrilsabine.com/series/gotrt

Find maps, more stats and details about the next book.

Book 5: Crystal Mine

Book 6: Cursed Harp

Book 7: Treasure Seeker

BOOKS SET IN THE SAME WORLD AS THE GUARDIANS OF THE ROUND TABLE SERIES

Adventurers Guild Handbook (Lore Book)

Legend Of The Ancestral King (Lore Book)

Lost And Powerful: Myths Of Misplaced Staves (Lore Book)

Disclaimer

This is a work of fiction. Names, characters, businesses, places, events and incidents are either the products of the author's imagination or used in a fictitious manner. Any resemblance to actual persons, living or dead, or actual events is purely coincidental. The opinions expressed or beliefs held are those of the characters and should not be assumed to be the opinions or beliefs of the authors.